Lights of Boston Harbor

Nakala Akasie

A Point of Light
Pleiadian Publishing

Pleiadian Publishing
WhenAngelsSpeak5@aol.com
PleiadianTraveler.com
Copyright © 2023 by Nakala Akasie

Lights of Boston Harbor is a work of fiction. Names, characters, places, and incidents are products of the author's imagination or are used fictitiously. Any resemblance to actual events, locales, or persons, living or deceased, is entirely coincidental.

Interior Design: Marcia Breece
Cover Design: Marcia Breece
Copy editor: Ray El

ISBN: 978-1-942445-10-4
Library of Congress Control Number: 2023910789

Contents

ALSO BY NAKALA AKASIE

When Angels Speak: The Awakening
A Pleiadian Endeavor

Awakening: The Gift
The Accounts of a Pleiadian Traveler
Book One

The Sacred Contract
The Accounts of a Pleiadian Traveler
Book Two

In the Light of Day
The Accounts of a Pleiadian Traveler
Book Three

Mirrors: Holding the Vision
The Accounts of a Pleiadian Traveler
Book Four

Fifth Sphere: Attainment
The Accounts of a Pleiadian Traveler
Book Five

Advanced Dowsing
Building a Strong Foundation
By Nakala Akasie and Ray El

God oversees our creations—the endless patterns of Light as they swirl, take shape, and connect with other patterns of Light, all to be used for the highest good.

— We are One

Chapter One

Driving through Boston at night during this winter storm is unavoidable. Some of the street signs are rocking and twisting like the wind is coaxing them to come out of the concrete to take flight. Claire sucks in a breath and swears. Even with the street lights illuminating the intersections, the heavy mist and fog obscure the details making it impossible to see the pot holes. Claire thinks of the patches of black ice that are hiding in plain sight and feels the anxiety continue to mount. Her head throbs. If only she could grab an aspirin. But she doesn't dare reach for her purse, not now. In order to get home safely she tells herself, *stay alert.* She knows, no matter how careful she is, driving in this stuff is a crapshoot.

Claire is having trouble staying focused. What happened at The Manor where she works as a nurse, took her out of her comfort zone into a world that even she couldn't dream up. After the experience though, she can't disregard what happened… and she can't make sense of any of it either. She wonders if she ever will. It's all too weird. Her mind reels, examining each scene again and again.

Claire is familiar with the set up: the angels stand vigil in the patient's room when a patient is about to pass from the physical realm. Claire is accustomed to this, but this time, one of the angels spoke to her. This time, one of the angels made a request of her.

Driving in favorable conditions in Boston will wear on anyone's nerves, but tonight is different. Bubbles of suspicion and dread have made a home in her gut. The energy feels different and continues to plague her as her mind whirls to free itself from the onslaught of questions. Why was she the one who was in that room at that particular time?

Claire thinks about her two patients who made their transition earlier that evening. How beautiful the events had been. Then as she began her drive home, a string of incidents occurred, that were impossible to predict and turned increasingly daunting and dangerous. It's becoming more difficult to emotionally recover from these episodes. She's worried about what might be waiting for her around the next corner.

Could it be that the tables have turned somehow and now there's some sort of malicious energy that has singled her out, wanting to trip her up, hurt her, and maybe kill her?

As she drives, the landscape is surreal. Has she somehow slipped into another dimension? Is the Earth merely an illusionary construct covering up what is really going on here? Nothing is as it seems.

Claire is familiar with the signs; she's still flying high on adrenalin and knows she isn't grounded. Her thoughts are outrageous, but still there have been so many near accidents. To be driving at night under these harsh weather conditions isn't a smart thing to do. Miserably, she tries to convince herself that once she processes the incredible yet bizarre experiences everything will return to normal.

Out of nowhere, a blue van swerves in front of her, causing her heart to skip a beat. "Shit," she exclaims. "That driver must have hit an icy spot." Then, in the beam of her head lights, she sees the movement of a small furry animal that looks like an opossum, scurrying across the street. When the headlights of an approaching car momentarily blind her, she feels she's being propelled out of her body unable to cope any longer. She's mentally and emotionally spent feeling the succession of incidents, however insignificant they may have seemed at the time are building a momentum. Her gut aches from the tension. She thinks she should pull over and sit for a few minutes to catch her breath and calm herself. Instead, she keeps driving. She just wants to be home, where she can close her eyes and rest, knowing that she's safe within her four walls… for the time being, anyway.

When she stops at the traffic light, she breathes deeply and is drawn in to the movement of the fog, the array of dreamy textures. The light rays bouncing off the ice, shimmering in the mist, as if disguising important details that would help keep her safe. The image reminds her of paintings by famous impressionistic artists, Claude Monet and Vincent van Gogh. She sighs, seeing the mist gradually changing into a mix of sleet and rain that will freeze overnight. *Nice,* she groans. *It's going to take me more time to get to work in the morning.*

Instantly, it seems, the light turns green, now her thoughts are distracted by the rain drops and the reflection of the street lights, like a million faceted diamonds twinkling in every direction at once. On any another night, Claire would consider the scene straight out of a fairy tale, but tonight, she's weary to the bone from her previous ordeals at The Manor. The lights bother her eyes, and everything looks dreamlike—garish. She no longer feels she is in her body.

Driving down the darkened streets, she can't shake the feeling that at work today she was being given some sort of crazy endurance test to see how far she could go without breaking. She feels as if she's about to go over the proverbial edge. Although, she considers, it could be some type of initiation. She doesn't know for sure, but she has a strong sense that her life will never be the same.

Even though Claire knows this route by heart, she struggles to keep her eyes focused. The last thing she needs is another incident. That last episode with the opossum was too much. To stay alert, she imagines Boston to be a theater of fantastical illusions. The street lamps are a disguise for tall star beings, shrouded in metallic uniforms and stationed at each intersection, guiding people to their destinations.

She imagines that the metal caps on the globes of the streetlights look like hats. Each being in the customary fashion tips his hat to greet her and to wish all travelers a safe passage.

Wow, that last idea was a doozy. Claire laughs at herself, and in the darkness, her laughter echoes, sounding a bit creepy, *but it's the perfect camouflage.* Her outlandish imagination is getting the best of her. Maybe she *has* taken all she can—she has finally gone over the edge.

Less than an hour has passed since Claire clocked out at The Manor. Her nursing duties are demanding, but tonight, her obligations far exceeded her usual twelve-hour shift. It was as if the stars had aligned specifically to place her in intimate, however shocking, ordeals for the shear purpose of challenging her.

No longer is she thinking rationally. Her mind is numb. All she wants to do is get home safely, take a hot bath, and get some rest. As she finally approaches her street, a wave of relief washes over her. At last, home, safe and sound, or so she thinks.

Chapter Two

Slowing to turn into her driveway, Claire hits a patch of black ice. The chrome bumper of the vehicle parked on the street catches her headlights, creating an eerie illusion. It's her neighbor's red Ford truck.

Like a vision, she sees him out in the summer heat, wearing nothing but his faded shorts and his Red Sox baseball cap, washing and waxing the truck. He's good looking enough to catch her eye, but his personality isn't. Before she had a good understanding of the magnitude of his odd and unpredictable behavior he caught her outdoors and flagged her down. She had politely approached him only to be blasted by his monotonous chit chat. She learned to tune him out then avoid him altogether.

Her heart is pounding wildly, and she knows she's sliding much too close to the truck, but she doesn't react to the situation. Instead, she watches the event slowly unfold, capturing her attention like a terrifying scene in a movie.

Knowing she's no longer in control of her SUV, she watches her car slid sideways, closer and closer to the parked truck. She wonders if she'll keep sliding until she hits it. Normally, in a situation like this, she would be afraid, but not tonight—tonight, she feels nothing. With an unexpected, ugly thud, she hits the curb, jolting her forward and back to reality. Turning, she sees that she has missed the truck by mere inches. In disbelief, she mutters, "Will it ever end?" Letting out a sigh of relief, Claire carefully backs up to realign her car to drive onto her driveway and under the protective shelter of her new carport.

Boston winters are the worst, she muses. Claire thinks about the many times she has had to tread carefully on ice or to wade through knee-deep snow on the sidewalk just to get to her front door. Pulling herself back from her reverie, she assures herself that she'll be inside in no time, however, she sits there, not wanting to leave the warmth of her car.

Claire had juggled the numbers every which way to no avail to have a freestanding garage built to compliment her home. She had requested three estimates, but the bids came back with totals higher than she expected, causing her to wonder if they padded their bids banking on the idea that her beauty was all there was to her.

In large cities like Boston, younger, single women should be doubly careful when they hire workers. With her small frame, fair skin, freckles, and pixie bob haircut colored red with blonde highlights, some people may take her to be someone not educated or experienced enough to exercise sound judgment. Claire, looking easily ten years younger than her forty years, would appear to be a likely target for that type of rip-off.

Not this time though. Claire had hired an architect, and he had drawn up a blueprint clearly showing the building supplies that were required by code. She carefully researched every phase of the construction, what materials would be needed and got the fair market prices for the raw materials. She also delved into what goes into pouring a foundation and the going rate for construction workers and electricians. She had a trusted friend in the roofing business who told her what a garage roof should cost. Claire had gone the extra mile to prove to each contractor that she knew what she wanted, and was aware of what the cost should be, so they could not take advantage of her. Even so she could not afford a real garage, not yet anyway. Disappointed, she opted for a modest carport and a cement driveway. At least it had three sides that partially shield her from the blustery wind.

By the time Claire arrives home, her neighbors are settled in to their warm, cozy houses, sharing a nice meal or sitting in front of their televisions. Not being the least anxious to step out of her car to make the final dash to her door, Claire stares into the darkness, watching the faint shadows dance on the corrugated, steel walls. She takes several slow, deep breaths and feels the last surge of adrenalin taper off.

The howling wind seems to be in fierce competition with her thoughts this evening. Gladly, she gives in, and listens for a minute, wanting nothing more than to forget the unbelievable events of the last few hours. She tells herself that opening the car door isn't such a big deal, but she remembers leaving The Manor—how the wind had savagely whipped at her clothing and numbed her face. Each breath cut as if inhaling tiny razor blades. Right now, however, Claire sits feeling disturbed. She knows that she should be grateful that she arrived home safely but she's unable to feel any emotion. She tells herself that gratitude will motivate her into moving, to make the transition from her warm car to her beautiful home, but gratitude isn't what she feels. *Lately,* she confesses to herself, *I have felt a persistent heaviness, slowly eating away at me. I want a family.*

Claire knows that no matter what she thinks or how she feels, sitting in her car isn't going to change anything. Outside, the air will still be freezing and, inside the rooms will be completely quiet.

The temperature has dropped into the low teens, keeping everyone indoors. The neighborhood resembles a ghost town. There are times, like today, when Claire thinks there must be a warmer place to live—a better place. But then, she questions if any other place could possibly offer what Boston offers. Here there are numerous museums, art stores, river ways, Fenway Park, Harvard University, and Boston is rich with history. Then, there are the restaurants with every imaginable cuisine. But most importantly, Boston Harbor and the Atlantic Ocean. She can't imagine living anywhere else.

Just get on with it, Claire, she tells herself. *As soon as you get inside, you can light the fireplace. It will be warm in no time. Run the bath water and take out some vegetable soup. All you need to do is heat it up.*

In the glow of the porch light, Claire fumbles with her keys. Her fingers are cold and stiff, but she forces herself to take in another frigid breath and tackles the lock again. The click of the deadbolt, for some reason, reminds her that she's alone, there's no one waiting for her to come home to.

Once inside, Claire breathes easily, instantly noticing the stark contrast in the temperature and environment. Here, in her home, she has all the modern conveniences, and the air is warm. Even at 62°, it feels luxurious compared to the frigid cold outside. Vigorously, Claire rubs her hands together and wiggles her fingers to warm them faster.

She's mindful of her aching feet after her grueling shift at The Manor, a high-rise facility with a wide range of services geared toward seniors. In reality, it's a high-end retirement/nursing/hospice center offering comfortable living accommodations for those nearing or requiring end-of-life care. The Manor maintains that they are a top-rated Boston care facility for the elderly and disabled.

Although Claire is dead tired, she doesn't move inside any further, she stands with her forehead resting on the heavy, oak door. For several minutes, she remains there, as though she's glued to the wood. Marveling at the depth of her fatigue, she surrenders to her exhaustion and sinks further into the door, feeling that she's now a part of it. Claire whispers reassuringly to herself, "There's no need to rush. You are home now. Take your time."

Ironically, even though she breathes more easily now, Claire still feels little motivation to move. All the while, she senses her legs growing heavier, and her feet screaming for her to take the weight off them—to sit down. At once, as if someone other than Claire has taken control of her body, she turns to slip off her shoes. Instantly, she feels the cold tile floor and shivers. All she wants is for the aches to magically vanish. Just a few more minutes, she thinks, and she'll be there.

Although Claire loves her job, being on her feet all day is becoming too much. Feeling her feet and legs throbbing, she wonders if her job is truly worth it. Of course, she knows the answer—she loves her job. But it's times like these that she seriously questions her career choice, her sanity.

Claire thinks about how she purchased her home after her aunt left her a large sum of money. She remembers being stunned as she sat beside her father in those fancy leather wingback chairs while the attorney read the stipulations of her aunt's will. She had not seen that one coming.

Excited by this unexpected gift and the opportunity it yielded, she immediately did the necessary legwork to find a home with strong bones. She loved the oak woodwork, its charm, its quality. She marveled at the craftsmanship and the home's character. The stone used for the fireplace and exterior was quarried here in Massachusetts. Some people would think her home dark and drab, outdated, but she loves the architecture and the style. *No,* she admits to herself, *it isn't the fanciest or the largest house, but it's all mine.*

It should feel good to come home after a long day at work. Home is a refuge, after all, and there are no pretenses—it's what you make it. The only person Claire must answer to is herself. There's no one calling for her to get them something or do this or do that and, above all, no beeping machines for her to read and recalibrate. But there are times she feels the walls closing in on her, and the silence is deafening; she feels out of place and that gets on her nerves.

Funny, Claire thinks of the door and its function. Odd as it is, she doesn't believe doors are thought of... considered or appreciated enough. A door's job is to allow passage, although the ideology surrounding doors is so much more.

Claire wonders if she may have finally fallen off her rocker. Why does she think of these silly analogies anyway? But, instead of answering her question, she continues ruminating.

Doors are symbolic of entrances and exits, keeping someone or something in or out. Claire asks herself, *Am I the only one who thinks of these things?* Doors are worldly creations of our desire to separate or to keep things together. When it comes to our safety or even our comfort, it depends on how well built the door is. Even the strongest door can break down or incur irreversible damage when it's severely mistreated or not given the proper care and maintenance. *In this regard,* Claire concludes, *doors are like people, her patients.*

Vigorously, Claire shakes her head, working to empty it of the senseless comparison. These thoughts are preposterous, considering all that happened today. Suddenly, she laughs out loud and says, "Who cares? How can my life get any more outrageous?" Claire exhales slowly in preparation for her final step, making the transition from work to home complete. She takes another deep breath, exhales, and feels her body shudder as it releases unwanted tension.

Taking a step, then a few more, Claire notices how the aqua carpet feels luxurious under her feet. Like every other day after work, she walks straight to the fireplace, lights it with a push of a button, then climbs the stairs to the bathroom. Again, she laughs at the absurdity of what she went through today. This has not been at all like any other day.

Focusing on adjusting the temperature of her bath water and adding some lavender oil, Claire reminds herself that she only has one more day before her weekend. Surely, she can make it through another day. Claire prays that there will be no more episodes. She so wants to *forget*.

The running water captivates Claire until she remembers the nice bottle of wine in her refrigerator. Calculating the water depth, she decides to go to the kitchen to retrieve it. Once there, she reaches for a lead crystal wine glass, a treasured find from the thrift store down the street. She feels the cool, smooth glass, momentarily admiring the floral design that is hand cut into the glass.

Like a record playing in the background, Claire hears

her mother's voice cautioning her, "Now, Claire, do keep your senses in order. We cannot afford another accident." She clearly sees a tear run down her mother's cheek and Claire's bottom lip quivers. Her mother is afraid, but regardless, she loves Claire and is merely reminding her to be mindful, to not forget and become careless. Nevertheless, these words spoken so long ago still make Claire angry. Claire wants her mother to know the truth… that *it was NO accident*. But she orders herself, *I am sure not going to be the one to tell her.*

Claire's younger brother, Steve, had gone and got drunk. He was seventeen. The news reporter indifferently described him as the latest fatality at Boston's historical Longfellow Bridge stung badly.

What perplexed Claire though was how he had driven his car through the steel guardrail into the Charles River at a very high speed without as much as denting another car. He must have decided at a precise moment—done it impulsively. *Such a wasted life.*

Since Steve was under age Claire thought their parents knew that he was drinking and depressed. But one day she mentioned to her father that Steve had been saying strange things, did he know that Steve had been getting drunk? Claire regrettably had decided not to reveal that she had heard Steve talk about ending it all. No, she's positive, it was no accident.

No one, to Claire's knowledge, could speak to her mother without her bursting into tears. Claire's mother was never able to accept what Steve did—that he had done it intentionally. Claire knew. Her father had known. How come her mother didn't?

Ordinarily, Claire fills her wine glass before imbibing, but tonight, as she holds the cold bottle in her hand, she feels the defiance rising, then absolute exhaustion sets in. In one swift motion, she places the wine glass on the counter, pulls the cork out of the bottle with a loud pop, and lifts it to her lips as she hears her mother say again, "Claire, dear, please do try to be on your best behavior."

"Whatever, Mother," Claire whispers, disregarding her vow to use only those words that mean to teach and to protect. Passionately, she swallows a mouthful of wine, knowing it will only take a moment to take the edge off.

Laughing, she sees her mother shake her head in disappointment. "Nope, Mother, my actions are not at all ladylike. But who's to tell? Oh well, right now I just want to forget. Never mind all of that."

Tightly holding the wine bottle to her breast, she sees a vision of an old man sitting on a wooden park bench, hugging a liquor bottle as though his very life depends on what's inside it. He's making a spectacle of himself now. Waving his hands to get the attention of those who pass by, beckoning them to come closer. They do not. Indignant, they shake their heads and quickly turn away. The old man is quite perplexed. He can't understand why people will not come to him, why they will not listen to what he has to say. Instead, they look at him like there's something horribly wrong with him, pity in their eyes.

The old man, quite drunk, wears torn, dirty clothing and speaks to those that pass by in gibberish, like it's some exotic language. The vision is so real that for a moment Claire holds her breath, believing she smells the stench of his filthy body and the stale liquor on his breath. Eerily, the vision ends.

Slowly, Claire walks to the bathroom and turns the water off. Remembering her robe is hanging in her bedroom closet, she turns to retrieve it. With her elbow, Claire flicks on the bedroom light, having nothing on her mind except to undress as quickly as possible and to grab her robe. But before she opens the closet door, she feels her vibration quicken, the hairs on the back of her neck stand up, and her heart begins to pound. Claire knows the signs. Someone is standing behind her watching, no doubt about it.

Instinctively, she goes deeper to assess if she may be in any sort of danger. Time stops. Her thoughts are pointed and direct. She feels insecure. She's terrified. Claire wants to be small, better yet, invisible. She knows sooner or later, though, she'll have to face whatever—whoever is there. Postponing the inevitable doesn't solve anything; it only delays the outcome. As if abruptly flipping a switch, she turns to face her fear. Not meaning to, she gasps.

An unmistakable sweet gentleness washes over Claire as she recognizes the angel standing before her. He's the same angel Claire saw earlier at The Manor. Beside him stands Jerry. Like an artist preparing to paint her subject, she studies them—taking in their features, memorizing every detail. Then it hits her. *Jerry can't be here. He passed over earlier this evening. How is this possible?*

She takes a closer look at the angel to really see him, his features, his clothing. She also observes his manner. Yes, he's definitely tall, like he had appeared before, and he has a foreign ambience about him. Maybe he's Asian? No, she decides. Could he be Mexican or Spanish? She can't decide. His curly, jet-black hair has a healthy sheen and cascades down a little past his shoulders. And, as if his mother taught him to respect others, he holds his black felt cowboy hat in front of his belly.

Claire is moved to look into the angel's dark brown eyes. He pulls her to him, as if some sort of magnetism is at work. Unexpectedly, they become one. There's no sense of time or separation. Surprisingly, the angel says, "You know not who you are," as Claire travels to an inner realm that only knows love.

Even though Jerry is tall himself, the angel towers over him. The angel has broad shoulders and an easy smile. He makes Claire feel comfortable, yet she's unable to process what is occurring and almost laughs. What is happening seems all too preposterous. She wonders how this would look from another perspective.

Jerry's cheeks are flushed, his eyes wide with excitement, no doubt from his recent travels. Willing herself to relax, Claire takes a deep breath and exhales, doing her best to work through her present dilemma. Deciding that understanding any of this is probably pointless, she smiles, then chuckles.

Jerry no longer wears his ill-fitting blue cotton hospital gown. Now he's dressed in his well-worn bib overalls. She remembers that Jerry told her he worked for one of the railways until he retired some years ago. This attire is probably what he feels most comfortable in. She can't help noticing his clunky leather work boots. Oddly, his boot laces hang loosely on the floor.

Jerry was from the Deep South. Claire never found out why he was in the Boston area. Jerry had gone to Mass General Hospital complaining of chest pains, classic symptoms of a heart attack. He was transferred to The Manor for rehab after Mass General released him, stating they had done everything they could for him.

Claire knew his clinical history. The doctor had run a complete panel and prescribed medications. His diagnoses: advanced cardiovascular disease and diabetes type 2. They determined that Jerry had recently undergone several mini strokes and was in end stage renal disease. He simply was near the end of his life; surgery wasn't an option. The doctor gently explained the situation to Jerry, advising him to take the prescribed medication and to "make the most of the time he had left."

Never mind that, why are they here?

Claire is dumbstruck when, in his slow southern drawl, Jerry explains, "Ma'am, we all stopped by to give you a proper thank you for what you done for me. You were right kind, I reckon, to give me what you did." Claire couldn't help noticing that Jerry stumbled over his words a bit, like he didn't really know what to say or, maybe, how to say them.

Claire's heart warms. "Jerry, I'm surprised to see you here. Thank you for your kind words. But really, there's no need. I want to help in any way I can."

The angel speaks, his deep voice soft but distinct, "Claire, my name is Frank. Jerry and I both, want to personally tell you how much your song meant to us. Your voice..." he closes his eyes and takes a deep breath as if he were traveling back to that exact moment and reliving it, "...is quite extraordinary, beautiful really." He smiles.

Claire blushes. Stammering, she says, "You're much too kind." To avoid meeting their gaze she lowers her eyes, finding she's still holding the bottle of wine. Startled, she exclaims, "Oh, gosh. I forgot what I was doing." Claire sucks in her breath and chuckles, "I was getting ready to take a bath." She pauses, "After today…" Looking at the bottle again, she suddenly realizes how she must look to them. She cringes. *They must think…* then she stops herself. She doesn't need to make excuses. What an unbelievable day.

When Claire looks up, she watches them both shimmer and fade. Not knowing what to do or how to feel, for a few minutes Claire stares at the spot where they stood moments earlier, wondering if they might reappear.

After her bath and a bowl of soup, Claire's evening proceeds in a blur. Strangely, she no longer feels all that tired, although she dearly wants to forget the day's events. But how can she?

For years now, Claire has accepted that she sees angels who stand around her patients, waiting for them to take their final breath. But really, how often does a person actually get to talk to an angel and… dead people?

In awe, she shakes her head, noting that Jerry certainly did not look dead. She feels bewildered, but she doesn't actually know why. She exclaims aloud, "Weird shit always seems to happen to me." With that, she turns off the bedroom light and crawls into bed.

Chapter Three

Earlier that evening at The Manor, Claire silently slipped out of her patient's room like she's done so many times after *it* happens. She needed to look out the window overlooking the harbor. The scene, just moments before, had moved her to tears.

Brilliant reds, oranges, and yellows with tinges of metallic gold, light the evening sky. As if it were the sky's sole purpose tonight, it reflects on the water below, like a giant mirror to intensify its irrefutably dazzling display for all of life to behold. As Claire watches, the sun silently slips below the horizon to continue on its journey.

Each time Claire visits this end of the hall, she feels like the sky with its many colors is literally whispering her name, coaxing her to surrender her mundane ways to join with it in a powerful yet playful dance. If only for a short time, she aligns with the sky's spirits, becoming one with them. She lets go of thoughts of today's illness, disease, and death. Sometimes, it's all too incredibly heavy to carry for long.

Claire contemplates the risk she takes when she assists a patient after they suffer a collapse, such as respiratory failure or cardiac arrest, when she experiences an adrenalin rush.

Although an adrenalin rush can be lifesaving, it initiates a heightening of the senses. Certainly, being in this state makes it possible to do extraordinary things, but unfortunately, it can burn out some of the receptors in the brain, causing various health issues later in life. Health care practitioners are especially prone to this unfortunate consequence, yet the adrenalin rush is necessary as they assist patients and each other in dealing with life and death situations.

In this state, there's no room for error. Many days Claire experiences higher than normal stressors, resulting in a taut body. She knows, all too well, the importance of being relaxed. Hanging on to the thoughts and feelings ultimately results in an imbalance.

Her spirit longs for freedom from the ties of this world, to return solely to its true nature of pure love and light—where nothing is heavy or troublesome, where there is only love, kindness, and joy. In gratitude, her heart expands with the light-filled colors of the harbor, and she acknowledges their part in helping to balance her life. Claire thinks the lights are incredibly vivid tonight. She reaches for the window pane, feeling the smooth, icy cold glass. Focusing on the sensation, Claire sighs, releasing another layer of tension allowing the peace and serenity to build.

Watching the bright hues of orange with tinges of gold and magenta, changing to a deep purple and then red, Claire imagines herself once again as a child. The colors hold her spellbound in a magical place that she never gets tired of or wants to leave.

It seems like she watches the movement of the colors for hours, although only a few minutes pass. Like a curtain closing, the darkness crowds in, muting the beauty. Silently, the lights of the Boston Harbor Shore Path begin to flicker on, signaling it's time to return to her desk. What a different world it's suddenly become.

As one of the many registered nurses at The Manor, Claire appreciates the services made possible by her employers. It's big business to be sure, one of many facilities created to assist those in need. She laughs at how her employers present their services, "We make aging more practical."

The Manor is like a city unto itself. The lower floors are for people who want a community environment during their retirement years. All their needs are met, and they have the freedom to come and go as they please. The location of the building is equal to none because they have easy access to Boston Harbor, via the Boston Harbor Shore Path. When a resident requires a higher level of care, they are moved to an upper floor. Claire's station is on the fourth floor in acute care, facing the water front, where she plays an active role in the end-of-life phase.

Claire is particularly grateful to the architect for having the foresight to add glass panels, enabling everyone who comes to The Manor to enjoy the spectacular view. The water itself, is healing, mesmerizing the mind with its constant rhythmic motion. This ambiance offers an incredible healing balm to everyone, even if they aren't consciously aware of it. It's certainly a great asset for the medical staff who take advantage of the scene for a moment or two while on duty, letting the forces of nature wash away some of the pressures of the day.

As a nurse for long-term residents, Claire usually develops a loving friendship with her patients. Even so, their needs are extremely taxing at times.

Although her shift has officially ended, she must finish some paper work before she can clock out. One of her patients, Mary, passed away twenty minutes ago. After that, Claire needed some air. Everyone did. It doesn't matter how many patients they lose; the staff feels the impression of each one of these souls after they depart. Claire can't count the number of times she's reminded herself that dying is just part of life… and part of her job. It's inevitable. Everyone, sooner or later, leaves this world.

Sometimes, it seems that so many of the patients needlessly suffer. The excruciating pain they endure stirs the hearts of their caregivers unless they have become hardened to protect themselves from *feeling*. Claire admits, there are times she also feels it's too much to bear.

Over the years, Claire has noted the various types of *exits* the patients make. Like a memoir, each patient writes their own ending. Some are certainly horrific, including the upsetting and often traumatic details that remain fixed in the minds of those who witness the event. She prefers the less flamboyant, unobtrusive narratives, wanting to believe the patient is in the midst of deep inner contemplation—silent, while no one watches or interferes.

Claire has detected an unfavorable structure to these stories, a pattern to it all. The majority of her patients seem to endure the same afflictions: the dreaded life-altering broken hips, diabetes, arthritis and osteoporosis, bouts of pneumonia, heart disease, bladder infections, various cancers, and so on. She questions why that is. They come to the fourth floor of The Manor frail, like tiny sparrows with broken wings.

On occasion, there's a patient who makes a heroic recovery, moving from the fourth floor to a lifestyle either on the lower level at The Manor or somewhere else, certainly more to their liking. In celebration of those times, while rare, Claire equates them to rewarding milestones because these people are stronger—more resilient, able to mend, and to continue on with their lives. Yes, sometimes recovery is a very long road, indeed.

The flip side of Claire's job as a registered nurse involves assisting others during their transition from this world into the next. Some quietly slip out of consciousness, whereas others gasp for air, hanging on to life. For almost twenty years, Claire has worked on the fourth floor in the geriatric unit, assisting patients through life-altering episodes with intimate moments of victory, whether it means a life continued here or traveling on to the next realm.

The last ordeal with Mary lingers, fresh in Claire's mind, like placing a newly framed photograph on a wall, except the details are blurry and the picture hangs just a little crooked. She knows that the image must become focused and straightened for her mind to relax. She wonders about Mary's life, before she came to The Manor. Did Mary leave a legacy, something for others to remember her by? Or did she too, like Claire, live quietly, getting by from one day to the next. No family members came to be a part of Mary's passing. No one came to visit during her stay. Claire knows Mary had a son living somewhere on the East Coast. She shakes her head, wanting to clear it of the onslaught of intrusive thoughts.

For the most part, Mary kept to herself, remaining quiet except when she was with a younger nurse or attendant. Mary would give of herself, asking just the right questions about their lives. She had a unique quality, encouraging them to speak of personal and, sometimes, troubling scenarios while they cared for her. Claire marveled at Mary's insight, her wisdom and her inner strength, providing the caregivers with a safe haven to be encouraged and nurtured.

Claire overheard Mary offering advice to Sally, a young aide, who complained that her boyfriend gave more attention to his photography than to her. Sally felt he was obsessed with his hobby, overriding the time needed for them to build a strong, lasting relationship. Although Mary was nearing her last day on Earth, she patiently explained to Sally that in order to be healthy, people require their own space. They need room to develop and grow by exploring their own creative natures. "Despite that," Mary added, "there's a balance to all." Unquestionably, Mary's words helped Sally in some way.

So many times, Claire heard the staff talk about Mary's attitude and fortitude. There were others like Mary who shared their views to assist the nursing attendants in developing a broader perspective.

Claire observed Mary's expression at the very end. Her eyes fluttered open, her surprise transforming into utter astonishment when she saw the angel standing nearby. Then, at last, peace came. Claire will always remember those eyes… Mary's eyes.

Before the end, Claire saw Mary's lips move as if she were in conversation, but no sound escaped. Mary turned to look toward the foot of her bed and smiled as if she saw someone waiting there, someone she knew very well. Claire saw no one.

There were others like Mary. There were those who acted strangely, smiling at some invisible person or thing. She presumed they were being reunited with a loved one as they lifted their arms to accept their embrace.

Glancing at her watch, Claire confirmed that she needed to return to her desk to finish her notes for the doctor. Mary's body must be taken to the morgue. Nevertheless, Claire remains unable to move. She decides to stay late, like she does on so many nights. There's no one to go home to; her life is here with these people.

⌒

Claire married soon after taking this job in her early twenties. Her husband, Tom, made an assumption that deepened into an irreversible judgment. He decided that she wasn't committed to their relationship, to him. She began to feel he didn't have a heart. Of course, he didn't share her views. Who could? The events she was a part of, a witness to, were too eerie, too dramatic, and too intimate, drawing her to the conclusion that there was much more to this existence than what appears on the surface, than what she had come to understand, and, therefore, what she believed.

The first time Claire saw an angel standing near a patient's bed, she held her breath and stared. The angel looked like a woman of flesh and blood. But Claire knew when their eyes met and the angel smiled, she was not human. Claire felt the angel's love and knew her purpose was to take the soul as soon as it was released from the physical body.

That night, Claire went home, filled with wonder. She was excited, elated. Yet, at the same time, she was guarded and afraid to speak to Tom about the incident. She found out too late that he didn't relate; he didn't believe….

Tom thought…, no, he was positive, emphatic even, that she was working too hard. "Too many hours, too much pressure," he told her over and over. He did his best to coerce her into quitting her job, to convince her that she wasn't well. "Go see someone," he advised. "Claire, you're breaking under the never-ending demands of your job."

Now it was about him, his fear.

Tom spoke to Claire's parents, insisting that they *do* something because, after all, this was their daughter—whose hallucinating was probably drug-induced.

Claire finally shouted, "Enough." She demanded that he move out. In the end, they gave themselves permission to have different views, just not in the same household. Since then, all of Claire's attention had gone into her work—into helping others.

At first, she laughed at his assessment, his stern, unbending attitude, but all the while, she was crumbling inside. How could her own husband turn on her? Claire had believed that Tom loved her, would support her in all ways, and was committed to her for life. "Let no force separate us for any reason," he had vowed on more than one occasion. Driven to pit her job against her husband, Claire courageously stood up to him. She loved nursing.

Claire's mother, Margaret, turned on her as well. Every time they got together, Margaret scrupulously watched her daughter, making those faces, like she couldn't believe what was happening. Then Margaret began her notorious diatribes, shaming Claire until, for a long time, Claire stopped joining anything family oriented.

The rumors flew until Claire finally went to her parents and told them her side of the story. She never considered there might be a time when she would need to defend her choices to her own parents. During the encounter, her father protectively held his arm around Margaret's shoulders, keeping her close, as if his part in the matter was to not only comfort her but to keep her stationary during the altercation. There was a part of Claire that felt he was working to protect Margaret from her but she quickly dismissed that thought.

She only wanted her family's love and support. Claire begged them to hear her out, reminding them of who she was and of her integrity, noting that they had taught her to be an honorable and trustworthy woman.

She told them she wanted to live. She was not at all like her brother, Steve, who hadn't. Those words cut deep. She wished she hadn't caused the pain she saw in their eyes. It was then she silently swore she would never speak of Steve again.

"But Tom's explanations are so convincing," her parents appealed. "He's so charming. He certainly sounded sincere and believable."

Inside, Claire cringed. The tears began to flow, and then, in a quiet, desperate rage, "How could you believe Tom over me? I'm *your* flesh and blood—your daughter. You raised me! Have I ever given you an ounce of trouble?" But Tom had been very persuasive.

Claire took charge, declaring, "No one, and I mean *no one,* is going keep me from doing what I love. I love Tom, but not enough to quit nursing."

Later, her parents admitted they were naïve to listen to Tom's claim, albeit compelling. They assured Claire they were proud of her and begged for forgiveness. Claire, watching their eyes, found sincerity and believed they were indeed sorry. After that, everything went back to normal. Except occasionally, Claire's mother would get that look in her eyes, like she was worried—she didn't trust Claire.

～

Claire shakes her head forcing herself to return to the present. She has paperwork to finish. All the while, she feels that heaviness in her heart. Returning to her station, Claire quietly completes the required forms. As she types, she hears her replacement, Dianne, behind her, shuffling her feet and groaning, "Another one?"

Normally, Dianne is a supportive person no matter what happens on their floor, but tonight, she sounds sad, tired, and resigned. "Yes, just a few minutes ago, Mary Engel. I'm finishing her file now for the…"

Abruptly, a whoosh of energy runs through Claire's body, leaving her speechless. Then, an unusual prickly sensation takes over, causing her to break out in a cold sweat. She looks down at her keyboard, searching for something tangible to connect with. She sees her hands are clenched in tight balls like stumps of white flesh. She quickly moves them to her lap, hoping Dianne doesn't notice her odd behavior. Fortunately, just then Dianne turns to leave. She wants to go to the medication room to take inventory, getting her mind off the earlier death.

For some reason, during the episode, Claire is momentarily transported to a bench at Longfellow Park in Cambridge. The breeze is cool, blowing her hair about and ruffling the pages of her book. Suddenly, something moves through the area, leaving the air unnaturally still, silent, and miserably hot. An unexplainable puff of warm air blows across her face but she feels chilled. Not two minutes later, the fire department and an ambulance crew arrive. A man has collapsed across the park, and they are unable to revive him.

"Oh, God. Not another one, please," Claire silently pleads. But over the years, she has developed a reliable sense. This is a premonition of when *it* is about to happen.

Immediately, with the usual screech, the intercom blares, "Code Blue, Room 407." It's Jerry's room. Claire runs down the hall. She finds Jerry crumpled up on the vinyl flooring. Inwardly, Claire swears, recalling his eighty-first birthday just two days prior. Her heart sinks as she revisits his small celebration and remembers his smile when the nurses bring in a warm cinnamon bun, complete with a lit candle.

In general, Jerry had been relatively quiet, yet there had been a side to him that emerged every now and then. Observant, almost as if he worked to second guess or to memorize the nurses' routines, Jerry, at times, appeared to be a step ahead of the staff. Usually though, he presented himself as tolerant of his company.

Somehow Jerry got out of bed, rails and all, and fell. He's twisted up in the IV lines, and his gown is hiked up to his chest. He wears a diaper like so many of the patients do. Swiftly, Claire takes in the scene, making note that the side-rails are still raised. *How on earth did he get out of bed?* she wonders. "Never mind how he got out of bed," Claire mummers, "we will sort that out later."

Jerry's skin tone is ashen and wisps of white hair cling to his forehead. He's trying to say something as he claws at the floor. Rushing to his aid, Claire assures him, "We will get you up, but first let's get someone in here to help us."

Knowing that he may be on the floor for a while, she reaches for blanket while calmly explaining everything she's doing. "Jerry, I'm going to adjust your gown and get you covered up." Then she gently slips her hand under his neck and head to check for any injuries. "There now, Jerry, it's going to be all right. Hang in there."

There's a huge caution about moving him. Elderly bones tend to break easily. After his fall, Claire does not want to risk moving him alone. Talking under her breath she says, "Darn it all, where's the team? I know I heard the code, and it was for this room. Just because it's time for another shift to come on doesn't mean no one is accountable." Nothing makes sense.

Jerry is breathing, although he's highly agitated and confused. Yet, he has that look. Claire takes his vitals, noting the changes on his chart. It seems his body is getting ready, but she never really knows for sure. Something compels her to look up. She finds herself staring at a very tall man, looking like he's trying to blend in. Only this is no man. He's a tall angel, standing against the wall just beside the bed. He's so still, he could be made of stone. As best as Claire is able, she tries to keep her attention focused on Jerry, but she finds herself drawn, looking to where the angel stands to reassure herself that, yes, there's an angel here. And he's waiting.

"Jerry, look here. I'm right here. I'm Claire. You remember me? I brought you some juice a little while ago." She takes his hand, "Jerry do you see me?" He struggles to follow her voice, to find its source. She sees his eyes, wild with confusion, unable to make the connection. Kneeling closer, she hopes he'll be able to focus but she catches the unmistakable scent of death.

Promptly disregarding her intuition, she says, "Jerry, dear, I'm right here, I have you—Jerry?" She smiles, really big in hopes that Jerry can see her and feel reassured. "You have a visitor here. I think he has come to take you home." Looking up again, she sees the tall angel nod his head. Like so many times before when a patient is in crisis, Claire begins to hum one of her favorite songs. Almost instantly she sees Jerry eyes soften and his body relax.

When a patient gets disoriented and has that frantic look, it reminds her of a wild animal that's cornered, fearing for its life. All the staff is experienced with these situations and behaviors. As if to assure herself, Claire timidly glances at the angel, who stoically remains stationary almost as if he's nothing more than a piece of furniture.

To her utter astonishment, the angel winks, then smiles. Claire, aware that she's holding her breath, inhales deeply and feels the angel's presence—his love. Every cell in her body vibrates and tears gather in her eyes, threatening to spill over and run down her cheeks.

Abruptly, the angel announces, "Claire, Jerry likes 'The Old Rugged Cross.'"

Claire watches the angel's lips move and hears his voice. She thinks she notices a twang, almost a southern accent, causing her to wonder where he's from? The angel has her full attention now. Feeling light-headed, she nods, indicating she knows the hymn written so many years before. She barely finishes the song when she feels Jerry's body go limp. "Ah, there he goes."

Fully expecting the episode to be over, Claire looks in the direction where the angel stood moments earlier. She gasps. There stands both of them, Jerry and the angel, and they are engaged in an embrace. The angel looks over Jerry's shoulder, straight at her and winks. Nodding slightly, he says, "We do what we can to ease."

Suddenly, Claire realizes she's staring at a blank wall like nothing out of the ordinary has happened. They're both gone. She sighs, thinking that she has seen it all, but she hasn't a clue—it's just beginning.

Chapter Four

With her paperwork finished, Claire briskly walks to her car. She can't help noticing that the air feels particularly frosty, crisp, like another round of snow is on the way. She shivers as a blast of freezing air hits her face, momentarily knocking her off balance. She grabs onto her stocking cap and makes a mental note to get up earlier in the morning to allow more time to shovel snow and commute to work.

In the dark, every sound seems muted, like the world is incubating in preparation for a new day. It feels strange, as though she's wrapped in a layer of nothingness, or perhaps somehow, she has traveled to a different dimension. No longer tethered to the earth, she's momentarily protected from the city's harsh sounds and hard surfaces. Most people have already gone home. For that, she is grateful. While waiting for her car to warm up, she watches her breath make little clouds of various shapes.

The roads are somewhat slick, so she drives slowly. After her experiences at The Manor, she feels uneasy and a bit anxious. Nearing her exit, she approaches a stop light, praying that she doesn't slide through. Coming to a safe stop, she sighs in relief and releases the steering wheel, realizing that her tight grip is causing her hands to cramp. Although the streets seem to be relatively clear, she knows the next mile is even more treacherous. Claire suspects there are patches of black ice that she won't be able to see in the dim light.

The light changes, and as she reaches an acceptable, safe speed, without warning, a large animal darts out in front of her car. Slamming on the brakes, Claire propels forward against her seatbelt yanking her back from the inner world of another dimension—no longer safe in her protective bubble.

The action was so sudden, she wonders if someone went behind her back, convincing God that she doesn't belong in their parallel reality. With no hesitation, God raises His hand, sending her spiraling back into a world where she feels at times, uncertain and into a life that's too demanding.

Claire peers into the dark to identify what startled her so. In front of her car stands a big black dog. She sees the puffs of warm air emerge from his nose and mouth. "What's with these animals tonight?" The dog turns to look in her direction, as if curious to see what all the ruckus is about. Caught in her headlights, Claire sees its glowing, yellow eyes, and hears his deep snarl, she watches him bare his pointed teeth.

In disbelief, she blinks, telling herself that her imagination is working overtime. Again, she looks at the dog only to see its eyes staring back, as if it can see her face. She shivers. For one eerie moment, they connect on a deep level. She sees a ripple of confusion turning to disinterest before the dog scampers off, disappearing behind a wooden fence.

Almost as if she had been physically struck, Claire shouts, "Oh my God." Unable to stop the flood of emotion, she slams the steering wheel with the palm of her hand with a force that surprises then frightens her. Tears run down her cheeks. She is aware that she's sobbing but doesn't have the presence of mind to stop. Instead, she groans, "No matter, let them come." Like a torrent, the tears continue to fall until the rearview mirror reflects the lights of an approaching vehicle.

Claire knows that at work, she can do anything that is required of her and still keep her emotions in check. Her time at the window helps, but then there are *these* moments. After she wipes her eyes and blows her nose, she promises herself that as soon as she gets home, she'll take a hot bubble bath with some soothing lavender oil. That'll help her relax. The scene in Jerry's room haunts Claire in a beautiful, yet profound way.

The tall angel looked Indian or Hispanic with light brown skin, dark brown eyes, like liquid orbs, and a mass of long black curls cascading past his shoulders. He was definitely easy to look at. But it was his *Light* that took her breath away. She looked into those piercing brown eyes and felt the depth of his soul.

Claire muses that he was even taller than she originally thought. The angel dressed like a cowboy, complete with a black felt hat that he held against the front of his body. But it was his well-worn, highly polished black boots that held her attention, coupled with his snug, faded blue jeans, that revealed his long lean legs. His white long-sleeve shirt looked freshly pressed.

At first glance, she figured she was imagining things, making him up in her mind like Tom, her ex, had tried to convince her so long ago. But when the angel smiled in that slow, deliberate way, she knew he was real, and he loved his work—what he did for people. He knew how he affected them. She couldn't help but remember how he had winked at her, not once, but twice. She laughs at how absurd it all was.

Now, at home, sleeping is futile. Remembering the sound of the intercom blaring its message keeps her awake. Had she imagined that? No, she definitely heard it. Claire can't fathom who called it in. No one else responded to the call—not a single person.

As if she were watching from another vantage point, she

sees herself sitting on that cold, uncomfortable floor, tenderly stroking Jerry's face. Jerry wasn't even there. What she held was an inanimate body of flesh with no keeper. But she needed to somehow express her compassion for what occurred.

Even after seeing Jerry with the angel, she found it difficult to acknowledge that Jerry was no longer bound to his body. Focusing on how her body felt, she identified the exact moment when the chaotic feelings of compassion, turmoil, and, finally, defeat eased. She knows it was then the adrenaline coursing through her veins had let up, and she was finally able to accept Jerry's passing. Standing up, she smoothed the creases in her clothing, left the room, and softly closed the door behind her.

Her feelings are subdued, reflective of her experience in that moment. Nevertheless, she continues to feel somewhat troubled by the fact that no one arrived to assist Jerry. That's not like the staff at all. *What happened?*

Claire shakes her head and sighs. Feelings of indignation and self-righteousness overtake her sensibilities. What had happened could not be excused. Not being able to make sense of the situation, she decides to report the incident to her supervisor first thing tomorrow morning. That way, she can at last release it and get some much-needed sleep tonight.

Glancing at the clock, the glowing red numbers read 2:00 a.m. It reminds her of the dog's piercing yellow eyes. Claire sighs, turns over, and thinks, *Tomorrow is going to be a long day.*

Chapter Five

Waking up, Claire feels sluggish and disoriented. She rubs her eyes, recalling yesterday's events. Reexamining every detail from every conceivable angle, she's still unable to come to a rational conclusion why no one else showed up to assist Jerry.

A blast of cool air hits her full force as she throws off the covers. Claire shivers and swears. Knowing she's still tired, she forces herself to sound joyful, "Well, I might as well get on with it," as if she's trying to convince someone other than herself. She reaches for her robe, then swings her feet over the bed, easily sliding them into her fluffy, purple house slippers.

She tries to focus on her morning rituals, but images of yesterday's events surrounding Jerry persist. She laughs at how strange her life has become. *Claire, you have had some crazy things happen, but this time I think you hit the jackpot.*

Never before has she interacted with an angel. Her emotions are out of kilter. Her thoughts drift to how kind Jerry and Frank had been, taking the time to thank her. Again, she sees Jerry's rosy cheeks and wonders how he feels about no longer being on Earth but in a new realm.

From a different perspective, Claire feels as if she has been singled out. She feels uneasy.

What she experienced is a rare gift, but she needs time to understand and process it, allowing it to settle in and become a part of her. Then, as if watching reruns on TV, she sees Frank's face, watches him smile. He made her feel special, included, and most of all, loved. Feeling perplexed, she wonders what to do with all of this? Somehow, someway, she must put a stop to these random thoughts and redirect her energy. Rubbing her temples, she realizes how the event has affected her. Her head hurts from it all. Even so, her mind takes flight again, wondering what went wrong with the intercom's message.

Because she decided to talk to her supervisor, she wants to consider her options. Claire shakes her head, reviewing the situation. She can't help but feel she's missing a crucial piece of information. The pieces don't add up. Her team has always been reliable… until now. Claire swears, then stomps her foot. She could trust them with her life. *Why hadn't anyone responded?*

Grabbing her clean scrubs, she walks to the bathroom. Looking into the mirror she sees the light gray shadows under her eyes. "Ugh," she moans. *It's a good thing I woke up when I did because making myself presentable is going to take a little more time.*

Having short hair makes her morning routine much easier. Usually, there's no need for much makeup, just a bit of mascara and blush is all she needs.

Breakfast is a green smoothie, filled with lots of nutrients to boost her immune system and keep her energy balanced. She eats a piece of whole grain wheat toast, smothered in chunky peanut butter for something to *stick to her ribs*. Claire chuckles at the idiom.

Every time she hears that phrase, she envisions her family, sitting down for Sunday breakfast with her father's habit of reading his newspaper at the dining room table. Occasionally, he would peer over the top of the paper, his eye glasses perched on the tip of his nose. He would clear his throat to catch their attention. Deepening his voice to mimic a TV broadcaster, he ordered, "Now children, make sure you eat all of your breakfast so it will stick to your ribs."

She and her brother would burst into laughter. He had made meals fun. Then, feeling a wave of sadness, she thinks of her father—how much he meant to her. It's difficult for her to believe that her father is gone, and she'll never see him again. Tears gather and threaten to spill over. *I sure do miss him,* she sighs.

Packing her lunch, Claire looks at her kitchen as if seeing it for the first time, and evaluates how she feels in it. She has lived in this home for over five years now. The previous owners painted the walls white for a quick sale, and white they stayed. Claire loves this place, yet it has become nothing more than a place to rest in between shifts at The Manor.

Maybe I should paint the walls and get a dog for company. Thoughts about a dog make her heart ache. *What am I thinking? I don't have the time to take care of an animal or to paint. Maybe I should just buy a house plant.*

She feels a deep yearning in her heart. She admits she wants someone or something to spend time with. It's funny how the idea surfaces from time to time, the idea of having a male partner... or maybe a little dog... to keep her company. Then in the very next minute, she's off to work.

Every day, Claire takes the same route to The Manor. Today is no different. But today, she has a reason. Perhaps she'll see that mutt hanging around where she almost hit it. *By the grace of God,* she whispers, reflecting on how close she came. Speculating that it must be a street dog, she *knows* that he was cold and starving. *Maybe I should bring some pieces of meat, in case I see him again.* She decides to drive through the neighborhood, slower than usual, but she doesn't see the animal. *No dogs out this early,* she tells herself.

Arriving at work today is typical. She stops at *The Coffee Cup* located on the first floor for her morning coffee. She pushes the button for the fourth floor. Like most mornings, before she clocks in, she visits the end of the hall to look out over the harbor while she sips her coffee.

Feelings of serenity flood her soul. "What a peaceful place this is," she murmurs. Then she sees it has begun to snow and watches the flakes gently fall. "This is going to be a glorious day. Thank you, God, for those who watch over these people. And please, God, give me the strength to help my patients for their highest good."

First things first. Claire clocks in, intending to find her supervisor before she starts her rounds. At The Manor, it's easy to become distracted and then before she realizes it, her shift is over. As always, the patients are "handed off," so to speak. The nurses coming on duty are updated on who has a change in care, any labs that were ordered, new admissions, and so on. Of course, they are informed when any of the patients have passed. Every day there's a new set of circumstances. To do their jobs, they must stay well-informed.

Before Claire has a chance to find her supervisor, she notices a man with a gray winter coat draped over his arm, his salt and pepper hair unkempt. He seems to be waiting for someone near the nurses' station. She has never seen him here before.

Feeling conflicted, she tells herself this is exactly why she had planned to see her supervisor first. On the other hand, she concedes, someone in need always takes priority. The faraway look in his eyes instantly reminds her of the dog she saw last night.

Regardless of her morose feelings, she sounds cheerful as she introduces herself. "Hi, I'm Claire. You look like you can use some help." She notices the dark circles under his eyes, his two-day old beard and crumpled clothing. As though he had read her thoughts, he rakes his fingers through his hair.

"Oh, I see the sun is in your eyes. I'm sorry." Claire moves to his side, alleviating the problem a bit.

The middle-aged man holds out his hand, "Hi, I'm Gary Blanchard. The attendant downstairs sent me up here." Claire watches Gary's eyes darken with feeling. "I'm… oh God," he takes a deep breath. "I'm here to see Mary Engel. She's my mother."

Claire cringes. The people downstairs have not been updated. Usually when there's a death, the information doesn't slip through the cracks. Naturally, she feels a measure of responsibility for the mix-up. Politely, taking his hand, she says, "Gary, um, I'm sorry to tell you, your mother passed last evening."

Instantly, his posture changes, his face pales, and his eyes dim. "Oh, I tried my best to get here. I was notified that she was failing. Job, traffic… I drove straight through. I tried… I should have come sooner. Oh God, I knew it."

Gently, Claire touches Gary's arm and says, "Just a minute Gary, don't move. I'll be right back."

Claire looks for someone to cover for her. "Derrick," I have a family member in the hall. He appears to be from out of town and is in shock after I gave him the news. You know, Mary, the one who just passed last night? It's her son. I'd like to take him downstairs and fill him in on the details and offer him a shoulder. Do you mind if I leave for a few minutes?"

"No problem, Claire. I'll hold down the fort until you're back." Like a soldier, he salutes her.

Giggling, Claire says, "Thanks, Derrick. You are a keeper."

Claire finds Gary just as she left him. "Gary, hey, listen, why don't I take you down for a cup of coffee or tea and tell you about your mother?"

Gary strains to read her name tag, gives up, and fishes in his pocket for his readers. "Claire is it? Sorry, I'm not real good with names. Yes, I would like that."

Claire, smiling, walks him to the elevator. "There's a nice coffee shop downstairs. They have some pastries if you're hungry. You probably walked right past it." Then she laughs as she looks down at her hand still holding a cup, completely full.

"Looks like you're a chain drinker then?" At first Gary smiles at his corny joke. Then, realizing how he sounds, shakes his head and frowns. "Wow." Clearly embarrassed, he apologizes.

Claire's face turns crimson. She isn't sure why, though. She feels a bit awkward, watching Gary work to ground himself. Not knowing the correct way to respond, she hesitates. Taking a chance, she chuckles, "Well, some people may think I am."

Suddenly, Claire understands that she's reacting to Gary's masculine energy. She tells herself to stay focused on helping him. Embarrassed by her thoughts, she cannot help but imagine what Gary would look like when he cleans up a bit. She swallows, forcing herself to concentrate on the reason they're together.

By way of apology, Gary murmurs, "Sleep deprived here. Is it showing?"

Shrugging, she smiles. "I totally get it. No apologies necessary." Without Gary asking, Claire explains, "I just arrived for my shift when I spotted you. And yes, it's okay for me to take you downstairs. Sometimes we're able to offer a bit of guidance to those who are new around here."

At the counter, Gary orders a coffee, black, then they find a quiet table back in the corner. "I'm so sorry for your loss, Gary. Truly, I am. I had gotten to know Mary, your mother, quite well. She was a sweetheart. We're going to miss her."

Reflecting on last night's events, Claire pauses, wondering if she should share any of the intimate details with him. Trusting her instincts, she begins, "I was with her when she passed."

Visibly distraught, he looks down at his coffee and groans.

Claire sees tears in his eyes. "Gary, in those last few moments, she was calm, at peace. I saw her…." She pauses, acknowledging the effect her words may have on him if she continues.

Solemnly, he raises his eyes to meet Claire's. Feeling his pain, she patiently waits until he's ready.

"I want to know. Please tell me. What was it like?"

As Claire speaks, seemingly of their own accord, more significant memories of her interactions and observations of

Mary gather. She does her best to paint a beautiful picture of Mary from her admission until her death. She makes sure to include details that she knows will be comforting, like how the staff enjoyed her smile and how she doted on the younger aides as if they were her own children.

"She was a delight, Gary, but she was also in pain. She had days where she withdrew." Wanting to ease Gary's grief, Claire pauses again, "These things cannot be foretold." Claire watches Gary's face and his body language for signs of discomfort while she speaks of his mother's last moments.

Wistfully, Gary states, "I *was* on the way. Just not quick enough." Regretfully, he adds, "Damn it anyway."

Claire gently lays her hand on his forearm, "The look on her face was pure peace, Gary. I don't know who came to get her, but she looked so beautiful."

Gary swallows, hard, working to suppress his emotions before he dares to speak. "She was a teacher, you know? She loved young people. She adopted me when I was five."

"Ah, that explains the name." Momentarily confused, Gary asks, "What?"

Claire responds, "Oh, you have different last names. That's all I meant."

"Yes, she encouraged me to keep my given name to honor my parents. They were killed in a car accident. She thought it would help me remember them, to stay linked somehow. She knew how important it is for people to have an awareness of where they come from. "Claire, what do I do now? Where do I go?"

Realizing that his questions are symbolic, she responds by saying, "One day at a time, Gary." She waits a short while before addressing The Manor's protocols. "Your mother, her body that is, may be downstairs. You should see the social worker for the details. She'll know the directives such as which funeral home has been selected and so on. The Manor takes care of those things."

"Of course," he replies.

Claire sees Gary's eyes cloud over with emotion. "Gary, we also have a chapel downstairs. I can go with you if you like."

"Would it be possible for me to see my mother?"

"It depends solely on where they are in the process. She may already be at the funeral home. You should check with the social worker." For a second time, she asks, "Would you like me to take you downstairs?"

Slowly, he shakes his head, "No, I want to do this alone."

Deep in thought, Claire watches Gary get up and walk to the elevator. Turning to look at her one last time, he steps onto the elevator. Feeling the weight of the world on her shoulders, Claire sighs. She forces herself to stand, knowing that her work on the fourth floor will not wait. Wishing she could play hooky, she chastises herself, *You can't sit here all day, Claire. Time to get to work.*

Walking past Cindy, the barista, Claire gives her a nod and waves, "See you later, then?"

Cindy smiles and sings, "Same place, same time."

Returning to the nurses' station, Claire finds Derrick sitting at the desk, waiting for her. Claire waves, "Hey, I'm ready for the files."

He motions to a stack of files, indicating that they are ready for her.

Derrick, seeing Claire's contemplative look, decides to roll out her chair for her.

"Derrick, you are much too kind. That was Mary's son, the woman who passed last night. He wasn't able to get here in time." Claire frowns, "What a shame."

Their eyes meet. Claire sees Derrick's compassion and her heart melts. "You know, Derrick. I really like you. You're super easy to be around and work with."

Looking deeper in her eyes, he says, "Claire, have a seat."

"Derrick, you look like there's something troubling you. Can I help?"

"Oh, I was just going over the charts from last night. This one, Jane Campbell in 417, has been ringing the buzzer every few minutes. I was trying to think of a way to help her relax into her time here. Honestly, I was looking for an easier day than yesterday."

"Oh, me too. Last night, we were hopping. Two passed, one after the other. That last one, Jerry was a code blue. It was all so bizarre." Claire pauses momentarily before she mentions, "No one else arrived to assist."

Claire remembers that Derrick was working last night as well. Becoming suspicious, but remembering that the code was called after their shift ended, could he have still been here? Nervously, Claire shakes her head and sits down. "I had some weird stuff happen with that one."

Genuinely surprised, Derrick's eyes widened, "What? I didn't hear it. What time? Umm… No one responded?"

"Not one soul. Oh, it was after 7:00. You may have already gone by then. I plan to visit the supervisor ASAP. The usual assistants should have responded." They gave each that *look* that meant lawsuit.

"The odd thing is, Dianne was here. I saw her just before the code was called. Then, I immediately went down to 407. She never showed up, nor did any of the team. It was just plain weird. Then…" She narrows her eyes, as she studies his expression. As if she had crossed some invisible chasm, her eyes lock onto an unruly ringlet of red hair that keeps falling over his eyes.

Almost in a trance, she watches his repetitive movements, becoming aware of a softness, a vulnerability to them. Unintentionally, she looks deeply into his eyes, connecting to his soul. It reveals his childlike innocence and a deep compassion for humanity. As though she's caught committing a crime, she quickly looks away, feeling the heat rise throughout her body.

Repeatedly, he pushes the lock of hair aside. Feeling his openness, she nearly discloses her encounter with the angel in Jerry's room last night. She realizes better than anyone that it's simply not a good idea to talk about those things to anyone unless you know, for sure, they have had a similar experience themselves. She had learned that the hard way. Tom had done her a great favor by teaching her that valuable lesson.

Silently, she thanks Derrick for his uncontrollable hair. Derrick did have a nice head of red hair, thick and curly. He isn't married. She lets her mind wonder; the young ladies probably like it. He probably got teased as a child, though. Secretly, she wants to ask him about it. Her hair as a child had been strawberry blond (more strawberry than blond), and she had been teased plenty. Now she colors her hair, she believes to satisfy her creative nature.

Growing uneasy, Derrick's eyes darken, "What, Claire?"

"Oh, it's nothing. It isn't important." She can tell he wants to know what's going through her mind, but she doesn't feel comfortable having that conversation. As an excuse, Claire points to the stack of files and changes the subject. It was Claire's good fortune that Derrick made it a rule not to pry.

Later in the break room, Derrick approaches her. "Claire, you know what you said about the code last night, that no one responded? A while ago, I ran into Brett and asked him about it. He told me he didn't hear it either. We must have already gone like you said. He knew of the passing of the two patients, but nothing about the code."

Dismayed, Claire replies, "But I heard it come over the intercom, Derrick." She stands and walks to the refrigerator to look for something. A blast of cold air rushes out, hitting her face, and all thoughts of getting something to eat vanish. She takes a bottle of water instead. Her mind races as she retraces her steps last night, those leading her to room 407. No one had responded to the call because there hadn't been a call.

"Oh God," Claire's voice cracks under the strain. Her heart sinks. Even so, she knew she heard it. *How could she be the only one?*

Suddenly, Claire remembers her earlier encounter with Gary at the nurses' station. It was as if God had placed that man in the hall at that exact moment to prevent her from going to see Betty, her supervisor. A stream of gratitude envelopes her.

She knows that, somehow, God is working in her favor. Even so, Claire is more than concerned about the incident. Beads of sweat gather on her brow and under her arms. She feels nauseous and dizzy. She has grown familiar with the angels—with them *waiting*. Never mind that. The masculine voice booming over the intercom was the last straw. Her mouth goes dry.

Returning to the table, Claire forces a smile and takes a sip of water. In cases like these, the nurses follow the unspoken rule: keep your mouth shut and mind your own business. She intends to do just that. They say nothing more about the room, Jerry, or the code. Thankful does not begin to describe how Claire feels at the end of the day as she realizes that no one died, and no codes were called over the intercom. For the first time in days, Claire leaves The Manor when her shift ends.

All day the weather steadily grew worse. If nothing else, she can count on Boston with its never-ending rain and snow. Being more cautious than usual, she drives home, taking the same route, halfway hoping to see that mutt run out in front of her again.

Chapter Six

Claire has the next four days off. She has the luxury of sleeping in, although it doesn't matter, she still wakes up at the crack of dawn. Lying in bed, tossing and turning, for almost an hour doesn't change a thing. Slowly the sun's rays brighten the room until she gives up hope for more sleep. Yet, she remains in bed, thinking about what she has recently experienced and how she'll fill her day.

She still wants, no, needs to get some answers regarding the code blue alert. Again, Claire replays the scene at The Manor. This time, for some reason, she feels it's important to identify the emotions associated with each segment. When she heard the intercom, she felt the expected rush of anticipation, then anxiety. She was eager to get to room 407 in time. She ran down the hall as fast as she could, feeling the adrenaline rush, the push to get there to save the patient.

When Claire saw Jerry lying on the floor, she was all business. As always, she followed the protocol for assisting her patient. As a result, she held her feelings in check so she could concentrate on doing her job professionally. Yet, she felt a high measure of compassion for what Jerry was going through. She saw his confusion and fear. And when she saw Frank standing there waiting, she felt a sense of wonder, hope, and even excitement. That soon changed into suspicion, dread, and resignation, finally evolving into peace and grace. Through the experience of feeling those emotions, she comes to understand the fullness of the situation. Thankfully, Jerry's fate was in God's hands, not hers.

Passing over is a very personal and intimate event. For those who do not go into fear, it may become a beautiful time. She wants to help the patient feel safe, comforted, at peace. Claire is positive she did her best in easing Jerry through his transition. Even so, she still feels an emptiness that she labels as grief. Undoubtedly, one of the reasons she feels this way is because she was left with a lifeless body. Jerry was there, then boom, he was gone.

Examining the steps and emotions surrounding her experience gives her a fresh outlook, helping her realize that her awareness is expanding. She knows her mind has to have time to rearrange itself, to accept new information, which moves her into a new reality. But she also understands changes of this nature are a shock to the system.

Feelings of agitation resurface as she digs deeper. Part of the uneasiness results from not being able to peer into her patients' minds, to know what they understand about leaving their body, and how they feel about the process. Are they frightened? Are they elated? There are usually family members and friends who are left behind who will miss them. With Jerry, there were no family members present. Nevertheless, Claire knows from past experience, there will be those who mourn.

On many occasions after a passing, Claire has observed the family members' facial expressions and body language. She heard them cry out for their loss. Her heart ached to comfort them, to ease their pain. She couldn't help feeling the emotions associated with the loss of a loved one.

Fortunately, Claire knows about the angels who come to assist during this time. She senses her patients go to a far better place where they are loved and looked after. It seems paradoxical that she grieves at their passing. Perhaps what she feels is empathy for those who are left behind.

Reviewing the latest episode causes Claire's thoughts to run amuck. She gives herself permission to feel the agitation and pain that has been growing inside her. She allows herself to feel it and lets it go, until there's nothing left. Claire shakes her head in disbelief. The idea of those two, Frank and Jerry, appearing in her bedroom like that. She wonders what she'll encounter next.

Abruptly, she declares, *I am done. There is nothing more to think about here. I will keep my mouth shut. No one needs to know a thing.*

Chapter Seven

Having four long days all lined up, like a white picket fence isn't what it appears to be. It should be a time to relax, to do something fun or to spend time with family, friends, or a spouse. Isn't that what people do on their days off? In Claire's reality, though, having time for herself is like sitting in a big empty hole with nothing to do.

In Boston, there are all sorts of museums, parks, waterways, restaurants, and theaters. Of course, in order to partake in these experiences, people must venture outdoors, but traveling in the winter in Boston's traffic is something she wants to avoid. Claire concedes that she needs to do something constructive—so she has to stop obsessing about this *thing* at work.

She decides to paint her kitchen and dining room. She has incorporated some teals here and there. What she needs is a contrasting color. Yes, being involved in physical activity will take her mind off *things*. Feeling motivated, Claire jumps out of bed and gets dressed so she can go pick out her paint. She keeps in mind those splashes of teal in the curtains and canister set that she bought months ago. It's time to complete the transformation.

When she arrives at the paint store, she decides on two hues of peach, painted desert as her main color with copper river as the accent. She's confident the colors will feel warm and inviting with the rich wood tones (and the teals). By the time she buys her supplies, Claire is beginning to feel encouraged, confident, and even inspired, knowing that this is only the beginning. She vows to continue to seek out ways to stimulate her life.

Getting into a painting job takes some thought and a whole lot of effort. Claire wants to concentrate solely on what she's doing. She wants to be off the grid so to speak. But once a nurse, always a nurse. In case of an emergency, she knows she'll make herself available. "Ah, it'll be highly unlikely that anyone will want to contact me," she says as thoughts of her mother creep into her consciousness. All morning, she looked forward to at least getting some paint on the wall to see what the new colors will look like. Feeling tense and impatient, she suddenly sighs. It hadn't dawned on Claire how much preparation is required before results are actually seen.

Catching herself, Claire laughs. She wants instant gratification. *Ah, but humans are a funny lot,* she thinks. It's peculiar that it took her forever to finally accept the need to change something in her life. And then, when she finally does, she wants prompt results. What a hoot. Today she's feeling impatient about painting her kitchen and dining area, which she has avoided for the last five years.

Comparing the importance of this paint job with her nursing profession gives her a measure of clarity. It's a matter of priority and what each *craft* contributes to her life. Both enrich her life in different ways and different degrees; although, her job is her livelihood—how she pays the bills. To Claire, her job is far more important in that respect than painting walls.

After this last episode at work, she thinks her job may very well be in jeopardy. She may be called in to the supervisor's office and questioned at length for not calling for assistance when Jerry fell. All the while, she believed that others were coming and what she did in that moment was correct. She felt that she did exactly what she should have done under the circumstances.

Like a raging river, a flood of questions runs through Claire's mind. How is it that she knows when a patient is about to pass? To be sure, she reads the patient's vitals and by their appearance, knows when death is approaching. But this wasn't the case with Jerry. She got these feelings when she wasn't even in the same room. How did she hear the code when no one else did? How can she see angels waiting when no one else can? Now, she's seeing patients after they have passed. What's next?

Not only does she feel utterly overwhelmed and exhausted from not understanding the mechanics of it all, she feels like she's being pushed against a wall with no way out. With no one to hear her but God, her voice rings out, "Ha! The wall! To the angel, Frank, God! Please guide me to relax and still my mind to receive your loving grace—to know without a doubt that everything is working out for the highest good."

Talking to her coworkers or to her supervisor, she reasons, isn't an option. Not this time. "I could sure use a friend; someone I can confide in." But there isn't one person she trusts enough to speak to about any of these encounters with heavenly *spirits*.

Pausing to study her latest predicament, she recalls a handful of coworkers who, on rare occasions, have witnessed her premonitions. They describe these incidents, her ability, as a gift. *More like a curse,* she thinks. Claire throws the roll of tape on the kitchen table and marches outdoors for some fresh air.

Irritation has gotten the best of her. She needs to rest, but she keeps pushing herself to continue. She barely notices the ice and snow that cover the picnic table. Staring at the old sycamore tree's bare, gnarly branches, bordering her neighbor's lot, she sees the layers of ice and snow, reminding her of the icing scallops on a wedding cake—hers.

Slightly distracted by the sound of peanut shells dropping from the nearby squirrel feeder, she looks up to find the brown squirrel's beady, black eyes fixed on her as he furiously chews his meal. She notices a surge of energy being channeled through her body and, unexpectedly, hears herself sob. The pent-up stress has finally let loose, as if it has its own set of rules.

Now, from a different perspective, she sees herself grabbing the edge of the picnic table. Noticing the ice, she thinks she'll recoil from the freezing snow that covers the sun-bleached wooden bench. But, easing down, she only experiences a slight sensation. She doesn't notice that her pants are becoming wet and cold. Instead, something different begins to overtake her. *What is happening?* Her body is literally singing. Although she isn't in tune with that part of her that measures her outer physical senses, love and peace overtake her as she begins to relax. In her heart, she knows she'll get through this latest ordeal.

Someone is telling her she is loved and that everything will right itself. All she has to do is *believe.* She has experienced these types of episodes before, although she doesn't recall any of them being this strong—this powerful.

Maybe God knows that she feels heavy, burdened. She's worried that her job could be in jeopardy if anyone gets a notion to poke around. Now God is letting her know that somehow this is all going to go away. She'll be alright. It isn't necessary to invite trouble.

Going inside, Claire feels lighter, more resilient, and she knows that everything is as it should be. Just as suddenly as her physical senses had turned off, now they turn back on. Seeing her numb, red arms makes her shiver. Then, like a button has been pushed, she realizes her sopping wet jeans are stuck to her freezing legs. All she wants to do now is change into some warm, dry cloths and eat a hot lunch.

After lunch, Claire returns to her painting project, where she pushes her body as far as she can. With every stretch, bend, and twist, her body tells her that it would be wise to finish for the day.

She acknowledges the pain she'll surely feel tomorrow. But the walls are gorgeous. Now, at last, she has a little something to lift her spirits. Already her dining room feels cleaner, lighter, promoting a sense of newness as if she's being offered a new beginning. Taking a deep breath, she focuses on her heart and the gratitude resulting from her decision to make this change.

Her thoughts again shift to work, to her patients, to the place where she feels needed—whole. She wants to believe that she has seen the last of any unusual activity, yet a part of her feels apprehensive.

Chapter Eight

Driving to work after four days at home, Claire scans the snow-clad landscape, looking for the pup. At some point, she stopped calling him a mutt, but today, still there's no sign of him. Why does she continue to look for that dog? The sky is gray, thick with moisture. More snow is sure to come as the weather reports predict. She only has a few blocks to go before she turns onto Seventh Street.

Feeling depressed, she blames the weather, then her fatigue from her four-day weekend. She longs to feel happy and excited to return to work. Searching for something that will lift her mood, she recalls those beautiful moments of bliss three days ago when she stepped out her back door in the freezing cold and sat on the ice-covered bench. *Everything will work out,* she tells herself. Even so, she wants answers. Until she gets them, she'll remain cautious and alert. She needs to be sure that she always correctly hears what she's to do. But then, the code blue announcement, had been correct. She went to Jerry's room because she was the right person to help him.

Just as she finds an empty parking place, she has a queer feeling in her gut, signaling that something is amiss. Someone is watching her. She thoroughly scans the area, seeing nothing out of the ordinary.

The Manor has a parking garage that's connected to the main building by a breezeway. She feels relatively safe here in the parking facility. Nevertheless, she decides to stay put for a few minutes, waiting for the feeling to pass. Shutting off her music, she concentrates on the energy, what her body is telling her. Nothing happens. Shrugging, she disregards her instinct and turns off the engine. Then, she sees him.

Frank is standing directly in front of her car. How can that be? There was no one there seconds before. Frank holds up his hand, signaling that he wants to talk. Flabbergasted, she wonders, *How does he do that*? It's as if her mind is playing tricks on her. There's no way he could have walked up to her car. She would have seen him approach. Casually, Frank walks around to the passenger door, opens it, and gets inside, letting himself settle in beside her before he comments, "Nice Toyota. Blue is one of my favorite colors. I feel the color is rather calming. Claire, how do you feel about the color?"

Still not comfortable with his *arrival,* Claire stares at him for a few moments before she answers, "It's dependable, uh, the car that is. Uh, Frank?"

Frank turns to face her. *Did he just wink at me, again?* The expression on Frank's face tells her that he is totally aware of her inner thoughts. Then he smiles. *Oh, my God, is he nice looking.* Claire knows her face is reddening. She watches him rub his hands together, working to warm himself. He's wearing a gray, wool, winter coat. *Do angels get cold?* In the same instance, Frank declares, "Claire, it is cold. Wow." Then, casually he asks, "Do you have a few minutes to spare?"

Claire doesn't answer him out loud. Derisively, she thinks, *Of course I do. I always come in 45 minutes early.*

Reading her thoughts, Frank laughs. "Claire, I know you have a specific routine. I am just easing you into our conversation." Looking straight into her eyes for emphasis, he says, I am aware how everything that is happening is affecting you."

Nervously, Claire laughs, "You think? I do have a few minutes, and I'm glad you came to talk. I have questions." She stammers as she repeats, "Boy, do I have questions."

"Claire, you have been working with us for some time. You know that."

In her mind, she hears herself say, "*I do?*"

"Yes, Claire, I believe you do. Nevertheless, you are somewhat aloof. You feel afraid. I am here to assure you that everything is as it should be. We have everything under control."

He pauses as if in thought. "You are troubled about the code you heard directing you to room... Jerry's room."

Now he has her on the edge of her seat.

"You heard it alright. You aren't losing your mind. Far from it. But only you heard it. I gave you the code, Claire."

A wave of shock sweeps through her, "Wha... what? How can that be?"

"Claire, I sent that message to you. Be not afraid. You are ready for more."

Eyes wide, Claire glares at Frank, "More? More of what?" Before he has a chance to answer, Claire pushes her coat sleeve up, uncovering her watch, "Frank, I think I should go in."

Clearly seeing the time, she knows she still has a few minutes. The only thing running short is her courage. Mentally and emotionally, she is spent, and the day hasn't even started. She doesn't have the strength to listen to Frank right now, no matter how what he says might affect her. Turning to stare at the windshield, she says, "I have to go," hoping Frank does not know that she had just lied to him. *What am I doing? I never lie.*

Feeling compelled, she turns to look into Frank's eyes. She perceives that he's drawing her in, and the tears gather as she feels his reassurance—his love.

"Claire," she hears him say her name, but she's having difficulty concentrating. Frank speaks slowly with that twang again. *Where is he from?*

"You are here in this moment for a very important reason. I am asking you to go to work now and know, with all of your heart, that everything you experience is a gift. You are committed to your work. Everyone knows this. But I want you to remember...."

Tears run down her cheeks and he waits a moment for her to calm down. He seems to know that she needs some encouragement and a little more time. "You are in service to assist those who are having a rough go of it. It is this service that touches you, that feeds your soul. Then with more meaning, he repeats, "You are ready for more."

Pulling his coat tightly around him, he opens the door and steps out. She watches as he takes a few steps and then vanishes. Almost annoyed, she mutters, "Why does he keep doing that?"

It isn't until Claire buys her usual coffee and walks down the hall to the elevator that she feels warm enough to unbutton her coat. No one else is in the elevator, so she decides to raise her coffee cup high into the air to begin the day, "Here's to another day of… surprises. Here is to another day of…" Interrupting her toast, the elevator comes to a halt. When the doors open, there stands Alex, one of the nurses on the fourth floor.

Claire has always liked Alex. Over the years she has watched him mature, become more handsome, and that grin of his is adorable. The staff finds his uplifting manner infectious—she finds it alluring. He never brings his problems to work. Instead, his manner creates balance within the nursing staff. Alex keeps his slightly curly dark brown hair meticulously clipped and he always arrives clean shaven, smelling fresh. He is tall, she thinks about 6 feet 2 inches but has never asked him. She wonders if he has a membership to the gym because there isn't an ounce of flab on his body.

As long as she has known him, he has given her space, never pressuring her to do anything that she would be uncomfortable with. Gradually, they have become good friends. He has a way of making her feel comfortable, at ease. She can usually tell how Alex is feeling by watching his body language. There are times, though, when she looks into his deep blue eyes and connects with him in such a way that it scares her. She doesn't want to make any more mistakes.

Chapter Nine

Seeing Claire standing in the elevator, Alex gasps. He grins, sheepishly. Pointing to her hair, his expression swiftly changes to one of mock horror. "Your hair? What have you done?" Then he bursts out laughing, "You sure know how to keep surprising me."

Not in the least offended, Claire laughs, "Oh, you like my new hair color? It's called Blowout Burgundy."

The elevator door closes, and Alex turns to face Claire. He smiles like an attentive lover. Putting his arm around her shoulders, pulling her close for a hug, he says, "We make a perfect team. Don't we?"

"Do we get along?" Pulling away from Alex, Claire laughs, teasing him. "Seriously, you have to behave yourself. You know others are watching. We don't want to make anyone jealous, right?"

Alex removes his arm as they step out of the elevator into the hall. "Really, Claire, I've missed you. It's been a couple of exhausting weeks. We should go out after work, get a beer." He looks deeply into her eyes. "You think?"

Claire nods. "Oh, Alex, we do have to catch up. You're back to work, right?" Before speaking about anything personal, she launches into work-related stuff. "Hopefully today will be a slow day. It's been crazy around here.... How are you? How is your brother?"

At the mention of his brother, Alex's good cheer vanishes. The sudden shift reminds Claire of Frank, and she sighs.

"Charles, oh, he has *it* alright—cancer of the spleen, lymphoma."

Looking closer at Alex, Claire clearly sees the telltale signs of exhaustion, red eyes with dark shadows and tiny lines. His skin looks dry, he looks older than his forty-two years. She hears defeat in his voice when he says, "His doctor wants to remove the spleen ASAP. I want to go back out to help him with recovery."

Hearing him talk about his brother reminds Claire that Alex is still human, and one who harbors certain fears and misgivings.

"Only, I'm not sure if I can swing another absence. You know how they frown on taking off like that. Then there's the financial aspect. I have a mortgage. But Charles… I know, doesn't have full insurance coverage. This is going hurt bad."

Claire's mood darkens at the thought of Alex being away for another extended period of time. Genuinely disappointed, she asks, "Oh, how will we ever do without you?"

Realizing that, to him, she may sound needy, even possessive, she changes her tone. The last thing Alex needs is a coworker giving him a guilt trip. "Of course, you should go. I'm sure your brother needs you there. He's family. I'm sure they'll approve your request."

As they walk to the nurses' station she says, "It's time to get at it. Later then?"

"Yes, of course."

Chapter Ten

When Claire joins her coworkers, she notices the mood is tense. She chalks it up to a busy night. But then Janet, one of the less experienced aides, rushes toward her with wide eyes and her coloring unnaturally pale. Claire knows that beginning a day like this sets an undesirable tone, making it more difficult to be relaxed and find her own rhythm.

Janet is a cute girl, barely twenty-two, slender, with long blonde hair that she keeps up in a loose knot. "Claire, that new guy in 407 is complaining that someone is bothering him. But there's no one there."

"Room 407, a new patient? You said 407, right? You know I've been off for a few days. I have to catch up and read some charts. What's his name? I'll visit him as soon as I review his chart."

Frowning, Janet says, "Claire, he smells really horrible," as she pinches her nose. "I get close and want to, ah… well you know… throw up. He needs a shower or at the very least, a sponge bath. But seriously, I can't bear to be anywhere near him."

Annoyed, Claire says, "Janet, we've had patients like this before."

"Claire, not like this we haven't. I'm sorry, but he's really *old*, and the smell… well it's just awful."

"What's his name?"

"Um, Harry Delany."

"Janet, you aren't usually like this. What's going on?" Considering Janet's age and experience, Claire had taken her under her wing and mentored her like she always does with new aides. Claire saw great potential in Janet, being ambitious and quickly developing a good rapport with most everyone. But sometimes… well, Claire makes a mental note to speak to her later about her presentation.

"Okay, Janet… *Janet?*"

"Oh, sorry, Claire. His smell is in my nose and on my clothes. I need a shower. Oh, God, it's so bad. He's crazy as a loon."

"Janet, you must watch what you say. Come with me to Harry's room. We can sort this out together." It is obvious that Janet wants no part of Claire's scheme, but she has no choice. Claire is her superior. Not in the least discouraged, Clair grabs Harry's chart, motions to Janet, "Follow me."

She intends to do a quick read-through as they walk down the hall. But before they reach 407, they hear a loud, metallic, clatter coming from Harry's room. Something fell. They look at each other. Thinking their patient may be hurt, they hurry their pace.

They hear a man shouting, "I don't want to go, and I don't have to. End of story. Now get out," followed by another noise that sounds like something hitting the window blinds—hard. Eyebrows raised, Janet and Claire look at each other. Claire can't imagine what's going on.

Entering the room, the stench hits Claire full force. She sees that Harry is still in bed and alone in the room. The blinds are helter-skelter. She glances at Janet who is backed against the door.

Claire swiftly assesses his mood, along with his body size and probable strength. She feels it's safer to stay by the door, but she needs to see if the window is broken. Quickly, she steps to the foot of the bed and gags, knowing it's only a matter of time before she'll lose her breakfast. She must get out of there, now. She sees water dripping from the blinds, and the water pitcher lying on the floor. Putting her hand over her mouth, she gags again and walks toward the door.

Janet, with her forearm over her nose and mouth, quietly whispers, "See, I told you so."

Claire holds up her hand as she turns to face Harry. She says to him, "I'll be right back. I have to check your chart."

In the hall, Claire opens the chart and carefully reads it:

Harry Delany: Caucasian

Age 62

Height 6' 4"

Weight 260 pounds

Disabled. History of mental illness (psychosis, neurosis), incontinent, advanced heart disease (heart arrhythmia, two heart attacks, one major), mini strokes.

Career: car mechanic, retired.

Family: Widower, two adult children living in the Boston area.

Notes: Reason for admittance: confusion and physical violence. Augusta Delany (daughter) provided the report.

Oh nice, there's the violence. Well, wonderful. Life is always full of unexpected surprises.

Hygiene is an issue. *Understatement.* Complains of not being able to relieve himself, incontinent, but refuses to use diapers.

Maybe an undiagnosed bladder infection? She takes note of his admission and release dates from Mass General Hospital.

Notes: EMTs transfer patient to The Manor.

Claire, scratching her head, wonders if Harry should be at The Manor at all, which is geared more for end-of-life situations rather than for someone who is mentally unstable.

Why didn't they keep him at the hospital? We could easily request a transfer, but if Mass General is full, then… well, we would have to wait.

Brainstorming, Claire recalls who is scheduled today. Who could better handle this situation? *Will Harry respond better to a man or to a woman? Maybe he'll behave for a younger woman?* Nope, Claire knows Janet can't do it. She settles on Alex or Chris, but it may take both of them. Maybe Alex can talk to him, man to man?

Right now, the important thing is to get Harry cleaned up and settled in. Doc won't tolerate this. He'll be in soon, she's sure. If Doc can't stand to talk to him, he won't be able to make an evaluation. Honestly, she doesn't know how Harry has gotten this far in the process without bathing. This may be one of those times that a patient was dumped. *Well, there's nothing like a challenge first day back on the job.*

Janet looks like a frightened jack rabbit ready to run. Claire laughs and shrugs, "Well, young lady, we have a wild one on our hands, don't we?" Reaching out, she takes Janet in her arms to give her a quick hug and whispers, "We got this kid. Follow my lead."

Janet nods.

"It's time." They take several deep gulps of air, before walking back in.

Claire speaks deliberately and louder than usual, all the while, keeping her eyes glued on Harry's facial expression, especially his eyes. "Mr. Delany. Hello, I'm sorry for the interruption. My name is Claire, and this is Janet. I believe you two have met. I see you have come to visit us." She waits for Harry to say something, anything, but he remains silent.

"So, I hear someone is bothering you. Is this correct? I want to take care of any and all problems quickly. We want you to be as comfortable as possible during your stay here. Do you know where you are?" She pauses. "Mr. Delany? I need you to answer my questions. Do you know where you are?"

Irritated, Harry yells, "Yes, I'm in the ER."

"Mr. Delany, no, you're at The Manor. We're a nursing facility, kind of like a hospital, but more of a rehab. We will be working with you until the doctor does an evaluation to determine where you should be."

Claire looks back over the records to confirm the date he was admitted to Mass General and when he was released. "Originally, you were in the ER, and Mass General kept you for a short stay." Working to lighten the mood she says, "These places all look the same. Don't they?"

Harry narrows his eyes and frowns.

"If needed, we're geared for longer rehabilitations. It appears that Mass General thought you would be more comfortable here." Claire emphasizes, "You're here to get better. We want you to go home if at all possible. Please cooperate with us so we can make that happen."

She wants to address the matter of the intruder, hoping to gain a sense of trust. "We want to identify and remove the person who is bothering you. But I want to make sure that I have a clear description. I wouldn't want to scare anyone needlessly. We have other residents to consider."

Harry looks her over before saying, "Look… Claire, is it? I can read your name tag." With wide open eyes, he continues, "I don't know what to do. This guy followed me here from work. He says I have to go with him. I asked him what for?" His voice grows louder and angrier. "You know what he said? It's time. It's time. Ha. 'Time for what?' I asked him. He comes in here like he owns the place and orders me around. I don't like it, and I don't like him. Not one bit!"

Somewhat baffled, Claire is determined to get to the truth of the matter, "Mr. Delany, you said he followed you from work? It says in your chart that you are disabled, retired. Did Mass General document your history incorrectly? This man was at your work? Where do you work?"

"My car repair shop on Nineteenth and Elm. I still have it. I go in there to check up on the men. I still have my business to run you know."

"What does this man look like? I certainly want to take care of this for you. In fact, why don't I get Alex in here and you can give him a description." Claire smiles, "I bet Alex will catch him in the hall, then we can call security."

Harry nods. As Claire turns to leave, she says, "I'll be right back." But, instead, she acts like she remembers something and turns around to face Harry again. "After I talk to Alex, why don't we get you a bath and a clean gown? I think some hot tea might be good too."

Then she shifts her voice, using soothing tones to entice like a mother would when she wants her children to eat—anything. "Would you like some breakfast? I bet you're famished. Today we have scrambled eggs, hash browns, and bacon with multigrain toast. Oh, maybe you would rather have biscuits and gravy with a bowl of fresh fruit?"

Opening his eyes wide, Harry says, "Oh, that sounds good. Could you bring me some biscuits and gravy? Oh, and I want some black coffee, too."

"Of course, Mr. Delany. May I call you Harry?" Suddenly, acting suspicious, Harry looks down at his blanket and begins to pick at some invisible lint. "Oh, it's okay Mr. Delany.

"We'll get you set up and taken care of real soon." At that, they turn to go.

From behind, Claire hears Harry mumble, "Claire?" Then louder, "Hey wait! You can call me Harry. That's okay. I know that guy is out there just waiting for you to leave. He's tall, real tall. Looks like an injun."

Harry's words stop her in her tracks. She turns to face her patient. She's afraid to ask because she already suspects it's Frank. "An injun?" *Indians are easily mistaken for Hispanics.* "What was he wearing?"

"Blue jeans and those pointy-toed, black boots."

Claire, faking it better than she had in her entire life, knows exactly who's bothering Harry. "Ah, Harry thanks. That's really helpful. I bet we can find him real soon." Claire takes a quick look at Janet and motions for her to follow.

After shutting the door, she leans against the wall for support and stands there, filling her lungs with fresh air. "Oh, my God, Janet. You were so right. He positively reeks."

Janet cautiously replies as if she's embarrassed to mention it, "Claire, I saw your face when Harry Delany said the guy looked like an Indian. Your face turned white."

Claire's head is spinning. "I was out of air. I truly thought I was going to pass out." Quick thinking on her part.

"Claire, one more thing," Janet says, "Harry isn't supposed to have bacon or gravy."

"Janet, dear, this one time, let's forget about his diet. Getting him clean and settled is our priority."

Finding Alex is easy. Explaining the situation while purposely withholding information isn't. Claire wants to tell Alex what she knows, but at this stage in their relationship, she deems it unwise. All she can figure out is that Harry's time is about used up.

Alex agrees to get a full description of the intruder while he helps Harry bathe. They decide that Claire, in turn, will look out for Doc to inform him that Harry is currently noncompliant. She wants to assure him that they're working on that. Doc will know exactly what's up.

Being busy taking care of other patients the rest of the day doesn't stop Claire from thinking about Frank and Harry. *Doesn't Frank know how he's affecting Harry? Of course, he does. Harry is throwing things at him.* Knowing that Frank is not part of Harry's psychosis definitely helps her understand his behavior.

Later, Claire sees Alex at the nurses' station and asks him how he got on with Harry. Before answering, he raises his eyebrows and makes a big production out of clearing his throat, "You owe me big time, Claire! I think a beer after work might make us even."

Claire bursts out laughing, "Sure, I do owe you. How about dinner? Tonight?"

Grinning, Alex says, "I'll be waiting right here for you so we can leave together."

Bending her elbow so they both can see her watch, Claire taps it. "See there? Our shift is almost over. Be on time, mister or I'll be eating and drinking for both of us."

Alex has a peculiar glint to his eyes as he states, "I'll catch up with you later."

Claire wants to check on Harry one last time before leaving for the day. Opening the door to 407, she feels uneasy. What will she find this time? Heck, a lot of days she feels this way, no matter which door she opens. Then she remembers the symbolism of doors—gateways to other worlds. Walking in to greet Harry is so much more pleasant this time. Claire can actually breathe. "Hey. Harry. Remember me, Claire?"

"Oh, yeah, right, Claire. Come to check in on me?"

"Right, Harry. Are you feeling better? I know that Doc visited you this morning." Claire quickly checks his chart. "I want to remind you that it takes time to become accustomed to new medications and to get the full benefit from your treatments. You may have symptoms that make you feel uncomfortable and sleepy. Have you noticed anything like that?"

"I'm tired almost all the time. And I haven't felt good for a long while so… well, I plain don't feel good at all."

"Harry, I'll make a note of that on your chart right now. We'll take care of you, and the doctor will adjust your meds if necessary." Trying to bond with Harry, Claire keeps talking, "Oh, I wanted to ask about that Indian guy. Did he come back? I want you to know we alerted security, and they're being more vigilant about visitors. I haven't heard anything more. Have you?"

"No, I haven't seen him again. And I didn't hear anything about him either. I don't want to see that injun again, ever!"

"Well, Harry, I have an idea. If he shows up, and I doubt he will, but in case he does, would you ask him what he means, *it's time?* It's obvious he isn't going to harm you. He would have already done that, don't you suppose?"

Harry furrows his brow, "I know he won't hurt me, but he wants me to go with him. I know what he wants. I just didn't tell you."

"Oh? Do you want to tell me now?"

Tears gather in Harry's eyes, "He says my time here is done. But... my kids... I..."

Claire's heart swells with love. She's relieved that he can trust her. "Harry, you just rest for now. We can figure it all out tomorrow. Do your children know you're here?"

"I don't know. They won't talk to me. They hate me."

"Harry, why don't I call them and tell them you're here? Would that be alright?" Harry's eyes shut, and she hears his rhythmic breathing as if the Sandman, had come to magically put him to sleep.

"Good, Harry, you rest." Claire says under her breath, "Tomorrow we'll see what we can do to fix this." As Claire turns to go, she finds herself three feet from Frank. She looks up and whispers, "You scared the daylights out of me."

"Don't worry. He'll sleep through our talk. And Claire, for the record, I'm not an injun." He flashes his smile, melting Claire's heart.

"Frank, we need to talk."

Chapter Eleven

"**F**rank, I know you help people cross over. But in Harry's case, you seem to be the crossing *the line.*"

"No, Claire. I am doing exactly what needs to be done. It isn't all about healing physical wounds. There are emotional wounds that require healing as well. Remember I told you that you are ready for more? This is what I meant. Together we are going to help this family before Harry leaves this sweet Earth. He knows it is his time, but he doesn't want to leave with his children hating him. His words, not mine. His children are merely protecting themselves from his inconsistent behaviors.

"In the past, as a father, a husband, and so on, he has displayed many unusual behavioral patterns. His thought projections are unpredictable, you see. He realizes this, yet to date, has been unable to correct them. Here is where you and I will assist in his healing, allowing the family to lay down past hurts as much as possible that is."

When Claire doesn't respond, Frank continues, "Claire, it is time you understand your function in an expanded manner. As a nurse, you don many robes. You are aware of the various and unique methods of communication. You practice these as you engage with your patients and others, and individuals with very specific needs."

"You are a nurse to heal the physical wounds, and a psychologist to aid with your patient's mental and emotional clarity. You even act as a mother who dotes on her children.

Sometimes, you take on the role of a student or daughter, allowing the patient to counsel you.

"You are a peace maker, a friend, a confidant. You are a true healer who, in fact, acts as a chameleon to support the soul in healing in whatever area is required.

"In this case, you will be assisting Harry in finding clarity, to understand why he pushes people away… why he feels threatened and vulnerable to such an excessive degree. This causes him to withdraw at times, while at other times he strikes out with harsh words or even with physical violence.

"He wears his own robe, a suit of armor to protect himself. In reality, he is distancing himself by pushing people away. Subconsciously, this makes him feel safer and somewhat impervious to disturbances of his psyche. The thing is, this robe of his isn't working. It's made of negative energy, which is pervasive and destructive. It is eating at his soul.

"Negative energy as does positive energy attracts more of the same. You see how it works? This suit, his armor, must be melted away, enabling his heart to open in order to trust himself to love. Our jobs are to assist in mending to the degree that forgiveness happens in the hearts of Harry and of his children, you see?"

Deep in contemplation, Claire realizes that Frank is a wise angel. What he presents is for the best, and she's in the perfect position to assist. But how? "Frank, how much time do we have? Harry's doctor is working on his medication. You know he has heart disease." She throws her hands up in resignation. "He has many chronic ailments, Frank. We really don't have a lot of time, do we?"

"Dear Claire, we have time enough. You'll see."

Curious to know if Frank is able read between the lines, impatiently she taps the face of her watch. "Frank, my shift ends in seven minutes. I want to be on time tonight."

He smiles knowingly. "Ah, yes, Alex."

She raises her eyebrows. "You know?"

Frank puts his right hand on his heart and says, "I know."

The *way* he says this fills her with amazement, but for now, her objective is to get to the nurses' station.

Giving Frank a sideways glance, she leaves the room. Claire begins to worry about going out with Alex smelling like Harry. She sniffs at her uniform. The stench is in her clothing and on her skin. Horrified, she reaches the unsettling conclusion that she has grown accustomed to Harry's smell. She laughs, *Oh well, if I stink this badly, I can't imagine how Alex must smell. It has been a long tedious day with not only Harry, but a few others who are also struggling. God love 'em anyway."*

Chapter Twelve

laire finds Alex waiting for her at the nurses' station. "Alex hey. I could use a hot shower and clean clothes. I've been in Harry's room."

"I hear you," Alex replies. "It's been one of those days for me too." He gives her a pointed look, then grins, letting her know he holds her partly responsible. "It's all part of the job, *right?*" Then, he winks.

"Um, how about we change the plan? You come over to my place after you shower. In the meantime, I can take a shower. We'll both feel so much better. I have a pizza I can pop into the oven and some salad fixings. How about you pick up a six-pack on your way over?"

"Oh, does that ever sound like a good idea. It's a deal. I'll be at your place between 8:00 and 8:30." Looking at Claire strangely, he asks, "Is that too late?"

"No, but we are scheduled to be here bright and early in the morning. Just want to remind you," Claire teases, but deep down, she's testing the waters. "You may want to bring your PJs with you."

"Oh, right, a slumber party. You know, Claire, I *am* a night owl." Then, as though he's done it a hundred times before, he slides his arm around her waist. "Besides, I travel light."

Claire looks into his eyes and sees a sea of emotions. Smiling, he adds, "You know we make a good team. Walk out with me?"

As they walk out, Claire notices that his curly, dark brown hair is beginning to gray at the temples. *Some guys just let things take their natural course,* she muses, *not trying to conform.* Quickly, she steals a glance, wanting to absorb everything about him. She watches how he carries himself. She's never looked at him like this before.

Alex has exceptional posture. His gait indicates that he's sure of himself, confident. With him, she feels natural and safe. He accepts her as his equal. But, even so, *will he treat me the same once he learns about the angel sightings and now the visitations?* She sighs.

There's a part of Claire that wants to confide in Alex, but she quickly rejects the idea. Up to now, she has told herself, there hasn't been a convenient time to talk. Certainly, at work there's no privacy. Now she sees that is a lame excuse. She wants to see if he'll fully accept her for who she is. At work, they're always rushing from one patient to the next. Sure, they have gone out to the pub a few times. One year, they joined a bowling league with several of their coworkers and had a great time. Why hadn't they continued bowling? She couldn't remember.

What Claire admires most about Alex is his inherent compassion and work ethic. He loves to help people. Sometimes he goes out of his way to lend a hand. She wants to know him better. But at work, she draws a line, making it clear that work is work. It's not a place to mix business with pleasure. Regrettably, she brought her work experiences home to her marriage, and that destroyed it.

Finally, Claire is opening up to the idea that she wants more—needs more than just a work relationship with Alex.

She can count how many times she has been attracted to other men. Over the years, she's had a few flings, but nothing ever came of them. Her marriage fixed that. She wonders if she'll ever trust anyone again. It always comes down to the same thing, by revealing too much, she'll likely jeopardize the friendship. Yet, if she can't be totally honest about who she is and her experiences, then is it really a friendship in the first place? *Is it time to try again?*

Like a true gentleman, Alex walks Claire to her car and tells her that he'll be over soon, then turns to go. Claire hadn't planned to, but she grabs his arm and says, "Wait, Alex. I'm serious about you staying over. Bring your toothbrush." She blushes. This is one time she's grateful for the freezing cold air. Feeling awkward, she abruptly releases his arm and turns to open the car door.

Casually, Alex puts his hand on top of the door frame, preventing her from shutting it. "Are you sure?"

"Oh, Alex, I have a spare room." Then she winks at him. *Let him be the one who wonders.* She knows there is sexual energy between them. Until now, she has successfully sidestepped those feelings and Alex as well.

Chapter Thirteen

On the drive home, the memory of what Frank said about Harry's suit of armor comes to the forefront of Claire's mind. Shocked, she realizes that his analogy applies to her as well. She swallows hard, then whispers, "I understand, Frank." Like Harry hiding behind his armor, she sees that she has been hiding behind her nurse's uniform and there's no reason to continue.

Once home and sitting in a nice, warm, relaxing bath, she thinks of Alex. She reminds herself that they have known each other for a long time, yet do they really know each other well enough? Claire sighs. She's felt Alex's energy for such a long time. Alex always jokes around with her as if he's testing her. Maybe it's time to do something about it. Certainly, she doesn't feel like having another roll in the hay and leaving it at that. She decides to see what happens.

Frank had said, *You are ready for more.* She blushes as images of Alex and her together play in her mind. Surely Frank's statement only applies to assisting her patients.

Then telepathically she hears someone say, "Do not compartmentalize my words, dear Claire. You are ready for more."

She knows it's Frank, but how? Not now. Claire assures herself that she'll get to the bottom of this later. Alex is due to arrive any minute.

Claire quickly dries off and dresses. She tidies her hair and dabs on a touch of jasmine perfume just as the doorbell rings. When Alex steps inside, she immediately notices how nice he smells. He smoothly says, "Hi sweetie. Here, take these, I want to get out of this coat." Handing her two bags and a bouquet of yellow roses, he swiftly takes off his coat.

Claire, noticing his expression, wonders if it's the frigid temperature or the fact that she asked him over. He appears relaxed, yet he seems a bit anxious. "Where do you want it?" Seeing her puzzled expression, he laughs and slowly says, "I'm referring to my coat, Claire."

He caught her. She was dreaming. Claire's face turns crimson. She swallows, "Ah, I wasn't quite sure, for a moment what exactly you were referring to."

"Okay, then." Their eyes meet and she feels a rush, the longing she has been pushing down, deep inside, for what seems like eons.

Claire smiles, taking his arm, guides him further into her living room. "Come in. Make yourself at home. I'll just hang your coat in the closet." She turns, "the pizza will be ready..." she's at a loss for words. It's as if she's seeing all of him for the first time.

Tonight, he has on a navy-blue pullover sweater and nice fitting blue jeans. "Oh my..." She stands there for a minute, not sure what she wants to say, then, "Alex, you look nice—real nice. Come in." Realizing she had already said that, they laugh. "I just put the pizza in the oven. Hope you like pepperoni, just in case, I have another one, veggie, has tomatoes, onions..."

Alex looks at her, very seriously.

"What?"

"Claire, I love pepperoni. That bag has the wine, I figured this is a special occasion. That's the reason for the wine and the flowers. Here, let me have that other bag. Where is your bathroom? I can put it in there."

Finding it difficult to speak, she points and replies, "Up there, to the right."

"Why don't you find a vase for the flowers. I'll be right back." He pauses, "I have something else to give you."

Under her breath, she murmurs, "I'm not sure how many more surprises I can handle." As soon as she hears Alex coming down the hall, she sings out, "In the kitchen, Alex. I want you to see my *new* kitchen and dining room."

Alex whistles low, "Looking fine, Claire. I didn't know you were an artist."

Claire throws her head back, laughing, "Oh, you don't know the half of it." *Not the half of it, Alex. I sure hope you don't run like Tom did.* With childlike anticipation, she says, "What is it you have for me?"

Taking her in his arms, he whispers, "Oh, a little of this…. I have been waiting such a long time, Claire."

She breathes deeply and whispers, "I know. Me too."

Breaking the embrace isn't easy, but then her stomach growls, reminding her of the pizzas. "I should get the pizza out of the oven. I'm sure it's ready." Pointing to the cabinet on the right of the sink, she says, "The wine glasses are in that one."

"Right."

Heading for the oven, all she can think of is, *I am ready for more.*

Chapter Fourteen

Talking between bites, Alex asks, "Claire, this isn't one of those frozen jobs, is it? I love the sauce and the crust is perfect. Very tasty."

"Oh, it's homemade. I love to cook. On my long weekends, I make extra. I used my mother's favorite recipe." They drink the wine until it's gone, both completely relaxed now. Claire nervously begins, "You know, Alex, I've wanted to ask you over for a while, but our schedules or something always conflicted."

"Yes, I wanted to ask you out too, but I was pretty sure you would say no."

Claire laughed, "Yep. I probably would have said no. I don't know what changed. Today I felt different, more relaxed. I feel comfortable with this. Not to put you on the spot but how do you feel with us together like this?"

"Heck Claire, it seems I've been waiting for eons for this moment to arrive. I am real good, thank you."

"I like your home. You've made it inviting."

"Thanks, Alex. I enjoy decorating. I'd like to do more to the place. I suppose I'll get around to it someday."

"Hey Claire, there's something I wanted to ask you.

Derrick told me you seemed troubled by your experience in room 407 last week. If there's a problem with any of our co-workers I'd sure like to know about it."

"What are you talking about?"

"Oh, the intercom, code blue for one of the patients. What happened, Claire?"

Instantly, she feels guarded, defensive. But she takes a deep breath. "First, tell me what you heard."

"Well, wasn't much to it, except that you responded to a call that no one else heard. What was that all about?"

"Right, well, as you probably know, I get these feelings when a patient is about to make their transition." She looks into his eyes to see if he's about to make a judgment. He appears to be neutral. He could easily be faking it and pumping her for information to see if she's certifiably crazy. Her face turns hot and red. She feels suspicious and afraid. She stops talking.

"Claire, it isn't uncommon for nurses to develop a keen sense of intuition concerning their patients."

"Well, right, but the other night, I was ready to leave. My shift had finished, then I heard the intercom. I heard the intercom, Alex. So, I went to 407 and found Jerry on the floor. At first, it looked like he'd fallen, but the rails were still up. He was all tangled in the IV lines and extremely confused. When I got down on the floor to assess him, I uh… …" She can't finish her sentence. She wants to tell Alex what happened that night, about what she saw, but she can't, not yet.

"So, you heard the intercom with a voice and everything?" he said with wrinkles between his eyes.

"Right! And you know what else?" She suddenly feels stronger. It's now or never. If this is going to be a deal breaker, then she wants to get it over with—the sooner, the better.

Instead of approaching it in a serious manner, she makes a joke, "I saw this really tall angel standing there waiting next to Jerry. You know what for, right? He was waiting for Jerry to... *Alex?*" Claire decides to quit acting. "Too much, right?" A single tear slips down her cheek. She shakes her head and keeps talking, "If you want me to stop I will."

Alex says nothing.

Claire's voice quiets as she continues, "Sometimes, I see angels, waiting for the patients to leave their bodies. It's the most beautiful experience. Yet, to talk of these things, well, I haven't, not to anyone, not until now."

Alex doesn't speak right away. She thinks he'll need some time to process what she's revealed. Politely, Claire excuses herself, thinking they could both use a moment alone. Returning the empty wine glasses to the kitchen, she can't help think Alex could be sneaking out the door. She can't decide which would be worse, if he left without saying goodbye or if they had a real conversation about things that happen at work.

Returning to the living room, she sees that Alex is still there. He's waiting on the couch for her. Claire feels a ripple of fear run through her.

He looks up and motions for her to sit next to him, patting the cushion. Taking her hand, he gently guides her. They sit in silence for a few minutes.

"Look, Claire, neither one of us is a stranger when it comes to death. Death is very much a part of our lives. Geez, we face it almost every day." He chose his words carefully. She knows it's his nature to be articulate, never wanting to alienate anyone because of the way he says something. She so admires him for this quality.

"Many of us have experiences with our patients that we would never talk about unless we felt we could trust the other person. These experiences defy logic. Claire, I trust you. Can you trust me?"

"Alex, there's more," Claire sighs.

"Yes, Claire, there's more, much more." Before they

begin to talk again, she wants to know in her heart that she trusts him completely. She thinks she does, but there remains a tiny part of her that holds back. "Alex, I think I want to go to bed. It's been a really long day." He nods his head in agreement and asks, "Where do you want me?"

"With me. Just with me."

Chapter Fifteen

Claire can no longer deny how she feels about Alex. Somewhere along the way, she fell head over heels in love with him. No doubt, she admits, she has always been attracted to him. They share a definite chemistry. Until now, she had avoided taking a risk, saying she wanted to remain friends.

Sitting in the corner posing as a wall flower isn't easy. It's time to stand up and move into the room, admit that she wants love, romance, companionship—someone to share her life with. But, being vulnerable is scary. Claire has been playing it safe by avoiding her feelings and staying out of relationships. She doesn't want to be hurt again.

All this time, fear kept her from getting serious with Alex. Her heart was calling out for love, yet she was not able to trust another man. She could not love or be loved. She felt her heart's desire with such intensity that it wasn't easy to describe in words.

He's right here. He's so easy to be with. We're molded to fit together perfectly.

She's no longer able to ignore what is right before her. Those fears are no longer holding her back. For the first time in a long while she feels free.

Over the years, in every conceivable situation at work, Alex proved himself to be trustworthy, someone she could rely on, and trust. Claire reminds herself that she wants someone she can confide in and feel completely safe with outside of work.

Last night, they were both tired. Nevertheless, sleep was the last thing on their minds. They crawled into bed beside one another, their desires spilled over into the early morning hours. Their bodies literally aching to touch, to be touched and caressed.

Claire thinks, *Alex is a good lover, slow and attentive. No doubt about that. Yup, to a T, he fits my idea of the man I want to share my life with.*

On her drive to work, Claire ponders her relationship with Alex. The idea that Alex is forty-two and never married nags at her. His lifestyle suggests he may have some sort of serious flaw. Once, he told Claire that he was much too busy for that nonsense. "Women are unpredictable, making them unreliable; more trouble than they're worth." His comment was dipped in sarcasm, like an ice cream cone coated with chocolate. As he was saying this, he looked Claire straight in the eye. She knew he was baiting her, testing her, and she saw straight through him. Then, he discretely winked at her and chuckled.

Although, Claire wonders, could he have been telling it like he really saw it, just covering it up with humor? *Did I misread his intent? Maybe he just wants to play the field?* Like a pendulum, Claire's thoughts swing back and forth, but she makes no effort to stop them.

It's easy to understand why the single nurses had gone after Alex in hopes of luring him into a relationship. He was comfortable to be around and had a kind face, his smile genuine. With his engaging personality he made friendship effortless. Then, there were the married ones; they loved to flirt with him as well. Alex is a charmer, always knowing the right thing to say, to please. Claire never discouraged his banter, yet she always made it clear that she wasn't available, wasn't interested in a relationship outside of work.

There had been a few times that good looking men with admirable qualities came her way. Always, she managed to find a plausible excuse to part ways, which ended up leaving her feeling ungrounded, restless. She convinced herself they lacked integrity or maturity, tricking herself into believing those escapades were a healthy way to release tension. In the long run, a relationship didn't seem to be worth it.

Actually, those relationships were shallow. Deep down, she wanted genuine passion, someone she could trust enough to be crazy in love with and share a profound commitment with—a partner who not only had great listening skills but enjoyed meaningful conversation as well. The man she ultimately chooses must have the awareness that there's more to life than ending up stiff and cold in the ground, no longer able to think or feel.

The breakup with Tom left her doubtful that there were any good men left in the gene pool, those who believed in God and were open to the mysteries of life. So she used her career as a shield, alienating everyone worth dating. How could she get involved with someone who had a narrow perspective on life and death?

Claire, you are ready for more. What exactly did Frank mean?

At The Manor, while the staff works to get Harry back on track, Frank remains elusive. She wonders if Frank will give her some direction. There must be something else she can be doing—should be doing. So far, Harry's only visitors have been a couple of friends from his car repair shop. Still, Claire anxiously awaits some sort of sign to show her how to assist in mending his family relationships.

Harry came to The Manor in such bad shape—physically, mentally, and emotionally. He was a broken man, angry and frightened. Heart attacks, incontinence, strokes, and finally, seeing ghosts can do that to a person. From his perspective, it seemed he had little to be hopeful about. Claire wonders if Harry thinks he's hallucinating? To think you're seeing ghosts that aren't really there *will* make you crazy. She wants to ask him about the *injun* again.

The staff understands that it's highly improbable that Harry's body will heal completely. In fact, it's only a matter of time before his passing. With that hanging over his head, Claire is surprised to see a slight but significant shift in his attitude. Some of the staff have commented that he's cooperating with them and acting a little friendlier. He's also experiencing longer periods of clarity. And he no longer complains about the person who bothered him when he first arrived at The Manor.

Claire feels confident that the worst is behind them, although Harry, to date, continues to reject bathing. Claire shrugs. She has witnessed this countless times before. He may be exercising his will as an attempt to keep some control in his life, regardless of how uncomfortable it may be for him. Claire sees how he works the requests the staff make until there's some sort of trade agreement that makes him feel like a winner in the end. Yet, for the most part, Harry appears to feel safe in their care. All they can do at The Manor is continue to give him first-rate care.

For several days, no one has passed on during her shift. For that, she's grateful. At work, Claire sees Alex in the hall, but she doesn't have a chance to connect with him on a personal level. They're both working twelve-hour shifts. She has one more day, then she'll be off for four days. She wants to ask Alex if his leave to go to Phoenix was approved. If he's going, she knows he'll be leaving soon. Finally, a little after three that afternoon, she feels caught up enough to actually go sit down with a cup of coffee in the break room. Before she goes, though, she walks down the hall to look out the window.

The sky is overcast and the harbor is foggy like so many days this time of the year. All of the boats are docked. *What a peaceful waterscape.* She studies the colors she would use to paint the water, the boats, the dock, and the sky. Maybe she'll dig out her oil paints, although, she sighs, she needs a new canvas.

Turning from the window, Claire shrieks as she almost collides with a shorter woman, with expressive features but a little younger than her. "Oh, excuse me!" Being friendly, she says, "I was just contemplating painting the scene. I sure could use a diversion about now."

"You're a nurse here, I take it?" the visitor asks.

"Yes, I am. My name is Claire."

"I figured as much with the scrubs and the name tag. I'm Bridget. Glad to meet you. I'm here to visit a resident."

"Oh, may I ask which one?"

"Harry Delany. He's my father-in-law."

Instantly, Claire knows her sign has just presented itself. "Bridget, have you seen Harry yet?"

"No, I'm waiting to meet my husband. We thought we would go in together."

"Harry's doing much better now. I'm sure you'll have a nice visit. It's time for me to go, though. I need to take a long overdue break. Maybe I'll see you later?"

In the break room, Claire is determined to take a full thirty minutes. Of course, she sighs, the coffee is cold. Going through the motions, she puts on a fresh pot then decides to have a burrito as well. Just as the microwave beeps, Alex walks in. "Hey there, Claire, it's a little slower today."

"Thank God! I sure need one. I wanted to ask you about Charles. Has the doctor scheduled him yet?"

"Yes, the thirteenth. In eleven days."

She walks over to the microwave and takes the burrito out. Disappointment sets in, "That's a long time to wait."

"Doc wants him stabilized; his white blood count is too low. It's a waiting game, and his surgery is considered high-risk." Alex sighs heavily as if he's carrying an extremely heavy burden.

"Yes, of course. They want the circumstances to be in their favor as much as possible. Alex, did you get the time off you requested?"

"Not yet... should know though, after this weekend." Alex pauses and looks at Claire. Then abruptly, his eyes brighten and his manner lightens, "By the way, are you booked for this weekend?"

"Booked?" she laughs. "That's a funny way to put it. No, I have no solid plans. Although, I do want to go to the art store and pick up a canvas. I have an idea for a painting. Alex, I really need a hobby." Alex suddenly looks serious. Clearly, he has something on his mind.

Claire hesitates before continuing, "I dabble in oils and water colors. Painting my kitchen and dining room the other day sort of inspired me."

"Did it now? I have always enjoyed the Museum of Fine Arts. Maybe we should drive over this weekend, make a day of it?"

"Yes, I'd like that. Maybe we could try that Greek restaurant out on Broadway? Oh, and go over to Fenway Park. I love that drive along Charles River."

Alex puts on his best Cheshire cat grin like he has just completed a huge accomplished. "Then it's a date?"

Fully realizing what just happened, Claire whispers, "Yes."

They sit for a while in silence, gearing up for another round of nursing. Breaking the stillness, Claire says, "Alex, I need to get back to my patients. Can we talk later to figure out the details?"

"Oh, hold on a sec. I have an idea. Why don't we plan a road trip? Go somewhere together?"

Wow… she almost wants to tell him to slow down a bit, but instead, the excitement takes over. "That's a great idea, but you'll be going to Phoenix soon, right?"

As if a terrible storm has just blown in, Alex's eyes cloud over, "We'll see. Later then?"

Claire nods, then makes her exit to go to room 407. As soon as she turns to go down the adjoining corridor, she notices a pressure in her solar plexus that turns into nausea, then light-headedness. Immediately, Claire wonders if it's a result of the burrito she ate. "Oh God, was that thing bad?" She makes them herself, using fresh ingredients, then immediately freezes them. She nixes the idea, remembering that she has recently eaten two out of that batch and felt fine. She shakes her head *this cannot be caused by that burrito.*

Suddenly, she stops walking and falls back against the wall with a loud thump, slowly sinking down to the carpeted floor, using the wall as a support until the sick feeling passes. Surprisingly, as quickly as the symptoms appear, they vanish.

Positive that she had broken out in a sweat, she wipes her brow and neck. "Shit! What was that?" Out of the corner of her eye, she sees a movement. Still on the floor, she looks up to see an eerie image of a patient ambling past her. He's elderly, wearing a green hospital gown and pushing a portable IV pole. Claire stares at the image, working desperately to make sense of what she's seeing, but the image remains fuzzy and ethereal.

Determining that the figure can't be attributed to her vision but instead to an apparition, she curses, "Damn it, lucky me!" She reassures herself; everything is okay. She continues to watch the elderly man as he shuffles down the corridor until finally, he disappears into thin air. Thinking she would like to call it a day, she looks at her watch, calculating the time left on her shift.

Alex, hearing the noise in the hall, jumps up and looks around the corner. Alarmed to find Claire on the floor against the wall, he says, "I heard a strange noise it… like something hit the wall out here. Was that you? Did you fall?" Then he sees her face, pale and withdrawn. "Claire, what happened? You're as white as a ghost."

"Thing is, no, I didn't fall."

"Can you stand?"

Looking up into Alex's eyes, Claire holds up her hand for him to take.

"What happened then?" Alex asks.

"I'm pretty sure I just saw a ghost patient go down the hall, right in front of me. He was hooked up to an IV drip." Working to compose herself, she involuntarily backs up against the wall again. Laughing to hide her true feelings, "Obviously, too many hours on duty. Are you seeing ghosts too?" They looked at each other.

Claire thinks, *Here it is, the dreaded deal breaker.* Claire wants nothing more than to run and shut herself in the nearest room and never come out again. She doesn't want to look at Alex, to see his concern. She just wants a way out.

Alex studies her ashen face, seeing the fear, he asks, "No, no ghosts. Really, are you okay?" At first, Claire doesn't answer. She tries to keep quiet and think through what, if anything else, she should say. Then, suddenly the words gush from her, "Well, as good as I can be after *that!*" In tears, she looks straight into Alex's eyes and says, "This type of *thing* is precisely what ended my marriage." She bit her lip, tasting blood.

Abruptly, the words pour from her, "Got to go, Alex." She can't manage anything else. She walks down the hall, feeling more than bewildered; she feels resigned. *That should do it alright. Alex is off the hook. I'm off the hook. I'll stop by after work to buy my canvas. No need putting it off now.*

Claire's plan to go to room 407 changes. She needs to make a pit stop in the ladies' room. Looking in the mirror, she sees the tears, confusion, sadness, and the blood. She really liked Alex. She'd been so close to telling him how she felt. Wanting to wash away the shame for something that's out of her control, she wipes her tears away, dabs at the blood, and takes several deep breaths. Hoping, if she splashes some cold water on her face, she may at least look normal.

Telepathically, she hears, "Claire, turn on the faucet, the water will help you feel better."

She waits for a few moments until she's satisfied with her color and composure. Then, Claire turns to leave, again she hears, "Claire, you have to get back to work. You have a job to do."

Claire says, "Frank?"

Chapter Sixteen

Without thinking, Claire walks to the nurses' station instead of room 407. Clearly, a change of plans is required. Unquestionably, she's not ready to face anyone after what just happened. All she wants is to sit and rest at her desk for a few minutes to gather her wits.

The other nurses are all leaving to care for their patients. Claire is relieved that she won't need to talk to anyone. Hoping that none of her patient's buzzers go off, she sits down, leans back in her chair, and closes her eyes to tune into her energy. She asks herself if she should go home sick. As soon as she opens her eyes, something unusual catches her attention—a medium-sized envelope is lying on top of her keyboard. Funny, she doesn't remember seeing it before.

The cream-colored paper is beautiful and obviously handmade by a very skilled artist. Her name is elegantly handwritten in a gold-metallic script. As an art enthusiast, she appreciates the overall presentation. Stunning, it's…just stunning. Absentmindedly, Claire runs her fingertips over the embossed lettering. She admires the calligraphy, wondering who it's from. *What's the occasion?* Finally, she turns the envelope over, ready to open it, when she sees the note—

Read when you get home.

How odd. Okay. Hastily, she tucks it in her pocket, then decides she shouldn't put off taking Harry's vitals any longer. Maybe his family has gone by now.

Several doors before reaching room 407, Claire hears loud voices. Instantly, she recognizes Harry's voice. *Bridget is here with Robert,* she thinks. *Oh great, Harry and Robert are at it. What more, God?*

Initially, Claire feels that remaining discrete would be the best option. Let them have their privacy. But instantly, she reacts to the raised voices and changes her mind. Like a mother bear watching over her cub, she boldly swings the door open and walks in, announcing her arrival, "Harry? Is there trouble?" Her gut tightens, seeing the tall man standing at the foot of the bed with his fists clinched. This must be Robert, Harry's son.

With ruthless determination, Robert abruptly turns to stare at Claire. At first, his stance doesn't change. Momentarily, he does not realize who has entered. The veins in his neck bulge; his body language is hard. Looking into his eyes, Claire sees contempt for all in his wake. Fear sweeps through Claire's body. But she will not back down. This is her domain after all.

She knows she must use caution. She places her hands on her hips, a posture that no one can mistake. She means business. She refuses to let him intimidate her; she won't back down. *Ah, the Delany temper… wonderful.*

Claire sees Harry's agitation. An important part of her job is to keep the residents calm and to protect them. Working to defuse the situation, she turns to meet Robert's unruly demeanor head on. As she looks into Robert's eyes, she unexpectedly points out the positive, "Harry, you have visitors!" Seeing Bridget, she joyfully says, "Oh, Bridget! You made it. This must be your husband?"

Still holding her coat, Bridget searches Harry's face, then

Robert's, looking for a clue of how to proceed. She's perplexed by Claire's greeting and equally hopeful that Robert regains his composure. The last thing they need is to have security escort them out.

Bridget looks into Claire's eyes before saying, "Claire. Hi. Oh, yes, we made it alright. This is Robert. I have the feeling we should be going." Claire hears the tightness in her voice like she's pleading, yet she hears relief as well. Bridget continues, "You have to check him, right?"

"Yes, it's time to check his vitals. We have to make sure our man here is doing well." Claire makes a notation in his chart that his blood pressure is elevated. "Maybe you two can take some refreshments downstairs in the cafeteria and come back in a few?"

After they shut the door behind them, Claire casually says, "Harry, you need to breathe deeply several times. Your blood pressure is up. Look, at me, Harry. Breathe with me, okay?" Together they take several deep breaths until the numbers begin to drop and level off. "There we go. Good job. Harry?" No answer. "Harry, do you want your family in here? You seemed to be upset when I arrived."

"I don't know what I want." He pauses for several moments to calm himself before saying, "Every time we talk, we end up yelling. He tries to tell me what to do like I'm a stupid little kid. He has no right! Then, I get mad as hell and yell at him. I deserve some respect, you know. I raised that kid!"

As he speaks, his heart rate spikes again. "Harry, stop. Look at me, breathe with me. Think of something you like. How about the boys down at the shop? How much you enjoy being with them? Or maybe think about walking in the woods, swimming in the ocean, or warming yourself on a bench in the park?"

Still working to get Harry to focus, Claire raises her voice for more emphasis. Kneeling down beside his bed, she continues, "Mr. Delany? *Harry!* I know that you must be frustrated by what happened with Robert just now."

When she gets his attention, she reaches for the monitor

and pulls it toward him. She explains, "See this machine?"

Harry nods.

"You see these numbers in the upper right corner? That's your pulse, your heart rate. We call them bpm or beats per minute. We want to keep the numbers between 70 and 100. I know you can tell by the way you *feel* when your heart rate escalates. But maybe if you look at it, study it…" her voice trails off as she watches his facial expression. He needs extra help with this. "So, Harry, what do you think? Should we practice this technique, or do you think it doesn't really matter if you're calm?"

Harry stares at her, like he wants her to leave. He swallows, then bellows, "I have said this a hundred times before, I do not like being talked down to. I have no use for anyone who tries to make me feel guilty!"

"Harry," Claire patiently explains, "You know that I have no reason to do that. What I do want is to see you make the improvements necessary in order for you to go home. It's in your best interest to learn to breathe, not only when you're faced with some sort of adversity, but to breathe to heal your body. More oxygen means the body is receiving what it requires to regenerate and to maintain itself." Claire sighs, wondering if she's getting through to him. Perhaps he's simply too agitated from the encounter with his son. "Harry?"

Finally, he looks at Claire like he's ready to listen. "Harry, listen to me. This is what I want you to do. I'm going to come back later. You know how busy we all get around here, but I'm going to make you a deal. I'll come back and *together* we'll practice breathing."

"Look Claire, I know you want to help me. But really, why?" Harry begins coughing and clears his throat. Claire notices the beads of sweat collecting on his brow. "I don't have much time left. Why bother with any of this? Why bother with me?"

"Ah, I get it. You're using the famous 'wear down the nurse routine' so we'll leave you alone. Ha. Well, guess what buddy. I know that one." At that, Harry glares at Claire until she laughs. "Harry, I like you! You are stubborn as a mule and tenacious! By the way, those are two traits I admire in a man. This means you are more apt to succeed when you put your mind to something."

Claire closes her eyes, taking a deep breath as she examines her feelings for Harry. He certainly is a challenge, but there's something about him. She feels a deep compassion toward him. Maybe she knew him in a past life.

"Harry, the goal here is to learn to relax. By learning to breathe slowly and deeply, you'll learn to control your beats per minute, keeping them within an acceptable range. I want you to practice lowering your pulse with this technique. Breathe deeply and slowly as you envision yourself in a place that's beautiful and peaceful, a place where you feel calm. Tell me what place that might be."

Surprised that Harry was willing to try this exercise, she watches him sink deeply into his fluffy pillow and close his eyes as he wills himself to remember something, anything, that made him happy. Claire sees his jaw relax and a slight smile emerges. His voice takes on a raspy edge, "When I was a teenager and went to the beach almost every day."

Claire asks, "Where was that?"

He looks thoughtful before he replies, "Oh yeah, a beach in San Diego."

"Oh, which one? What was the name of that beach?"

"Pacific Beach. Oh, yes, that's it. I used to hang out there when I was a kid. I really liked that place."

"Okay, then, perfect. You're now on your favorite beach. See yourself doing what you love." She sits on the side of his bed to join him. Closing her eyes, she exclaims, "The sand feels so warm between my toes, and the sun feels so good on my skin. I hear the waves crashing. The sea gulls are screeching. Harry, these birds are really noisy. I don't know...? They're a bit obnoxious. Oh, Harry, look at the kids surfing. Wow, this is a neat place. What do you feel...? What do you see...? What do you smell…? What do you hear?" Each time Claire asks a question, she waits long enough for him to remember.

Harry smiles. "There was a hot dog stand near Crystal Pier. Those were the best hot dogs!" Then He pauses before he continues, his voice filled with emotion, "I met my wife on that beach. She was so pretty. I see her long blond hair blowing in the ocean breeze.

"Back then, she was a little thing. I can still hear her laughing." He stops speaking as tears fill his eyes. Then he quietly says, more to himself than to Claire, "It won't be long now 'til I get to be with her again."

"What's her name, Harry?"

"Patti Jo, Patti Jo Malone. She died six years ago. Cancer."

"I'm so sorry Harry. She's Robert's mother?"

"Yes, and Augusta's."

"You have two children?"

"Yes." He pauses, then says, "I'm tired now."

"Harry, I know you're tired. But before I go, can you help me with something? Before I came in, the weirdest thing happened to me. I saw this man walking down the hall. The perplexing thing is that he was all fuzzy, and I could see through him. I think he was a ghost. I've never ever seen anything like that before. Did you see him, Harry? Has he been in here?"

Harry's eyes widen like he thinks she is off her rocker, then he slowly shakes his head, no.

Deflated, Claire says, "Oh I thought that way our man. You should rest. It has been a a big day."

Claire watches him close his eyes and listens to the rhythm of his breath slow down. He falls asleep. Satisfied, she turns to go and sees Frank. Knowing he was watching them, she waits for him to speak. He says, "Claire, we should talk."

"Right. Can it wait until I get home? Maybe you can stop by then?"

"I'll plan to."

Then he's gone.

Chapter Seventeen

Apparently, Bridget and Robert didn't stick around. Perhaps, today, that's all for the best. Fortunately for Claire, everything was routine for the rest of the day, and she was able to focus on her patients rather than on Alex. What he must be thinking of her by now.

On her drive home, thoughts of the dog, Alex, and what she would have for dinner swirl around in her head. She's surprised she thinks of the dog, she hasn't in a long while. She doesn't feel hungry but knows she should eat. She feels empty, forlorn, and love sick. Claire stops by the art store to buy a canvas, hoping that painting will fill the incessant void.

It isn't until she's home that she remembers the letter. Pulling the envelope out of her pocket, she again studies the heavyweight paper. Claire looks closely at the handwriting as if it might give her a clue as to who on earth gave her this. Claire is impressed at the graceful, old-world elegance of the writing.

She reaches for an afghan for extra warmth before she sinks into her rocking chair. Midway, she changes her mind, knowing from past experience that if she sits down now, she'll have a difficult time getting up later for a shower or even to fix her dinner. Instead, she opts for a frozen entree to bake while she showers. *Setting aside the mystery is best for now,* she tells herself.

She remains in the shower longer than usual, hoping to wash away the memory of the entire day. Seeing that ghost… she laughs, then she cries. She's not sure that a hundred hot showers will ever erase that image. *And Frank said I'm ready for more. Is this part of his plan?*

As the hot water pours down over her body, Claire uses the same technique that she does at The Manor to release pent-up emotion. She begins by imagining herself looking intently into a roaring fire. The glorious orange, red, blue, and golden flames leap high fed by the oxygen-rich air; the tongues meld and transform into different hues, shapes, and sizes.

Becoming one with the energy, she breathes deeply, acknowledging her fear concerning the ghost. She assures herself that what she saw was nothing more than an apparition, and it cannot hurt her. She empties her mind of everything that has happened and continues to breathe deeply. At last, she notices a release, then she moves into feelings of gratitude for the gift. She's sure there's a higher purpose for everything that happened today.

Searching her memory for more fear, she sees herself with Alex and the way she acted. She felt like a child, so insecure and exposed. She wanted to run and she did. Knowing that her fear stems from past experiences with her ex, she recognizes a pattern. She now knows the truth.

Claire is afraid that Alex will follow suit by finding fault with her, quitting the relationship before they even get started. She asks herself if she really believes that? Before she answers, she begins to breathe again and prays, "God, I know I'm afraid—that I feel vulnerable, and in some ways, sometimes, I just don't feel that I'm good enough to have a man in my life who will truly trust me and believe in me, who will love me for who I am. Please God, give me the strength to face Alex again, even if he decides that he doesn't want to be with me. Please, let us always remain friends. I trust that you have my back."

Continuing to breathe deeply, Claire fully relaxes, allowing her fears to be released and then affirms her strength and her willingness to try again. "God, please give me the grace and humility to face my fears and to admit them to Alex so we can start anew. I want to be happy again." She knows there's probably more to say, but the hot water is gone.

After dinner and dishes are put away, she can't find any more excuses to put off opening the letter. She wonders if she's deliberately avoiding it.

Once again, she picks up the envelope. For a few moments, she again admires the penmanship, immersing herself in its beauty. The letter doesn't want to slide out because it fits so snuggly in the envelope. Working to free it, she imagines the message wants to remain a mystery. She chooses not to force it, lest she spoil the contents. "Somethings are worth waiting for," she affirms.

Slowly, she unfolds the letter and smooths out its creases, again noticing the lovely script, which is identical to the envelope. She moves to the end of the letter. It's signed by Frank. Her heart skips a beat.

Dearest Claire,

As humans, your journeys are often fraught with adversity. Remember, though, nothing of great value comes without merit.

You are taking a personal journey. The road you travel is laid out to include many interesting vistas. There are all sorts of stimuli that pull at your attention, causing you to question which way to turn or how to go forward. At times, these options distract you from your higher purpose, sometimes for many years or even lifetimes. And there are times you question some of the choices you make.

Are they benefiting you? Are they preventing you from reaching your destination, the place where you can at last rest, the place you call home?

As you review your journey, you easily recognize those times that have been arduous and demanding; to the point, you felt worn to the very core of your being. You required rest before once again, you could pick up and continue onward. This, dear One, has always been the way.

Deep down, you remember that there were precious moments in life when you were truly happy, at peace. Because of these memories, you tentatively seek out inspiration to bring forth excitement, joy and new ways to expand your knowledge, resulting in satisfaction and contentment. Yet, there is more. You desire balance, an equilibrium of all feelings that are a direct result of careful consideration and decisions made.

In a nutshell, as a social being, you desire total acceptance and unconditional love, which allows you to experience the "treasure"—a wide array of positive emotions. These emotions give you fuel to continue your quest for happiness and eternal life.

Know that the road you walk is never traveled alone and is never-ending. You are guided, assisted by those who are residents of the angelic realm and by the ascended masters, your spiritual guides. Although you receive this guidance, ultimately, you draw from your own individual, unique store of experiences.

Always, you are supported by those in the angelic hierarchy. Contrary to your belief, the Godhead, The Infinite and Eternal Source of All Life, has always accepted and loved you unconditionally every moment of every day.

Dear One, it is because of the robe you have donned, your human form, that you, at times, feel frail and unworthy to accept the treasures that lay before you.

My purpose for these words is to show you a broader perspective. I am honored to be the one who entrusts you with this additional wealth, which you have earned by sharing an open heart while in service. To assist you in better service, you were chosen to receive this gift in the form of this letter. You are ready for more.

All experiences lead you down the path to knowledge and wisdom. All choices that you label good or bad or even indifferent are magnificent opportunities for you to use as a springboard to opulence, not only for yourself but for others and in all ways including love and companionship. It is through experience that you learn to choose what is best in all circumstances.

Look at your walk. You have chosen wisely the path of nursing because it serves as a catalyst for healing on all levels. You have attained the knowledge and wisdom to assist others, helping them move through their own lives as well as through the intimate passage to the afterlife, which is so often referred to as death.

As a healer, you are a facilitator who assists in bringing alignment to the four lower bodies, which consist of the mental, emotional, spiritual and physical bodies, and aid in the release of the soul from the physical body.

You are aware that healing takes place in degrees as well as on many levels, and that it is accomplished by the contributions of many modalities.

Your method is to love unconditionally, supporting your patients by offering a listening ear and, when appropriate, advice and instruction to aid in recovery. Using a healing touch, you transfer a higher frequency that stimulates the molecular structure to accept an increased flow of life force or prana.

And finally, you administer medicines specifically chosen for alleviating symptoms and for healing the physical body of identified disorders. Never do you judge. True healing is a result of unconditional love for self and others.

Look before you, Claire. See the beauty before you. Trust that your vision is clear. Walk on, dear One.

In Love,
I AM Frank

While she read, tears silently slipped down her cheeks. When the first teardrop landed on the paper, she thought the ink would run, but the tears dried and vanished as if never there. She was grateful the letter suffered no damage because it would later serve as a reminder of the blessings in her life.

With this letter, she feels as though her life is taking on a new meaning—a new direction. Examining some of her choices in life, she thinks of her current patients and how she might better serve them. She sees their many faces, knowing of their relentless pain and their desperation to be free of it.

Claire is sensitive to the fact that many of the patients are now shut-ins, no longer able to leave The Manor for any of the reasons others may take for granted, such as taking a leisurely stroll, shopping, or visiting friends and family. When some of the patients are admitted, they're completely withdrawn, the light in their eyes is dim, their energy is almost gone. It's an honor to be a part of a team who cares, wanting nothing but the highest good for their patients.

After a few days of care, some of the patients begin to smile again; their faces take on a healthier appearance. She knows it's not medication alone that assists their healing. Claire has made it a point to visit with the patients, not only to be social, but she understands that through this socialization, the patients have an opportunity to interact and communicate. This is important for healing.

To see a portion of light return to so many, if only a small degree is gratifying. Some open up and share bits and pieces of their lives or show an interest in hers, but that's not always the case. Some patients just don't get better. Even so, she continues to treat them as she would want to be treated.

Claire's phone rings. Glancing at the clock, she realizes that she has been ruminating for over an hour. When she sees who is calling, she hesitates. It's her mother, Margaret. Since Claire's father passed over, her mother has been depressed and a bit on the needy side.

"Mom, hi. Do you know what time it is? I was just about to turn in. You barely caught me."

"Claire dear, I certainly do know what time it is. I figured you would be up at least for another hour. Do you have tomorrow off?"

"No. Last day, though, before my weekend. What's up?"

"I want to go to the cemetery tomorrow. Remember, it's the anniversary…" Her mother stops speaking. Claire hears her sniffle and blow her nose, "Oh, Mom, I know. But I have to work tomorrow. Maybe you could ask someone else to drive you. How about your neighbor, Audrey. She might be able to take you. You like her, right? You two seem to find plenty of things to do together."

"No, Claire. This is different, too personal. Your dad…"

Claire hears her mother sniffling.

"Well, I just… I don't think Audrey would want to be involved in such an intimate affair."

"Maybe not, but you'll never know unless you ask, right? I'm sure she would give you your privacy."

"You're right Claire. She probably wouldn't mind. I'll figure out something. I may just wait until you're off so we can go together."

"Mom, I have tentative plans. *Claire don't lie here.* A friend from work asked me to go out of town this weekend. You know, road trip. We're about to firm up our plans."

Her mother replies, "Oh, where are you going?"

"Thinking of Philadelphia. There's an expo on home care." *Claire, what are you doing?* "Mom, it's late, and I have a couple of things to finish before bed. Are you okay? You sound like you've been crying."

"Oh, got the sniffles is all. I'm okay. I miss you, honey."

"I know, Mom. Let's make a date for my next weekend off. I'll take you out for breakfast. How would that be?"

Claire hears her disappointment. "That sounds really nice, Claire. I hope you have a good time on your road trip."

"Well, if I end up staying home, I'll call you. You know it's freezing cold out there. But if you still want to go the cemetery, I totally get it. I'll take you. Okay?"

"Sure Claire, good night."

"Night, Mom."

Claire disconnects, not understanding her motives for what she just told her mom. She just lied to her own mother. Claire feels a measure of shame; she doesn't have any plans for this weekend. She senses the heartache as she thinks about the ideas that Alex suggested. Placing her hand over her heart, she sobs.

As she lies to her mother, she begins to lie to herself. She tells herself that Alex will conveniently forget he ever said anything about going to the museum or on a road trip. She feels like she has lost her best friend. But she reminds herself that she can go without him; she can go anywhere without Alex. She loves the Museum of Fine Arts. *But I love him.*

Concerns about her mother's well-being seep in and take over. What can she do for her mother? If she does too much for her, she'll become dependent on her just like she did with her father. Claire wishes her father was still alive. Once again, the tears flow.

Chapter Eighteen

Near the end of Claire's shift, she reflects on how the pace at The Manor has increased with the admittance of two new residents who arrived earlier that day. She guesses, even if he wanted to, Alex had no free time to connect privately with her. In passing, he was pleasant enough, but she noticed that he was not his usual jovial, lighthearted self. She admits, she too was centered in her own thoughts, wanting to make the new patients as comfortable as possible.

Even so, there were moments when each caught a glance of the other. In spite of the hectic schedule, Claire wishes Alex would give her a sign to let her know everything is okay. Maybe it's just best to forget what happened, to forget about Alex.

Suddenly, she straightens her posture, and shifting her attitude, she declares, "Darn it all! I'm just feeling sorry for myself. For the last twenty years, I have survived on my own just fine, thank you!"

A vision of the dog flashes through her mind, and without any pre-planning, Claire decides to visit the animal shelter this weekend. Perhaps she can find a dog or a cat. She has heard that animals are more sensitive to the energies of spirits, making the perfect companion for her. Except, she contemplates, the long hours she works may be too much to properly care for the animal.

⸻

Claire feels like she's treading water, going nowhere in particular any time soon. She desperately wants to see results in some area. She telepathically calls to Frank. *Frank, where are you? This deal with Harry doesn't seem to be going all that well. Is there something I can do to speed up the process?*

At the end of her shift, Claire goes down the hall to look out the window. She loves seeing the lights reflected on the water at night. She can almost hear the water slapping against the boats docked there. The monotonous motion of the boats rocking back and forth in the harbor has a soothing effect on her psyche. There are no ducks, sea gulls, or pelicans hanging around the harbor in hopes for a handout. Not tonight. Before she turns to go, Harry comes to mind as if he had summoned her. She decides to look in on him one last time before she leaves. What she wants to do is not unusual for her because most evenings, she finds an excuse or two to stay a little longer.

Standing in the doorway, she sees Harry sleeping soundly. Quietly, Claire prays, "God, please watch over him and the others while I'm away. Please keep everyone mindful of their duties. Keep everyone safe." As she turns to go, she almost runs into Alex. "Oh. Alex! I didn't expect to find you here."

"Hey, sorry. I didn't mean to startle you like that. I'm surprised to see you're still here."

"You know me. I like to hang around. Nothing going on at my place."

Alex tenderly asks, "Are you ready to leave? Can we walk out together?" He pauses, waiting for her to answer. "Claire?" Taking her chin, he guides her to meet his gaze. "Shouldn't we talk? I thought we had a deal."

"What? You mean this weekend?" Claire waves her hand like it was of no importance. "Alex, you have *no* obligation whatsoever. I'm officially letting you off the hook. I know what yesterday looked like, but I'll not apologize for my behavior. It is what it is.

"That incident was really strange. Suddenly, I felt sick. I saw this guy, a patient, obviously deceased, with a drip line walking down the hall." She shivers, "Totally caught me off guard. The thing is…." She stops. She has no desire to explain herself to him or to anyone for that matter.

"Claire, it's okay. Look, I know you see stuff. Most of us know that you are *hooked up*. Shoot, I even see stuff sometimes. Although lately, I haven't seen anyone taking strolls down the corridors." Smiling, Alex holds out his hand.

All at once, her resolve crumbles into tiny bits and pieces, then it vanishes. She takes his hand, and in one smooth motion, he pulls her close and gives her a hug. "See there, this isn't so bad. Is it?"

Claire pulls away to playfully punch Alex in the arm. "You are a big flirt, Alex." She had been so sure he thought she was nuts. Relieved, Claire rolls her eyes, mocking him. Grinning, he takes her hand and kisses her palm. "Why don't we go for coffee and just talk?"

As if they had been planning it all along, Claire exclaims, "If we're going for coffee, I want a yummy sweet roll too… maybe a maple long john or a cherry Danish! Those are my favorites!"

Alex's face lights up. "You know, for a little thing, you sure can eat. What about Bova's on Salem? Open twenty-four hours. Pretty sure they have anything you could want. We can drop your car off at your house and take mine."

Her eyes twinkle at the thought of indulging herself after a hard day of work. This being the last day of her week, she's doubly grateful for Alex's suggestion. Ironing out her perceived troubles gives her a reason to celebrate.

Walking to her car, she has time to think. The frigid air brings her back to her sensibilities regarding the ghost she saw, followed by her confession to Alex. But really, why should she be afraid to talk about what has become a normal thing for her. She murmurs, "Why am I afraid? Is it that old childhood thing? To be different is to *not* be normal. We should blend in, not be noticed, not stand out. In other words, to be different is to be noticed. Good grief."

Thinking back, when Claire talked to her husband, she presented herself as unique, someone that Tom could not relate to. It was that distinctive quality that caused a schism in their relationship, finally ending it. Being different means she won't be accepted by some people, she realizes that now. It all makes sense.

She snubbed Alex because she was afraid of becoming an outcast. Being included and then unexpectedly excluded feels awful. She knows that. Claire groaned fully realizing that her ego had been in charge. Above all she wants to be honest. She's just beginning to let herself relax with Alex and it feels good—really good. But still, there are certain things that are better kept to herself, no matter how she feels.

Alex's statement replays in her mind, "We can drop your car off at your house and take mine." That would mean they would go back to her place after coffee. Does he have an ulterior motive? Ah, she thinks she's seeing the correct picture now. He probably just wants a roll in the hay. Just as she has the thought, she regrets it. *Nice Claire. How could I think that about him? He's the nicest guy I know.*

With what seems an inordinate amount of effort, she pushes her thoughts aside. She has created an ugly habit of examining what people say and assigning her own spin to it, thinking the worst, or more accurately, being suspicious of others for some reason. *Why can't Alex just want to spend time with me? What happened to having a good time with a friend because you enjoy their company?*

As it turns out, they buy coffee and pastries to go and drive to the waterfront. It's a beautiful night, although a bit chilly. After catching up on their days' events, they both confess they need a good night's rest.

Neither one of them mentions a sleep over, but it's on their minds. If they would be honest with each other, that's exactly what they want to do. Instead of addressing any feelings,

Alex asks, "Claire, do you still want to go to the museum this weekend?"

"I think I need tomorrow to rest and putter around the house, to just be. Maybe we can go in a day or two. How's that sound?"

"I think you're a wise woman. I need some time myself. This week has been a bear, but I have news—my leave was approved. I'll be taking two weeks off, and I have some preparations to do before I go. It looks like there will be no vacations for me in the near future."

Claire doesn't hide her disappointment, "Oh, I was hoping that…"

Alex jumps in, "I know. I know. We're barely getting started and then I go off again." Then he emphasizes, "I plan on being away for only two weeks. Claire, the time will pass quickly."

Being tired causes Claire to feel more vulnerable, out of balance. Being a bit emotional, she blurts out, "I hope so Alex. There are so many things we should talk about and then there are the things… " Claire's voice softens as she continues, "… that I want to experience with you." She laughs, "Oh dear. Are we really dating?"

Although the car is wrapped in shadows, she watches Alex's face for any clue of how he feels. Did she cross a line? Instantly, she relaxes as Alex turns to her. The kiss is light at first but quickly rekindles the longing she feels, the flame that's ever present.

As she pulls away, she sees his lip quiver ever so slightly. "Claire, what I feel for you now, I have felt for such a long time. I'm drawn to you and to your energy. I wonder if you're afraid that I'll drop you just like your ex did. Is that why you've held back for so long?"

Stunned by his level of observation, she's unable to answer him at first.

"Claire?" Alex continues, "Are you okay with us learning about one another in a very personal way?"

"Alex, I think I'm ready. I still have moments when I want to run, but I figured out what triggers that. In other words, I think I understand what I'm afraid of." She pauses, "I believe I can change the pattern, but just so you know, right now I'm cautious, real cautious."

"I have about a week before my flight. Part of that will be working. How about I call you day after tomorrow? Maybe we can at least go for a bite to eat?"

"Okay let's do that. I'll be thinking of ideas tomorrow while I'm … Oh. I forgot. I made a commitment to myself to go to the shelter this weekend to pick out a pup. Maybe you can join me?"

Nodding, he confirms, "Yup, you're ready. Call me tomorrow after you figure out what day you want to drive over."

With no hesitation, Claire asks, "What about tomorrow?"

Alex agrees, "Okay. I know we just talked about taking time tomorrow to do our own things, but you're right. If you want a pet, it'll need as much time as possible in its new environment before you return to work. The two of you should get to know each other and bond."

Suddenly, Claire is overwhelmed. "Maybe I should nix the idea. I work too many long days to have a dog."

"No, I think it's a good idea to at least see what they have. Know your options."

Claire agrees.

Pulling up in front of her house, Alex says, "Claire, it's best to not overthink these things. Listen with your heart."

"Oh, Alex, thank you for saying that. I guess you've noticed that I have that side of me that wants to pick everything apart—to analyze."

"A little, that's all," he smiles.

Claire keeps talking as she steps out of the car. "But realistically, it wouldn't be fair to a dog to leave it alone for so long during the day."

"I wasn't talking about the dog. I was talking about us."

"Oh, right. How did you know I was doing that, as well?"

"Just an educated guess, that's all."

Opening his door, he steps out, "Claire, wait, I have something for you."

Feeling the cold wind cut through her, all she wants to do is to unlock the door and get inside. She takes a few steps when she hears Alex calling her. She stops and turns around. Alex is trying to catch up with her. "I said I have something for you, Claire. Here take this." He holds out his hand for her to take.

"What?"

All the street noises become muted as he pulls her close. "I love you, Claire."

She's moved to tears and unable to respond to his declaration. After a moment, he releases her. "Claire, call me tomorrow, will you?"

Claire tries to speak, but there's a catch in her throat. She waits until she's calmer before saying, "Of course, Alex."

Chapter Nineteen

Morning arrives way too soon. Claire stays in bed for another forty-five minutes, hoping that she'll drift back into a blissful sleep. Not happening. She shifts her focus to getting out of bed and enjoying a hot cup of coffee. Throwing on her robe and slippers, she walks to the bathroom to splash cold water on her face. As she enters the kitchen, she catches the smell of freshly painted walls, reminding her of the journey that finally brought her to this place.

Long shadows play around the room, indicating that she has at least another hour before sunrise. She flips on the light, admiring the beauty that flows through her kitchen but acknowledging that it will take some time to get used to it. A swell of gratitude runs through her as she marvels at the appearance and feel of her *new* home.

Reaching to open the cabinet door to get a coffee mug, she suddenly feels an eerie sensation; the hairs on the back of her neck stand up. She braces herself against the cold countertop and takes a deep breath, waiting for the feeling to pass. When it doesn't ease up, she feels sure she won't get out of this one so easily. Under her breath she murmurs, "Just turn around Claire. Get this over with. There's nothing here that will harm you."

The self-encouragement doesn't work. Solely out of self-preservation, she postpones her *meeting* by focusing on the smells in the kitchen—the latex paint mingling with the coffee's rich, nutty aroma. She decides it's not at all appealing.

Accustomed to these peculiar feelings, she reaches for her mug. This time, she directs her attention inward and how it feels instead of focusing on her logical thoughts wanting to make her believe she's in danger. Taking her mug from the cabinet, she notices her movements seem exaggerated, even surreal. The counter-top is grounding her somewhat, reducing the sensation and making it more tolerable. She begins to breathe deeply, holding the prana in her body for four counts before exhaling. As a rule, this helps to relax her. She wants to sit down but she's afraid to turn and see what's causing this sensation.

In a hushed tone, she begins to reason with herself, "Claire, you can't stand here all day. Whatever is here can't hurt you. It's probably someone from The Manor."

Inwardly, she chuckles at the absurdity of her conclusion. With all her will, she turns to confront the source of her discomfort, finding an image similar to an impressionistic painting in the style of Monet, Pissarro, or Degas, only this is three-dimensional and semi-transparent. Before her sits an older man in a well-used wooden rocking chair, smoking a long stem pipe. As Claire watches him rock, she slides into a hypnotic trance that holds her prisoner for a few moments. She shakes her head to free herself of his supernatural grip.

The old man wears wrinkled khaki work pants, much too large for him, with a white, short-sleeved T-shirt. His skin looks like leather, dark brown with deep creases, like he's been outdoors most of his life, and he's rather thin. His bony toes are unnaturally white with gnarly long jagged toenails. His greasy hair is black, streaked with silver. His black eyes are expressionless. Because he's sitting, it's difficult to gauge his height, but he's probably less than six feet tall. Claire thinks he's in his sixties.

She shrugs, wondering what she's supposed to make of this. *Maybe if she speaks to him?* She greets him like he's her guest. "Hello there, I'm Claire. Who are you? Can I help you?"

The man smokes his pipe as he stares into the distance, never looking at Claire or speaking. He seems unaware that he's sharing the same space with anyone or that anyone is speaking to him.

Like a magic trick, the image shimmers and fades away, leaving her feeling a bit unsettled with several unanswered questions. Pushing the episode away as though today is exactly like any other day, she pours her coffee and goes into the living room to relax and to get the episode out of her mind. Chuckling, she thinks, *Well at least I didn't feel sick this time.*

Sitting in her recliner, her mind begins to systematically explore different areas of her life that evidently require further examination. Glancing at the clock, she sees it's still quite early and she's grateful for the luxury of time in this moment; she has the day off.

Her thoughts turn to her mother, who's likely sound asleep. *Heck, these days she sleeps more than she's awake.* Losing her husband has been tough on Claire's mother. For as long as Claire can remember, her father drove her mother everywhere. As far as she knows, her mother never had a reason to take the T or a bus.

She contemplates calling her mother. She agreed to call Alex and go to the shelter, but she's concerned about her mother. Even so, Claire acknowledges that she needs a private day to rest.

Instead of making breakfast, Claire runs a hot salt bath with some essential oils. Then she fixes bacon and eggs with whole wheat toast. By noon, she has completed all her chores. She finds a good book to keep her company but after reading three chapters, she's unable to sit still any longer.

Deciding to connect with her mother, she picks up the phone and pushes speed dial. After several rings Margaret answers. "Mom, are you still sleeping?"

"No, just sitting here looking out the window."

"Your voice sounds different somehow. Did you get out to the cemetery yesterday?"

"No, I didn't. I didn't feel up to it. I think I'm getting sick. I don't have any energy."

"I bet if you go outdoors, you'll feel a little better. Clear your head and your energy field. I always feel better after I've gone for a walk, even if it's a short one. Maybe burn some incense as well. You know, like you used to. No doubt that will make the house feel better. How long has it been since you've been out?" Claire normally asks questions, encouraging her mother to talk about what she's doing and how she's feeling.

"Um, let me think. I don't know, a week maybe? I needed some bread, so I went to the Corner Market. They also had some bananas that looked good."

"Do you still have any?"

"Any what?"

"Bananas."

"Oh, right, bananas. No, they're all gone."

"Would you like me to take you to the market?" Remembering her earlier lie, Claire explains, "We decided not to go to the conference after all, so I'm around if you want to go somewhere." She purposefully doesn't offer to take her to the cemetery. "I was also thinking of going to the animal shelter to look at the cats and dogs. Maybe I'll adopt a pet, something to take care of. I could use your opinion. What do you think?"

The line remains silent, no answer coming from her mother. "Mom? Did you hear me?" Then she hears her mother sob. "Oh, Mom, am I upsetting you?"

"Look, Claire, I just don't feel like talking now. Maybe we can talk tomorrow?"

"Sure. I love you, Mom. I'll call tomorrow."

"Okay, Claire."

Claire feels deflated. She expected more from her mother—she wanted more. She waits on the phone a while longer, hoping her mother is still there but realizes her mother has long since disconnected.

Claire's heart aches. A part of her feels like she not only lost her father, but she's losing her mother as well. She no longer senses any support from her. She knows her mother is grieving.

Setting her own feelings aside, Claire carefully examines their conversation. Her mother is not herself; her behavior is unusual. Claire remembers her mom being entangled, to put it politely, in a social network of activities with the community and the church. She was particularly involved in a quilting group. Her parents also participated in a bridge club and occasional dinner parties.

Claire wonders if her mother has even gone to church lately. Is she working on a quilt? She doesn't talk about any of those things anymore. Her father always drove her mother everywhere, supporting her. He was there for her. Now?

There has to be a way to encourage her mother to get out more, to break this pattern. But considering the stages of grief, with depression often being the first stage, maybe she should just let her be for a while longer and respect her choices. Hopefully, she'll work through this on her own.

As she thinks about what her mother is going through, she sees the similarities in what she went through herself when she divorced Tom. She, too, has continued a similar pattern that has lingered for quite a while.

Claire's entire life shifted because Tom wasn't willing to support her. All of their friends dropped away. She avoided Chinese takeout and watching murder mysteries as well. It's funny how people sidestep certain activities because it reminds them of something uncomfortable.

She knows there are times when people get stuck somewhere in the process of grieving. Looking closer, Claire lovingly admonishes herself for how long it's taken her to relax enough to move forward with Alex. As she reminisces, she notes that she definitely felt sad and somewhat betrayed. The word *abandoned* comes to mind.

Most days, she feels hopeful and excited for her future. She's no longer pondering the reasons for or results of the divorce. Then it dawns on her—*she's ready for more*. A wave of longing moves through her body. She definitely wants to speak with Frank about some of these strange things that she has experienced.

Feeling rested now, she contemplates either calling Alex or beginning her painting project. Buying that canvas motivated her into going forward. One of the upstairs bedrooms would make a perfect studio.

Satisfied that her plans are coming together, she relaxes, allowing the pleasurable memory of her and Alex to blossom. A ripple of joy erupts into laughter as images and sensations of their love-making whirl. They sure had a delightful night together. She shivers with an unexpected jolt of sexual energy.

There's no doubt that Claire loves Alex. They get along great. But deep down, she knows she has lied to herself for several years, she has loved him for some time. Without delay, Claire grabs her phone to call Alex. On the third ring, he picks up. "Hello."

"Hey there. How's it going in your world?"

"Pretty good." He sounds happy to hear from her. "I just did some laundry. Not too concerned with cleaning. I'll be gone in a few days anyway. Might as well save it."

Claire wrinkles her nose, imagining the worst, although she has never seen his place. Men can be such slobs. She reprimands herself for needless speculation. Feeling feisty, Claire dives in. "Well, are you rested, or do you want more time to sit around and stare at the walls?"

"Now, Claire, I don't stare at the walls. I surf the net and watch *HGTV, This Old House,* and *DIY*."

"What no sports shows?"

Pretending he didn't hear her, he exclaims, "Oh, and *MotorTrend*. I have to keep up on the latest trends and fixer uppers. I absolutely love to build things. Unfortunately, I don't have a suitable space."

"What? You don't have a spare bedroom?"

"Normally, Claire, you don't put a table saw and a stack

of wood in a bedroom. Pretty sure that would not do." Alex pauses. "I have an idea. Maybe a good one at that." Not wanting to disclose any clues so soon, he interjects, "What I mean is, I haven't got my shop set up yet."

"Do you want some help? You'd be amazed at my organizational skills and my strength. Oh... " pausing for added effect, "...and I'm a hard worker. Undoubtedly, we could whip your garage into shape really fast."

"Seriously Claire, when I get back from Phoenix, I think I'll concentrate on finding a place to work on my truck. My garage isn't big enough for my truck and a wood shop. Claire, where's all of this energy coming from? Just yesterday you said you needed a full day all to yourself. But here you are, oozing with ideas."

"Oozing? You can call it that if you want. I feel different, motivated, confident... and I slept well." She skips over the episode with the old man in the rocking chair. "And I rested this morning with a good book. I guess... well, I miss you." Not waiting for Alex to respond she asks, "Have you heard any news about your brother?"

"I called the doctor earlier." The line goes quiet. She waits, but nothing.

"Alex, are you there?"

"I had to stop and take a deep breath. Nothing new. I'm so worried about Charles. I have a bad feeling about it all. Prognosis isn't the best."

"We should pray for him, that he improves so the doctors can treat him or that he heals entirely, if that's God's design for him."

"It's difficult for me to understand how people become sick. Sometimes the illnesses are so devastating."

"You're right, Alex. I feel that way too." Not wanting to dwell on that, Claire changes the subject. "Do you feel up to going out for a bite to eat like you suggested, then swinging by the shelter? I checked their hours. They are open until 5:30. Would I be rushing you if I came by to get you in, say, thirty minutes?"

"Claire, there's nothing more I'd love to do. I've been snacking all day. A good meal sounds perfect. Are you thinking of bringing home a pet today?"

"I don't know. I'm not set up for a pet. I want a dog, but I haven't figured out the logistics. I have a small fenced-in area in the backyard, but I think I need a doggy door. The dog has to be able to get in and out on his own. So, really, I should wait until I get this sorted out."

"Claire, a doggy door is determined by the size of the dog. Why don't we go to the shelter and find your pet and talk to someone there about your situation? I'm sure this is something they can help you with. Normally after approval, you must arrange for the animal to be neutered or spayed as part of the terms of adoption. Although, it all depends on the pup you choose."

Claire repeats the key words. "Approval? Terms?" Sarcastically, Claire continues, "Great, I suppose they'll want to do a credit check as well."

Alex laughs, "Not sure on that one."

"Well, if we're going to do this, I'd better get ready and head over to pick you up."

"Ordinarily, I would agree, but I think this will work better; how 'bout I pick you up in forty-five minutes? There's this great diner near 53rd and Madison that I think you'll like. Wear that purple sweater. You look fantastic in it."

Claire wrinkles her forehead, "Uh, purple sweater? I don't have one, Alex."

"Yes, you do. Go look in your closet. I'm sure it's there. I'll see you soon." The line goes silent.

"Purple sweater? What purple sweater?" She walks to her closet and searches. "No purple sweater here. What's he thinking of?" Digging deeper, she finds some clothes she had totally forgotten about and then sees it—the purple sweater. "How did he remember this?"

Excited and mystified, she grabs the sweater, looking it over closely. It's a knit that clings to her shape and is cut low in the front. Claire whispers, "Alex. You are something alright. The color is really nice. How could I have forgotten this?"

As Claire finishes getting ready, she hears it again, *You are ready for more.* Chuckling, she says, "Yep, I'm ready for more. Sounds like my new mantra." Then the doorbell rings.

Chapter Twenty

Opening the door to let Alex in, Claire immediately surrenders to his clean scent and notices how nice he looks. She suppresses the impulse to reach up and stroke his clean-shaven jawline. *God, he looks good.* The tight lines and dark shadows have vanished. Alex looks much more relaxed. Claire swallows, "Wow, you clean up really good, Alex!" He's wearing light blue jeans and his navy wool coat with a navy knitted stocking hat and red knitted scarf.

In an exaggerated fashion, he runs his eyes up and down her body. "Yup, I knew it."

"What? What did you know?"

"You're gorgeous in that sweater." Then sounding like a teenager, he exclaims, "The color is so you!"

Nervously, Claire laughs, then twirls to show off her purple sweater. "Is this the one? Why, thank you, kind sir. You don't think it clashes with my hair color? Heck, I didn't even remember I had this sweater. Honestly, you only see me in scrubs. How did you know?"

Not waiting for an answer, she rambles on in her best Scarlett O'Hara impersonation, "I do declare, I have no idea how you remembered this ole thing." Claire suddenly blushes. For some reason, she feels slightly embarrassed.

"Remember bowling? You wore that sweater one night." He looks so serious, yet she can't tell. He must be joking.

"Bowling? Oh, right. Vaguely. Sure, Alex." Laughing, she lightly touches the front of his coat. "You are something else, Alex Malone."

His voice drops an octave, "Oh, I remember."

Alex slyly reaches around Claire, pulling her in so their bodies touch. Looking closely into his blue eyes, she sees them deepen, becoming more intense.

In a slow, deliberate manner, Alex pulls her even closer, more firmly into an embrace and kisses her. Claire's body zings. Unmistakably, she feels their love connection expand into something that she's never felt before. It throws her off-kilter. Unintentionally, she groans. She wants him, alright. Their passion will soon be out of control if one of them doesn't put on the brakes now. Ending the kiss, she meekly suggests, "Maybe we could stay home, fix some popcorn and watch old movies. After that…?"

"Claire, I know that look. Later, I promise. We will. Be patient."

Claire nods and smiles. After a few moments, she says, "I'm really hungry. Are you ready? I just have to get my coat."

Glad for a reason to leave the room, Claire walks to the hall closet, opens the door and just stands there. After a moment, she feels steady enough to get her things and sings out, "Just a sec. Almost there."

Returning to the living room, she sees Alex standing in wait, like her knight in shining armor. *God, is he gorgeous.* She sucks in her breath, pretending to focus on getting ready to leave, but nothing is further from the truth. Uneasily, Claire laughs, feeling sure that her knees will buckle. "Alex, I'm not sure how long I'm going to last." Her statement can be taken two ways, skillfully constructed to confuse, but the yearning is written all over her face, giving her meaning away.

"Claire, we don't have to go anywhere. Just because we're both starving and there's a puppy out there in need of a loving home doesn't mean we have to go anywhere."

She twists her face up to look into Alex's eyes. "Really?" Handing her coat to Alex, she asks, "Are you trying to lay a guilt trip on me or what?" Alex loves to play, and it shows in his banter, but he has his reasonable side too. It's when he mixes the two that she wonders.

"Okay, let's be serious here. Are you okay with going out to eat? You know how important it is to have a nutritional meal."

Mocking him, Claire rolls her eyes. "I think I love you, Alex Malone."

As she says his name, it's as if a bolt of lightning strikes. Excitedly, Claire raises her hands and exclaims, "Wait! Alex, you know Harry Delany, room 407? He was telling me a story about his wife, where he met her, and so on. Her name was Patti Jo Malone."

"Your point is...?"

"You may be related, of course."

Alex narrows his eyes as if to tell her, get a clue. "Claire, I have met dozens of people with the same last name. Very common name here, you know. Very rare to find any connection, though. I think you may be stretching this one. You know what I believe? You have earned a new nickname." Alex takes her hand and pulls her toward him. "Let's go, Stretch. Lock the door behind you."

Laughing, she says, "Yes, sir."

As they walk to the car, the howling, bitter cold wind whips at their bodies, making it difficult to communicate. Talking loudly, Claire says, "I've been looking for a way to help Harry make peace with his family, to help them find a way to talk to each other without becoming angry and defensive. Did you hear all that yelling a couple of days ago? Harry and his son, I swear, were ready to have a go at it. With his heart condition, that could have been the last straw."

"Seriously, Claire. You know the rules. Why, oh why are you getting personally involved with this patient? You know it's exceedingly rare that these types of relationships end well."

"Yes, I'm painfully aware of how these types of relationships fare, but being rare doesn't make them impossible." Not knowing how Alex will react, wistfully, Claire adds, "I was asked to assist him with the process of healing his relationships with his children."

No longer joking, Alex turns to look her square in the eyes. "What are you doing? You know it isn't a good idea to get emotionally involved with these people, our patients. Who asked you to help out?" He waves his hand, like he's trying to erase the entire idea. "It doesn't matter who asked. You should really look at this before you go any further."

Standing her ground, Claire states, "Alex, I really want to talk to you about this, please."

Reluctantly, he agrees, "Okay, no problem. Let's get to the restaurant. I promise you can have the floor. I'll listen with an open mind."

During the entire ride, Claire contemplates the different scenarios of how Alex may be related to Harry. Ha. It doesn't matter either way. She can use the topic as a doorway to get Harry and his children to talk about Patti Jo and to each other. The part she isn't sure about is if she should tell Alex about Frank.

Boston, being a large city, has plenty of restaurants that they have never heard of or eaten at. A coworker told Alex about this one, which offers a full menu. Right away, Claire decides on an Asian green salad, complete with mandarin oranges, almonds, shredded cabbage, and grilled chicken topped with fresh strawberries, and to go along with that, a cup of loaded potato soup. Alex opts for a more serious meal of steak, baked potato, and a fresh garden salad. Claire is absorbed in the aromas and tastes of her food. Feeling relaxed, she avoids bringing up Harry. It simply doesn't seem to be important anymore.

In this new place, Claire studies the color scheme and how it influences her emotionally. This leads her to a thorough examination of the overall layout and décor, and how functional the place is. Sometimes, she wonders why she didn't go into interior design instead of nursing. She looks at Alex and says,

"Nice decorating job. The ambiance is intimate, relaxed, yet not so much so that I end up wanting to take a nap. What do you think?"

Alex merely looks at her and smiles. She senses he knows she wants to make small talk instead of bringing up the subject that they had disagreed on earlier.

Claire marvels at how easy it is to be with him. Then, as if on cue, Tom pops into her mind. Tom. God! Flabbergasted, she wonders why she's comparing the two of them. There's no way around this. If she wants this relationship with Alex to work, and she does, she must push through her insecurities, be open with her thoughts and feelings. No more hiding experiences from Alex. If he can't take it, then it's better to find out now.

"Alex, the food here and the setting… you know, are excellent. Thank you for bringing me here." Not waiting for a response, she plows ahead, "I want to make sure that we can talk… I mean really talk. What I mean is… I want the two of us to fully communicate with each other before we go any further." Carefully, she watches his facial expression for a cue to when he wants to speak. He seems to be exercising restraint and patience, allowing her to speak without interruption.

"You know I was married before. It ended, rather abruptly because one day, I told him after work that I had seen an angel just before a patient passed." Her tone of voice changes. "His wonderful, supportive reaction? I quote, 'Claire, you have lost your mind.' He wanted me to quit my job and go see a shrink. He attributed what I saw to being overworked. He wasn't able to understand or accept that I love my job. He didn't even consider that I might be a wee bit different." She pauses for Alex to take advantage of the opening. Nope, he's remaining neutral. "So, we ended up divorcing."

She waits for Alex to say something, anything. He doesn't.

"I'm a little afraid to tell you some of the things that I've experienced and… wow," she pauses to catch her breath, "I'm afraid to not tell you. I want this, what we have, to work. I really like you, and I feel comfortable with you. I don't remember a time when I didn't feel this way with you."

Alex steeples his fingers in front of his chin. He smiles encouragingly as he gives her his full attention. "Claire, I told you I would listen to you with an open mind. I am. It's important that you bring me up to speed. Go on."

"Okay. The other day I had two patients pass, one right after the other. You were in Phoenix. The second patient was Jerry. I'm sure you remember him. Anyway..., I saw an angel standing in his room, waiting before he passed—the angel spoke to me, Alex."

Claire picks up her napkin to wipe her mouth. She wants a few moments to weigh her options. Does she want to continue? Then, disregarding her fear, she plunges ahead, "Someday I'll tell you the entire story. Anyway, that was the first time I've seen this particular angel. His name is Frank. Jerry was in 407. Incidentally, it's the same room Harry is in now." Claire frowns wondering why she felt it important to mention the room number. "Frank is the apparition that Harry was seeing when he was admitted."

Alex nods "Good to know."

"You remember, everyone thought Harry was pretty much insane. Well, of course, anyone would think that if they saw the way Harry acted. Everyone thought he was throwing things at an invisible person. Doc gave him antipsychotics, Alex. I hate that he was prescribed those meds." She looks at Alex, noticing a mask of empathy enveloping his face. "It was Frank the whole time. Frank was telling Harry that he had to go with him. Frank's the same angel who has been talking to me, coaching me. He's asked me… to assist in Harry's case.

"Harry described his apparition as looking like an injun, but Frank looks Hispanic to me. Anyway, Frank tells Harry it's time to go with him. Right? Harry refuses and throws whatever he can get his hands on to chase the guy off. What it boils down to is, Harry doesn't have much time to get his affairs in order, to work on the anger that rages inside him and with his children." Looking into Alex's eyes, Claire decides to stop.

"Claire, wow. I had no idea you were at this level of communication with the angelics."

"What? The angelics?"

"The angels. They minister to patients like Harry. Usually, though, people don't have a clue what's going on."

"You know? How did you know?" She's shaken to hear Alex talk like this. "You believe me? Oh my God, all this time? You knew? Have you seen them too?"

"A number of times, yes. Usually, it's out the corner of my eye—fleeting. One time I saw this angel walk through a door into a patient's room. She, the patient, passed within the hour. I haven't had conversations with any of them. So, this angel, Frank, approached you?"

"Yes, he came to my house that night, the day the two patients passed. He brought the second patient, Jerry, with him. They said they wanted to thank me." Grabbing a tissue from her purse, Claire wipes away the tears dripping down her face. "Frank has been coming to talk to me, telling me things, *and* he gave me a letter."

"Wait, he, Frank, gave you a letter, in writing?"

"Yes. I found it laying on my keyboard in the nurses' station, directly after that scene with the patient walking down the hall." She describes the penmanship and the paper without going into any detail as to the content. Then, Claire adds, "He knows about us, Alex."

"Ah, heck, Claire, *everyone* knows about us." He grins while doing his best to stifle a laugh. Shocked, Claire questions his statement. *Could what he said be true?* Claire is suddenly irritated that Alex would make light of this.

Alex sees his error. Taking her hands, he tenderly kisses them and apologizes, "Claire, forgive me. I didn't mean to poke fun. They, the staff, all know I love you. I've always loved you...." His voice has gone soft, his words growing faint, finally trailing off altogether.

Claire's face turns a deep shade of crimson. She feels utterly bewildered, "I guess I always knew. I just wasn't ready. I wasn't able to let go of the hurt. I wasn't able to let myself trust anyone. Not until now." Claire begins to cry again. She wipes her face with the tissue, "But the signs have always been there." Wearily, Claire sighs, "Maybe we should go."

"Before we go, Claire, know that I'm aware of these angels who escort our patients to another realm. I've also seen and I believe." He pauses, "Now, do you want to go to the shelter next or are you ready to go home?"

With determination, Claire says, "I'm ready to go to the shelter." Her voice trembles a bit as emotion overtakes her. "Alex, I'm going to want some company while you're away."

Changing the subject, Alex says, "I want to call my brother this evening, but it can wait until tomorrow.... Would it be okay if I stayed over tonight?"

Totally surprised, Claire hesitates as she studies his face. Looking deeply into his eyes, her heart takes over, spilling out its love. "I wasn't expecting that one. But yes. I want you to stay over." Then, as if to make light of her sudden gush of affection, she laughs, "By any chance, do you have your PJs with you?"

"Course I do. Truthfully, Claire, I was relatively sure that was the ultimate goal for both of us."

She shakes her head, wondering if this guy is able to read her mind or if he's joking.

Seeing her reaction, Alex softens his approach. "Claire, look, I know men in general can be rather aggressive when it comes to sex. Some, too many probably, consider their relationships as a quest or a sport like contact football—score! I want you to understand, I may joke around concerning all of this." He pauses for a moment as he watches her expressive eyes. "There are times to be playful and times to be serious. When a man and a woman come together, it's a beautiful expression of love. I believe the pure intention of loving and pleasing your partner is a rare gift. But our time together it..." He pauses, connecting with Claire's heart, "...is a precious exchange of energy. My intentions aren't superficial. My love runs deep. I ask you, Claire, to get to know me, the true me."

Claire can no longer hold her emotions in check. She's barely aware that tears are running down her face as she listens to him speak about love, intention, and purity, then asks her to know him. She aches, longs to be held by him, to hold him, to know him—all of him.

She tries her best to sound confident, "I want to, Alex. I truly want to." All the same, she remembers Tom used similar sentiments. *Look how well that ended.*

Tears once again gather. Feeling exposed, she bows her head to wipe her face and to clear her mind.

He stands up, "I'll get our coats. Be right back."

As she begins to feel more centered, she hears his voice, "Your coat, madam. I'll help you put it on."

Always such a gentleman. He's a keeper.

Chapter Twenty-One

"You know, I still wonder if looking for a pet is such a good idea. I'll be gone for far too many hours. Right? I know it depends on the age and training of the dog, but, well, I'm wondering about my mom. She sure can use a fur baby to take care of."

Walking to the car from the restaurant, she continues, "Since my father passed, she's been depressed, withdrawing from her social activities. I'm wondering if dog sitting on my days at work may help her and me too. Then I can pick him up and take him home to my place on the weekends. You know, a joint custody thing. What do you say we drop by my mom's place and talk to her about my idea?"

"She's your mother. You would know better than me. However, from what you've told me it sounds like she's grieving. Chances are if you ask her about dog sitting, she'll probably just make up some excuse to turn you down. Maybe you should just show up over there with the pup. See how she responds to it."

"Oh, I don't have any idea what she might say, I'm just wondering how I can help her through this. When my dad was here, she was dependent on him. He didn't encourage her to be any different. Maybe I shouldn't say it like that. They did most everything together. He drove her everywhere."

"Claire, people should be able to manage on their own, go places, especially here in this city. We have to be able to get around, be able to call people, know the transit system or, well, we won't be able to go anywhere. In other words, we end up being limited in our experience here."

"You're probably right. Let's go over to the kennel."

Feeling anxious during the drive, Claire admits, "I'm a bit nervous about these sudden lifestyle changes, and especially my ideas concerning my mom."

Then, Claire hears it again, "*You are ready for more.*" She mumbles, "Not sure how much more I'm ready for."

Keeping his eyes on the traffic, Alex says, "What Claire? Did you say something?"

"Oh, I didn't realize I said anything. I was thinking about something. Something weird keeps happening to me." She laughs, realizing what she has done. "Anyway, you remember Frank. The tall angel?"

"The tall angel?"

"Oh, that was how I thought of him before he told me his name. I was sitting on the floor with Jerry, looking up when I saw him. From that perspective, he really did look tall." She shrugs, indicating that it doesn't matter. "Frank said that I was ready for more. I keep hearing it, like a voice. Thing is, he never said exactly what I was ready for. And now, look what's happening—we're together, I may adopt a pet, I painted my kitchen, and I'm picking up my oils again. Somehow, I feel different, but I suspect, that isn't all of it."

She hesitates, not sure if she wants to elaborate but then, thinking it's now or never, she continues, "I'm hearing Frank talk to me telepathically and as you know, now I'm also seeing spirits."

"Umm, I know you see things that most people don't. You're referring to that old man in the hospital?"

"Yes. But there's more. Listen to me, *there is more*. What a trip. My entire life has become so bizarre."

"So, you've had more experiences with the patient or, ah, the ghost in the hall?"

In detail, Claire describes the man in her kitchen that morning. "Such an odd thing. He didn't even know that I was talking to him."

"You know, Claire, it may be helpful to get some information on this type of phenomenon. I've heard about these types of appearances or events. The energy can be imprinted in the etheric and replay itself in the physical. Odd that it would be in your kitchen. Although, your house is older."

"Most houses in that area of town are. You think that has something to do with it?"

"Might. Your house would benefit by being cleared. Maybe do a search at the library or on the Internet? It may be helpful for you to learn about these types of things and maybe how to communicate. Of course, if it's an imprint, you probably can't communicate, so maybe you can learn to clear the energy."

"Yeah? Sounds like really great ideas, Alex. I'll get on the Internet and see what I can find. Truthfully, I have no idea what I'm doing. I want to talk to Frank, but that's another thing, I don't know how to get in touch with him or even if I can. Maybe these guys just show up when they want to. You know?"

"Seems like from what little you've said, Frank gave you a clue as to what's in your future. It would be helpful to get additional information from him. So, he helps people cross over. What else does he do?"

"I don't know, except he requested that I help in some way with Harry. That's another subject."

Alex nods, connecting the dots. "So, Frank is the mastermind concerning your *involvement* with Harry?"

Being caught up with their conversation, Claire hadn't noticed that they were nearing the kennel. She had literally tuned out the voice on the GPS. She wonders how Alex can focus on their conversation and Alexa at the same time.

As they pull into the parking lot, it finally dawns on Claire what she's about to do. She reminds herself that she doesn't have to go through with this.

She looks to Alex for some reassurance. Their eyes lock.

"Claire, are you ready to go in?"

Feeling butterflies in her stomach, she smiles, opens the door, and steps out. Walking to the back of the car, she waits for Alex to catch up. "Alex, my stomach is giving me fits. Are you sure about this?"

"Look at me, Claire." Patiently, Alex waits until she faces him. "We're in this together. I want to be a part of this. Besides, the dog has to like me too. Wouldn't it be wiser if we do this together?"

Laughing at the image that dances across her mind, Claire blurts out, "What you really mean is that you want to make sure I don't choose a dog that will bite your backside when you aren't looking."

"Can you blame me, Claire? I've heard a few horror stories about dogs who growl and snap at any man that approaches his human companion. No lovemaking for them. That type of behavior can be a real downer, don't you think?"

"Sounds like you're really serious about our budding romance,"

"Well, yes, this is a big deal. This pup will be a part of our family. We all have to get along." Gently, Alex takes Claire's arm to guide her toward the animal shelter.

Walking through the kennel's door, Claire is instantly sad and concerned. Seeing literally dozens of dogs of all sizes and breeds locked up in cages, she wants to weep. Walking down the corridor, she tries her best to stay detached. "Alex, I don't think I'm ready for this. I feel like if I talk to any of them, they'll get their hopes up, then I'll let them down."

Just as she admits her feelings, she sees a little pup with a silky soft black-and-white coat. The dog's brown eyes are filled with hope. Claire, being drawn to the puppy, walks straight up to the cage and kneels down. She turns to see if Alex notices the dog as well. "Alex, look. She doesn't appear to be very old." The puppy jumps up on the side of the cage to greet her. "She seems kind, sensitive. I want to get her out. Can I? You think?"

Before she realizes it, Alex kneels down beside her. "She's

sweet, Claire. I'll find someone to help us."

Talking to the dog, Claire coos, "Oh, you are so beautiful. What's your name little girl?" The pup quietly whimpers as she enthusiastically wags her tail like she knows exactly what Claire is saying.

Claire hears Alex and an attendant are walking down the hall towards her. She stands up for introductions, explaining that she thinks this puppy is really sweet, and she would like to adopt her.

The woman, introducing herself as Stacy, reaches for the information sheet attached to the cage. "Well, this particular dog is quarantined for three days and already has a party interested in her."

"Oh, darn."

Pointing at the sheet, Stacy explains, "If you're still interested after the three-day period expires, providing the other party backs out, you can adopt her if you're qualified. If you want, we can get you prequalified. I would definitely recommend it. There are some papers to fill out. Your home has to be approved, just like you do. We're rather cautious about who takes our animals. We want them to go to the best-suited homes. I'm sure you understand."

"Oh, yes, certainly. You mean you check out the person's history, like a criminal record, and even have someone come out to the home?"

"We certainly do. For example, we don't want the animals to end up in puppy mills or abusive situations. To ensure their well-being, we have rules. As per the agreement, you'll have the animal neutered or spayed as well. We have a vet on staff, or you can use your own."

"So, there's a waiting period for an adoption to go through?".

"Yes, ma'am, there is."

"Oh, Stacy, I'm sorry. I'm Claire and this is Alex."

"I'm pleased to meet you both. As I was explaining, we can certainly begin the procedure, depending on how you feel.

It's a process. You don't walk out of here with an animal in a few minutes. We want to make sure there's a good fit, that your personalities compliment and that you have the correct environment for the pet. There's a lot to consider when choosing a pet."

Stacy pauses for a moment. "Undoubtedly, a pet is a family member. Of course, there may be times when you may not get along. You must train your pet to be obedient. Your pet, as all family members, must know the rules, what's expected. When everyone knows the rules, life is so much easier, you see? We also offer classes to help people learn how to communicate with their new pet. There are proven techniques that, when used consistently, ensure a well-behaved pet, a pet that feels relaxed, secure in its environment. Animals, especially dogs, want to *please* their companions."

Overwhelmed, Claire declares, "Oh, wow, I had no idea this would be so complex."

"Don't worry, Claire. It really isn't all that complicated. I'm sure you and your husband will easily fly through the process. We'll guide you every step of the way."

Blushing, Claire informs Stacy, "Well, for starters, we aren't married. Alex and I are both nurses at The Manor across from the harbor. We both work long days and in return have longer weekends."

Stacy looks at each of them. "You know, leaving a pet alone for long periods of time causes anxiety in some animals. With others, they can adapt and amuse themselves, or you can hire someone to come in to check on your pet. There are doggy day care centers too."

"To be honest Stacy, I'm looking into this adoption for a few reasons. One, yes, for a companion, but also because my mother was recently widowed and needs to be responsible for something to take care of, to love. Hopefully, this will draw her out of her depression." Claire's voice softens, "She needs to be needed. Maybe she can dog sit for me. These are just ideas right now."

"Claire, it sounds like there are a few questions to answer.

Who will be the main caregiver?" Stacy looks to Alex and asks, "Are you just the support person here or are you going to be involved as well?" Then she turned to Claire, "Do you want your mother to care for this dog occasionally or only while you're at work? I don't expect you to answer me now. Think about everything we've talked about. This is an important decision.

"As for this pup, her name is Daisy, and she's approximately eight months old. She was abandoned. No one has claimed her and, of course, because of the circumstances, we must keep her away from people to ensure everyone's safety. We'll give her a medical exam to certify she's healthy before we adopt her out. As part of the agreement, she needs her shots, and she must be spayed. That's an overnight stay, either here or at a vet that you choose. Would you like to begin with filling out an application?"

Suddenly, Claire feels like she's talking to a car salesperson. "Uh, I don't know. Yes, I think I want to get started and do the application to get approved. Is there a fee?"

Stacy grins, "Yes, there are set fees, but they are also donations, which may help out on your taxes. Just an idea."

"Oh, I'm not concerned with taxes. I want to get a rough idea on how much we're talking about with vet costs and so on. It's been a long time since I had a pet."

After Stacy gives Claire a rundown on the average costs, Claire remembers the doggy door. "Oh, and I want a doggy door installed before I bring home a dog."

"Excellent idea. We need to get you a dog before you do that, though. That's to get the right size door for the animal."

"Alex, let's look again and see if there's another dog we like. Stacy, excuse us. I'll let you know our decision in a few minutes."

Stacy holds up her hand and says, "One more thing, it may be more convenient for you to complete your application online. The website is listed on our brochure. Take your time. Have fun. The animals absolutely love the attention."

After thirty minutes, Claire determines that Daisy is the

only dog she wants. She's willing to wait to see if the other people back out. Then she remembers Alex will be leaving for Phoenix soon.

"Claire, I have a flight out Monday afternoon. I want to get the door installed before I go. We have four days. Maybe it'll work out. Don't know."

As they tell Stacy they're leaving, Claire says, "I'll fill out the application online. I sure would like to adopt Daisy. I feel a connection with her already, and she's adorable. I hope it works out that I can adopt her."

Stacy writes some notes before saying, "I learned a long time ago that if you are meant to be together, it will happen. Give me your number, and I'll call you if the other party decides not to adopt her for some reason. From what I remember… well, I won't go there. I'll just say that I feel confident that everything will work out perfectly."

Chapter Twenty-Two

Driving home, Claire and Alex explore how the adoption might play out before they agree there's just no way of knowing what may happen. They can only hope for the best. When they decide their time and efforts can be better managed, their conversation naturally drifts to what they want to do next as a couple.

Focusing on Daisy and the process of adopting a pet kept Claire's mind occupied. She didn't obsess over any of the challenges that she presently grappled with concerning Frank, Harry, or Alex. Now, it was the two of them—alone.

She isn't sure how to feel, making her a little uncomfortable, unsure of herself. Being with Alex is new; she's out of her element. So much time has passed since she actually dated, or had feelings like this about anyone.

Claire's heart suddenly fills with comfort and acceptance. She's sitting beside a cherished friend. She also feels the heat rise, knowing her face is flushed. She perceives so many conflicting emotions; she feels so vulnerable. She wants to be accepted.

Her ego causes conflict by bringing up insecurities, making her think she must behave in a certain way to please

Alex. The self-righteous part of her knows that she doesn't have to conform to anyone's view of how she should be. She can be herself.

What they have is not an ordinary friendship.

She drifts back in time, a time when she was with Tom and completely enamored with him—head over heels—until it all came crashing down around her. Maybe she was never meant to be with Tom. Only God knows what's best and certainly arranges circumstances to make sure she follows the correct path for her life.

She chose to be honest with Tom. Married couples don't survive if there isn't honesty. She was young, inexperienced, and, of course, naïve. She believed she was safe, and Tom would never let her down.

Claire examines Tom's reason for wanting her to quit her nursing career. True, he may have been concerned for her mental health. Although, she suspects that, deep down, he may have had other motives. After all, why would he have been so critical of her? Claire's conclusion is that he wanted to control her so he would not feel threatened.

Tom wasn't open to new spiritual ideas. When he found she wouldn't bend to his *suggestions,* he decided it wasn't worth his effort. Claire concedes that it was easier for Tom to move on than to mold her to his liking. What they had was not love. People are supposed to work things through together.

Alex appears to be different. He's open-minded and seems to be truly committed to making this relationship work.

"Alex, thank you. Your support through this pet adoption means so much to me. I sure hope I can get Daisy. If things don't line up, though, I'll gladly wait until you return from Phoenix when we'll have time to look again."

"The thing is, what we have is so new… well, I hope I'm not reading too much into it. It's as if we have a long way to go, yet, I feel we're already there. I need to get comfortable with not only the idea of *us*, but comfortable with us together. I still feel unsure of myself sometimes. I suppose, it's a matter of adjusting."

"I know what you mean. I feel the same way. We already know each other, we just need to adjust, or maybe we can…" He stops and makes an exaggerated funny face as if he's trying to figure out how to get his point across. "Ah, I have it! We can call it coming into this new way of being more *in tune* with one another."

Exploding in laughter, Claire asks, "Alex, did you by any chance take theater in college?" Still laughing, she says, "I do believe you missed your true calling, darlin.'"

Alex is totally shocked at her outburst. "Hey, I take that as an insult. What on earth are you…. I have no idea what you are talking about."

"Oh, you said, and I quote, 'we can call it coming into this new way of being more in tune with one another.' I heard the emphasis on *being more*. Alex, that was really good. Remember Frank said, 'You are ready for more.' Apparently, I'm getting more"

Almost as though he had intended nothing of the sort, Alex laughs, "Me? A thespian. No way." Alex has his hands on the steering wheel, Claire tenderly touches his arm, "Alex, let's go home."

"You're talking about your place, right?"

Realizing what she just suggested, Claire suddenly feels a bit bashful. Her voice drops in volume as she says, "I guess that sounded like we're already living together."

"Just this once, it did. But may I suggest that living together might make things less complicated all around. You know I bought a place with a garage. Hate to give up that garage." Shaking his head, he repeats, "Sure would hate to give that up." Then, he suddenly signals and turns to go back in the opposite direction.

Confused, Claire asks, "Alex, what are you doing? You have that determined look on your face."

"Yep, we're going back to my place. *Garage.*"

Alex refuses to talk to Claire any further about his actions, until they arrive at his home. "Here we are, Claire. I think it's time you see how the *other half* lives."

Claire's heart flutters as she says to herself, *The other half?*

Alex parks in the jam-packed, two-car garage and proceeds to give her the grand tour. It's nothing like she expected. There are no clothes on the floor, the bed is made, the toilet seat is down and covered, and the sink is spotless.

"So, this is it? Alex, I'm impressed—really impressed. You keep your place tidy." She's thinking immaculate, but really doesn't want to make such a bold statement.

"It's just me. It's easy to keep up. I have ideas, Claire. Lots of ideas. You like to decorate? Here is your chance."

"What are you saying?" Intrigued, she asks, "You'd like to hire me? Well, let's see…" Out loud, she systematically counts how many rooms and how many hours to give him an estimate before Alex stops her and drops the bomb. "Claire, I'm suggesting that you move in with me. We could ride into work together and well, I guess, you can use your imagination to fill in the rest."

Not believing what just came out of his mouth, she stares at Alex for a moment, dumbfounded. "Are you for real?" Seeing his expression, she's convinced Alex is serious. "Don't you think this is a wee bit premature?"

"Honey, we've known each other for what… fifteen years?"

"At least."

"Time to move forward. Remember the saying, 'you are ready for more.'"

Laughing, Claire says, "Okay, now you're taking Frank's line way too far. I'm pretty sure that you're plagiarizing his words. He may not appreciate it. Truthfully, though, I'm ready for more, but I want to stop and feel this first." Boldly, she adds, "I do love your place though."

Realizing the implications, she shyly asks, "Do you want to just live together, or do you want a more solid commitment?"

Claire's at the point where she wants to know how far he's willing to go with their relationship.

"To be clear, are you suggesting marriage and having a family together? Daisy is a great beginning, but what about children?"

"Claire, I know I want to marry you. The question is do you trust me enough to commit? Are you willing to be with me for the rest of your life? I know what I want. I figured it might be a good idea to live together for a while. Yes, I believe *you are ready for more;* nevertheless, will you accept more from me? I want to give you the time you need."

He's sweeping her off her feet. She whispers, "I am never going to live that down, am I? I mean what Frank said about me being ready for more."

Alex's voice becomes husky as it drops an octave, "Probably not." Looking deeply into his eyes, she sees they have gone soft. His lip quivers ever so slightly as he declares, "I love you, Claire." Reaching for her hand he asks, "Will you marry me?"

Claire is dazed, unable to speak. She had no idea he had come this far in such a short time. Sure, she has allowed herself to dream of the possibility of getting married and even having children. She's not getting any younger. They're not getting any younger.

From her point of view, they want to be together, and they enjoy each other's company. She finds herself choosing to do certain things because of Alex. Her decisions are contingent on how Alex feels, if he's available, and so on. She wants to include him in what she does. Not only does it feel right, but she also feels better as a person to have him with her—more complete.

Yes. Checking her feelings, she feels better as a person with Alex in her life. Even though she thinks these things, she still wants more time to adjust to the idea. Instead, the words gush out, seemingly of their own accord, "Alex, I love you, and yes, I will marry you."

He scoops her up and twirls her. Their tender kiss quickly turns into a fiery passion that neither one of them wants to deny. "Alex, how 'bout we try out your bed? I sure hope it's a king."

Alex grins, "I thought you would never ask."

Chapter Twenty-Three

Claire and Alex spend the remainder of the afternoon in seclusion. No phone, no Internet, no TV. Fortunately, Alex has plenty to munch on until they're ready for a more substantial meal.

Claire's old feelings of not belonging begin to emerge. She thoroughly enjoys their time together, yet she doesn't want to overstay her welcome. "Alex, I think I should go home. All of my stuff is there."

"What would it take to make you feel more comfortable?"

Ignoring his question, she asks, "Did you truly intend for me to stay this long?" Without waiting for an answer, she adds, "We both said we could use some rest this weekend. If I weren't here, what would you be doing?"

"Oh, probably the usual; thinking about the Apache or maybe practicing my drumming." Then he demonstrates an elaborate finger tapping on the side table. Claire watches his eyes; they are glistening. "Drumming? You play the drums? Oh, God, please no."

"Nah, just teasing, Claire. While you're here, we should get to know each other better. For instance, what kind of music do you enjoy? Do you prefer good old rock 'n' roll, opera, country, new age, pop, rap, hip hop, meditative/relaxing, classical, the oldies, gospel, the blues…?"

"Alex, you changed the subject. I was asking about me overstaying my welcome and having my own stuff around. This is your home. Are we going too fast here?"

"Didn't you just agree to marry me? Shouldn't we spend time together? Probably make it a little easier to learn about each other this way. Don't you think?"

"Okay, fine with me. Would you please take me home so I can gather some things to bring over here? I might as well be relaxed as we're getting to know each other. And to answer your question, I love all kinds of music. It just depends on my mood and, of course, the situation."

Without warning, Alex's jaw tightens. Something triggered him. Before her, his eyes glaze over, and he withdraws. Claire wonders what happened, where she stands. "Alex, I should probably go home. I'm sure you have things to do around here to get ready.…"

"Oh, something made me think of my brother. I feel like I need to call him. Do you mind? I just want to check in."

"Do you want to do that now? I can go into the other room. Maybe I can look around in the kitchen to familiarize myself with how you have things organized, or I could…"

"Nah, Claire. You don't have to leave. I do want to call, though. The sooner I call, the sooner I'll feel better."

A few minutes later, Alex hangs up the phone. Claire listened to the one-sided conversation, observing how his manner changed as he spoke to his brother. The entire time, he kept his voice even, his sentences short, like he wanted to control his emotions. Being fairly sure she understood the situation and that he could use some time to process the information, she remains quiet. She watches a crease in his forehead appear.

"Claire, you know we deal with this stuff all the time, but when it comes to my own family it…" He pauses, raking his fingers through his dark hair. "I'm afraid that he won't make it."

"Really? Did something change?"

"His white blood count has dropped even more. The meds aren't working. It sounds like they're going to try another protocol." Alex's voice sounds flat, resigned. "Charles didn't sound good. His energy is really low, and on top of that, he doesn't have a positive attitude. Doc says he won't do surgery until the numbers rise and Charles is stabilized. I knew from the beginning..., but now the blood count is even lower."

Alex slaps his knee, "I don't know what to do; I'm stumped. I've already put in for leave. I was really hoping this would go smoothly. Of course, his doctor has to follow what he knows is the best regimen, and I knew this was a possibility." Alex eyes lock onto Claire's, "You know, this means I'm probably going to have to reschedule my flight. Betty in personnel is going to love me for this."

"Isn't there anyone else in Phoenix who can care for him?"

"The only other option is to transfer him to a nursing home or to hire private care. I want to help him, but right now, there's nothing I can do." Quickly changing his mood, Alex says, "This sounds like your adoption quandary. We just have to wait and trust it will work out, right?

"You know, if I look at this from another perspective, maybe this *is* working out for the best. This way I can be with you when you get the pup."

Feeling embarrassed and somewhat guilty that Alex would even think that, Claire says, "Oh, Alex, getting a dog doesn't even come close to working out the details in your brother's situation."

"Well, I think it does. Both Charles and Daisy are waiting for specific pieces to fall into place before any of us will get more of the picture. Yes, we're talking about Charles' life, his health, but aren't we also talking about Daisy's as well? It's only a matter of degree. They're both going through a difficult challenge to find their way."

"You're comparing your brother's state of affairs to a dog's, Alex. You know I fell in love with Daisy, but she isn't human."

"No, but she has feelings. In her own way, I'm sure she's

insecure and afraid. Ah, at any rate, I can't control the outcome in either situation—neither of us can. We need additional information. In other words, we must wait for other people to make their choices so we can see how the events unfold. Sure, when things change and I can, I'll help Charles because he's my brother and I love him. You know, my brother will always take precedence over an animal. We have a bond, a history, but Daisy is important too."

Claire is stunned, but grateful for his ability to empathize with each party involved. But then she realizes, Alex is special and that's why she's attracted to him, why she loves him.

"Look, really Claire, if I'm here, I can help you with Daisy." Alex looks deeply into Claire's eyes. "This is something I want to do."

"Wait just a minute, Alex. We don't even know that we're getting Daisy." Claire realizes she used the pronoun *we. Boy, have I shifted my perspective.*

"Well, I'm practicing using a positive attitude—conscious language. That'll help us bring Daisy into our lives, right?" He chuckles, "Don't look so surprised. I heard you say *we* a moment ago. You remember saying that don't you, sweetheart?" Alex's face is animated, his eyes glittering with excitement. As he reaches to pull her closer, he whispers, "Might as well get used to it—to us.

"Charles is waiting at home for the surgery. Heck, he's waiting to get his life back, but that'll be a long process. For now, waiting is the wisest choice. It's kind of like me, I had to wait for a long time until a particular alignment came into place."

"What? Alex, what alignment are you talking about?"

"You, Claire, you." Alex places his hands on his heart and smiles.

Looking closely, Claire notices that his eyes are filled with tears. He doesn't try to hide his emotions. "Once the alignment came into place, my whole life changed. Look at me now. Look at us now. We need to have patience."

"Yes, I understand."

"Claire, I'm simply allowing everything to work out in God's favor. I'm not going to stress over it. I'm allowing it all to unfold."

"Ah, wise man you are, Alex Malone. Hey, since we're switching gears, perhaps you can help us out a bit?"

"Who are we talking about?"

"Oh, you know: Frank, Harry, his family, and me."

He puts his hands on his hips, looking up toward the heavens, taking a long, exaggerated breath, like whatever Claire has to say may end his way of being. Then, in a single instant, he changes his persona to that of a British knight. Taking a deep bow, he asks, "Dearest maiden, what does thou desirest of me?"

She taps her finger on her chin acting like she really has to think about it. "I want you to initiate a conversation about your name and where your relatives come from with Harry, and Robert and Augusta, Harry's children." She pauses in thought, "You know, it would be best if they were all together, but the chances of that happening, well, we'll see how that works out.

"Do you know your family genealogy? Surely you have someone in your family that lived in California. I'll find out where Patti Jo, Harry's wife, was born. I'm going to ask lots of questions. Maybe, when his son comes to visit, I can ask him if he knows anything." Claire is clearly excited now, "This will be fun!"

"I don't want to be the bearer of impending doom, but really, you're absolutely, positively asking for trouble."

Claire gasps, placing her forearm across her forehead, acting the part of the fair maiden in distress, "Whatever happened to your positive attitude, kind sir?" Placing her hand over her heart for dramatic emphasis, she says, "I happen to know in my heart that what we're about to embark on is an extraordinarily good idea. I'm sure what I'm proposing will reveal the answer that ultimately helps this dysfunctional family come back together again, help them remember the good times, and forgive one another."

"I trust your enthusiasm, Claire. You know, though, it's possible they didn't have many good times. What're you going to do then?"

"I don't know. To almost quote you, I'll allow it to unfold according to God's will." She waits a moment to see if he remembers her plight. Watching his eyes, carefully, Claire repeats her previous request, "Alex, will you please drive me home? You can stay over if you want."

With his knightly accent, he responds with, "Dearest Claire, honored I will be to escort you to your lovely home. Are the servant's quarters in order?" Claire grabs a pillow and throws it at him.

"Ah, all this time, I thought you were my knight in shining armor, but instead I find that you're but a lowly manservant. Have it your way. Bring the car 'round. I will be out in ten minutes."

"I'd rather be your knight in shining armor. Aren't the fringe benefits way better?" He winks, then turns to go.

Chapter Twenty-Four

On the drive home, Claire discovers that Alex likes the oldies. On occasion at The Manor, she has heard him sing a line or two. Never like this though. He has a strong voice. "Why didn't you tell me you could sing like that?"

"Who, me? I just mess around."

"Mess around, really?"

"You know, you aren't half bad yourself."

"Obviously, you're tone deaf but still able to stay on pitch—amazing. How is that possible?" *God, he has a beautiful smile.*

"Claire, you're one of a kind." With a devious grin, Alex mentions, "Did you know I have an old '59 Apache in the garage?" He purrs, "She'll be a perfect addition to our many exciting excursions."

"What's that? You said something about an Apache earlier."

"My '59 Apache is a Chevy pickup, short bed, bench seater, heavy on the chrome. You walked right past her!"

"Is that what was under the tarp? I love old cars, but I'm not familiar with the Apache. My uncle did custom detailing. He followed the car show circuit and so forth. I really loved going with him, but I haven't been in a long while. I didn't know you were into that sort of thing."

"I've been keeping it a secret, until the perfect time presented itself."

"Oh, you have, have you?"

"'Course, can't reveal too much about myself. They say being a bit on the mysterious side is very alluring." Claire thinks he's cute and chuckles, "They do, do they? So, Alex, are you just going to drop me off, stay over, or what? You probably have a suitcase full of stuff in the trunk for all occasions. I hope you have something warm. I keep the thermostat cooler than some people."

"I can drop you off, stay over, or whatever you want, Claire."

"Nah, don't put that on me. What do you prefer?"

"For starters, I want to look at the layout of your house and yard. Then, I want to look at the door to your backyard. Check it out, you know, for the doggy door. I think we can go ahead with it. You want a small dog, so no problem, we'll get a small door. Isn't there a pet store over on Henison? I think I should go ahead and get it installed. I don't think we're ready to combine households yet, but we have to be ready for Daisy."

"Why do you want to look at the layout?"

"Thinking ahead."

Uneasiness suddenly makes its way into Claire's solar plexus. "May I ask why?"

"Which place would be better to let go of. You rent right?"

Almost in a panic, Claire replies, "No, I own my house."

"I'm just wondering if we would want to sell or rent out one of the properties or what."

"Alex, I'm a little surprised, no, I'm flabbergasted at how quickly you're moving ahead. I'm not sure I'm ready for all of this yet."

"I'm just anxious to be with you, that's all. I love you. I want to live with you. Housing in Boston is extremely expensive. I just want to have the information handy so I can consider options. I want it to be as easy as possible."

"I understand. Sure, go ahead and look around. I think…, Oh gosh, I don't know about the door. Alex, maybe we should wait." Claire suddenly feels raw, emotionally unbalanced—doubt sets in. She feels these ideas are too new to be acting on. Alex is going forward fast and hard. It seems Claire has no choice.

Realizing getting a dog was her idea, and Alex had simply gone along with it, probably to please her, she cautiously asks, "Do you even want a dog? As sweet as Daisy is, she's going to be work. This all came about because I wanted a companion, someone to come home to. If I do this, and we get married, *we* will have to take care of her. Now things are changing. Alex, if we're together, I really don't think it's necessary? Do you?"

Curtly, Alex says, "What about your mom?"

"Mom? What has she got to do with this?"

"We should talk to your mom."

Claire is beginning to feel anxious and out of control. She's afraid Alex wants to take over. She doesn't like it, and she doesn't feel safe. "What do you mean?"

"As you mentioned, your mother could benefit from having a pet. You know how having a four-legged companion can reduce anxiety, stress, and depression. With an animal, she'll have to go outdoors on walks. In general, she'll be accountable for the needs of the pet."

Claire takes a deep breath, then another as she works to rebalance herself. "Alex, we don't even have a dog." Then it hits her. "Oh my God, you have a plan."

"Well, I wouldn't call it a plan, not yet anyway. These are ideas, Claire, just ideas. Okay? So, this is what I think. Adopt Daisy and then, because you love her and don't want her to be alone while we're at work, ask your mother to dog sit. Then," he breathes deeply, "… little by little, she takes Daisy as her own. She won't be able to keep herself from loving that little girl, which will assist her in healing her mental and emotional scars. We have each other; your mom has Daisy. Of course, that is, if you want to do that.

"You may want to stick with your original idea, to keep her with us on our days off. What I'm suggesting is a work in progress. You're in charge. You make your own choices, always. I'd love to have a pet in our lives, but I would love it more to have you. It's a no-brainer. I love you."

Alex waits for Claire to embrace his ideas. Because he has a keen sense for organizing and prioritizing the challenges that come his way, he knows there are times when it's wise to exercise a bit of patience until others have a chance to catch up. When Alex sees that Claire's staring off into the distance, he figures this is one of those times.

"You should probably think this through. Sort it out and see how you feel about it all. Maybe tomorrow you'll have an answer. We can always replace the door, but getting ready for Daisy would be a smart thing to do."

Claire likes his logic. It sounds perfect, yet she's resistant, hoping he's sincere about the option to decide for herself. Claire rubs her arms as if she's chilly, "Alex, when I feel rested, I'll be able to think more clearly."

Alex looks at Claire, as if he's studying her. "Claire, if you feel I'm rushing you, I can easily step back. Do you want to wait to see if the kennel calls before we install a door? What if I'm working and don't have the time. I just want you to have what you need if you get Daisy. It's one less thing to stress over."

Claire nods, letting him know that she at least heard what he said. "Alex, pull in behind my car."

The two of them walk through the side door together, but she feels totally alone. "Alex, I just want some time to get used to all of this. My mother should meet you and…"

"I have met your mother. Remember, bowling? Your parents came one time. They were both super friendly. Your dad said they thought it would be nice to meet some of the people you worked with."

"What do you have, a photographic memory? That was eons ago."

"Claire, I remember because meeting your parents was

important to me. I've been waiting for this for a very long time, remember?"

"My mother is different now, more fragile because Dad is gone."

"I think we should go visit her, especially now."

Claire feels awkward, put on the spot. She wants to find a way to convey her feelings without hurting his. "Alex, you have some great ideas, but I need to think about this through. I need you to slow down. Let me talk to her and prepare her. You barely proposed. Let's focus on learning more about each another."

"Okay, you need time; I'll give you time. If you need space, I can give you that too."

Her heart skips a beat and dejection creeps in. He sounds like he's on the edge of running out of patience. All she wants seems so simple—slow down. All she's asking for is a little more time.

Feeling frustrated, she gives in, "Go ahead and look around the house. I just realized how tired I am. I want to stay home tonight and get a good night's sleep. Tomorrow, I'm sure I'll feel more rested, and we can talk then. Maybe Stacy will call from the kennel, and I'll have something solid to go by."

Tears begin to pool in her eyes. "Alex, I sure could use a hug right now." In two steps, his arms are around her. "Ah, this feels so good, so natural." She breaths in the scent of him. Beginning to relax she whispers, "Now, everything is perfect."

"Yes, it is."

Regardless of her fatigue, Claire feels like there's an invisible force drawing them closer until, at last, they kiss. Their passion quickly reawakens, taking her to that special place. She moans involuntarily. She hears him speak but isn't quite sure what he said. "Alex, what?"

His voice has grown husky, "I want you, Claire." Then, suddenly, he pulls away. She sees him swallow hard before he speaks again. "Sweetheart, you're tired and have things to process. I'm sure you'll agree, we should wait."

She knows he's right, but even so, she feels a strong wave of disappointment. All the signs are pointing to being together. It feels so right. It's her turn to swallow.

Hopeful that she can steady herself better if she doesn't have Alex in her sight, she turns away from him. Her heart is beating faster than normal. As Claire breathes deeply, she purposely releases the hunger, the want, and the passion that she's struggling to hold in place. Finally, she dares to meet his eyes. "You, of course, are right. But wow." Shaking her head, she finds herself feeling anxious and begins to laugh, "That is some mighty powerful energy."

Alex starts toward her. Holding her hand up, she warns, "Don't Alex. I don't think I can stop myself again."

Alex's eyes darken as he admits, "I'm disappointed too. Of course, you are correct. I should go."

Forgetting all about his research around the house, she opens the front door, "Yep, you should go."

Chapter Twenty-Five

The following day, Claire, ready for a new beginning, decides to complete the online adoption application and then call her mother.

When she calls her mother, she notices that her mom sounds calmer than she had during their last conversation. Claire takes a chance, "Do you remember my coworker, Alex, from the bowling alley ages ago?"

"No, I don't believe I do. Why?"

"Well, because, I'm dating him. We've known each other for years and well…" Knowing she's repeating herself, she stammers, "…we're dating." She's still unable to tell her mother that they want to get married, that he asked, and she agreed.

"So, Mom…" Claire hesitates again, "…yesterday I visited the animal shelter. I'm really serious about adopting a pet. The only thing is, I feel bad about leaving a dog alone while I'm at work. I wondered how you might feel about dog sitting?" There it was, dead silence.

In that moment, Claire doesn't know how to proceed. *Dear God, please let me help my mother. Please press upon her that it may be good for her to open her heart, to take a chance on loving again, even if it's a small dog.*

"Mom?"

"Yes, dear."

Claire knows in that awkward moment of silence that she has somehow crossed an invisible line. She backs up to try to make them both feel better. "Anyway, I'm just thinking about it."

Claire scrambles, wanting to find the correct words to describe how she feels, "Mom, I'm feeling… well, it doesn't matter. It's just an idea." Then, at last, she says, "I found a female dog. Her name is Daisy, but the chances of getting her are iffy. I'm waiting for a call from the shelter. It's just a slim chance, anyhow."

"We have…" Margaret stops herself. As she speaks, Claire hears her mom's anger and frustration. "When am I going to get used to this? I mean, I have a fenced-in yard, that's about all I have to offer."

"Mom, let's just think about it. I may not even get the call, but she's a sweet little thing. Gentle. You would love her. But what about you? Are you feeling any better?"

"I'm better when the sun shines, and you know how often we get that these days."

"Pray for the clouds to move away."

Claire can almost see her mother nod in response to her suggestion. "Claire, you're such a good daughter. I do appreciate you." Then Margaret begins to cry.

"Mom, you know I love you. I sure wish you weren't alone over there."

"I have friends, Claire. I just don't want to visit any of them."

Feeling her pain, Claire whispers, "I know. I know."

Then, a veil of darkness lifts. Claire feels a measure of relief as she listens to her mother speak. The timbre of her voice changes, becoming a little stronger. Claire hopes that this is a sign of better things to come.

"When my mother died, I remember feeling this way, but I had your dad for support. God, I missed her though. And I still do. Although, not as much as when my dad died. This time

I feel like I'm in a deep, black hole, filled with muck with no possible way to get out. I feel stuck, wedged into this little pit, and everything around me is pressing against me. I can't move; I'm unable to free myself. The pressure is pure sorrow and pain.

"A horrible madness has been let loose in my mind and has taken over. God, I want this pain to end. Most of the time I feel dead, numb. I have no ambition, no drive. I don't have any desire to do the things I used to. I'm all alone. I imagine this to be hell."

"I hear you, Mom. I know, with time, the pain will ease. I'm sorry you're going through this." An unexplainable force comes over her, and the words gush out, "Mom, I'm coming over."

"No, Claire," she pleads, "I'm a mess. The house is a mess. Oh, God, Claire, please don't."

Claire hears the desperation in her mother's voice, but she knows she can't listen to any more of her pitiful excuses any longer. With a conviction she exclaims, "I'm coming over. It'll take me about forty-five minutes. I'll see you soon."

As soon she ends the call, the phone rings. "Claire? This is Stacy over at Find a Friend Kennel. I just finished reviewing your application. Great job, and I have news."

Claire's heart expands, "What? What is your news? I hope it's good news!"

"The other party who was interested in Daisy adopted another dog. They didn't want to wait any longer. Their adoption was time-sensitive—a present for their son's birthday. If you're still interested, we need to get you scheduled for a home inspection as soon as possible."

Letting out a huge sigh of relief, Claire exclaims, "Oh wow. I was holding my breath. Stacy, yes, I'm still interested. Any time tomorrow is perfect."

"Good. Then I'm scheduling you for a home inspection at 2 o'clock tomorrow."

"Perfect. I'm so excited. Thank you, Stacy. I was just going to pick up my Mom for lunch. I hope we can stop by to see

Daisy. I'd like to introduce my mother to you and the dog."

"Oh, yes, we would love to meet her."

In a rush, Claire calls Alex. "Stacy just called. I'm adopting Daisy! I'm going over to take Mom to lunch and then, hopefully, go over to the kennel. I just wanted you to know."

"That's great, Claire. What about the doggy door? You want me to pick one up and get it installed while you are out? Claire, you know I'd love to help you."

"Would you? That would be absolutely perfect. Thank you, Alex. There's an extra key in the carport near the edge of the door. It's sitting in a corner space. You should be able to find it with no problem. I'll call you later."

"Maybe we can do dinner tonight?"

Wistfully, Claire answers, "I don't know how this is all going to work out. I have to play it by ear."

As always, Claire knocks on the front door of her mother's home to announce her arrival, then lets herself in with her spare key. She sings out, "Mom? I'm here."

There's no answer. Claire doesn't see her anywhere. She walks straight to the master bedroom, finding her mother sitting on her bed and brushing her hair in slow strokes, almost as if she has traveled to another world. Her eyes are not focused on anything in particular.

Softly, Claire announces, "Mom, I'm here." Claire is immediately troubled by her mother's appearance. She's still in her rumpled nightgown, and it looks like her hair hasn't been washed in a while. Claire shifts her attitude. She'll not let this get her down.

Her mother finally acknowledges Claire's voice, mumbles, "Oh, Claire, it's you. I didn't hear you come in."

"Mom, why don't I vacuum and load the dishwasher while you're in the shower. I'm taking you out for a hot meal over at Nate's Diner. I know you love his meatloaf and mashed potatoes."

Claire watches her mother continue to sit as if she hasn't heard her. With authority Claire urges her to get up, "Come on, let's get you in the shower. I'll find you some clean clothes and lay them here on the bed." Her mother doesn't respond so Claire decides to use the sense of touch along with a commanding voice to see if that will encourage her mother. Claire uses this method to help uplift, inspire, and guide the residents at The Manor. It usually works.

Gently, Claire touches her mother's arm, "Do you want help, Mom?" Margaret looks at her daughter, "Maybe a hand."

Taking her mother's hand, Claire and her mother move toward the bathroom. "Mom, take a shower and shampoo your hair. Your clothes will be here on the bed."

Claire waits until she hears the water running to get started on the housework. Taking a look around, Claire agrees, the place is a mess. Her mom must be more depressed than she thought. It appears as if her mother hasn't done much of anything for a few weeks, if not longer. In that moment, Claire decides to check on her mother more often.

The living room is dusted and vacuumed, and all the dirty dishes are in the dishwasher before Claire hears the water shut off. *The place sure could use a thorough cleaning. No time now though.*

Looking pale and withdrawn, her mother reminds Claire of some of the residents at The Manor. She feels uncomfortable. They have switched places, and she's the one in charge now. Claire's afraid of losing her.

As if Margaret is one of her patients, Claire pushes aside her fear, "Mom, put some makeup on. I'm taking you out to Nate's for lunch. Want me to do your hair like I used to?"

"That would be nice, Claire." Patting Claire's hand, she continues, "You're such a good daughter."

During lunch, Margaret picks at her food. Claire is grateful for what she does eat and that she's out of her house. "That was really good, Mom. We have enough leftovers for another meal. How about we get some apple pie to go?" Claire, not waiting for her mother to turn down her offer, flags down the waitress to put in the order and to ask for a doggy bag.

"Mom, we're ten minutes from the kennel. I'd sure like to run over there and see Daisy. I got the call, and I can adopt her if I still want to."

"Okay, but I have to get home soon," Margaret replies.

Knowing that her mother is using her old standby excuse to get out of something, Claire asks her, "Oh? What are you doing this afternoon?"

Confused, her mother looks at her daughter and stares. She no longer knows what they're talking about. Claire immediately says, "Well, okay then. We'll go to the kennel together. It'll work out just fine."

As Claire drives into the parking lot, something connects. "Claire?"

"Mom, we're at the kennel to visit Daisy for just a few minutes. I'll take you straight home afterwards."

Entering the building, they hear all the barking and whimpering. Claire notices that her mom begins to look around. Maybe she's waking up a bit after her exceptionally, long, deep sleep.

Claire watches her mother pause at various enclosures and look at the dogs. "What a shame, Claire."

"It's a shame, Mother. I think Daisy is over here, unless they moved her."

Daisy, a few enclosures down, is sitting in the front of the pen. When her mother sees her, she takes the information packet to read the details and then asks, "Is this the one you were talking about?"

Claire chuckles, "I thought you didn't hear a single word I said about Daisy." Bending over, Margaret timidly greets Daisy. "Is that you, Daisy?" Then, looking into Daisy's big brown eyes, Margaret speaks to Daisy as if she were a person. "You know that Claire, my daughter, wants to adopt you, take you home to live with her. What do you think about that?"

Margaret pokes her fingers through the chain link enclosure, wanting to touch the dog. Sounding urgent she asks, "Claire, can you please get someone to let her out of this awful place?"

Claire doesn't have to go far to find a young man with

kinky auburn hair, freckles, and arms decorated with tattoos. His name tag reads Doug. "Hi Doug, we could use some help with Daisy over there. I'm Claire." Wanting to savor this moment, Claire briefly closes her eyes, feeling her heart expand. Proudly she announces, "I'm adopting her."

"Oh sure, Daisy, right. The little angel. Her quarantine was just lifted."

As they approach Daisy's cage, Doug takes note of the woman bending over in front of the pen and glances at Claire. "My mother," Claire whispers. Doug reaches for the information sheet to double check Daisy's status and to document what he's doing. "That's right, Daisy, we're getting you out in just a minute."

"Doug, this is my mother, Margaret McCurdy."

Still bent over, Margaret says, "Claire, give me a hand, will you?" Embarrassed, she looks at Doug. "Just a little stiff here."

Claire holds her hand out for her mother, "No problem." Doug introduces himself. "Mrs. McCurdy, I'm Doug." He puts his hand out to take hers. "I'm here to assist you with Daisy."

Unlocking the gate, he crouches down to speak to Daisy. "Look, girl, your family is here." He strokes her head, then skillfully hooks the leash to her collar and scoops her up. Handing the leash to Claire he announces, "In case you want to take her for a walk."

But not willing to give Daisy up quite yet, he continues to lavish his attention on the pup. Doug coos, "There now, Daisy." Daisy barks, and they all laugh. "She's a cute one, and smart— she knows what I'm saying." Noticing Margaret's keen interest, he asks, "Mrs. McCurdy, would you like to hold her?"

Claire's heart expands as she watches her mother's eyes light up at the thought of holding Daisy in her arms. When Daisy licks her nose and cheek before she settles in, her mother beams. It looks as though they belong together. "Claire, look at this will you? Miss Daisy likes me."

Claire smiles, "She sure does."

Looking directly at Claire, Doug smiles as he asks, "Who

is it that's adopting?"

Knowing where this is going, she laughs, "Well, I'm the one who filled out the application, but I think we may have a change of plans. Mom, do you want to take Daisy home?"

It's as if her mother has returned from her mournful travels. With pure delight written on her face, Margaret's eyes sparkle while she cuddles Daisy. "Oh, Claire she's a sweetheart, but I don't think I could manage her alone now, do you?"

Knowing how difficult it is for her to use the word *alone*, Claire wants to take her mother in her arms and hug her. Instead, she tells her, "Well, honestly, yes, I do think you can manage Daisy. But I can still go ahead and adopt her, and you can dog sit for me. Is that what you'd rather do?"

Margaret ignores Claire. She's talking to Miss Daisy like they are the best of friends. Claire turns to Doug and says, "Doug, it looks as if my mother will be adopting Miss Daisy."

Doug's eyes widened. Laughing, he says to Claire, "Does she know that?" Turning to get Margaret's attention, he asks, "Mrs. McCurdy, Claire says you're adopting Daisy. Is that correct?"

Margaret looks at him, then at Claire, and then at Daisy. "I guess so. Do you want to live with me Miss Daisy?" Daisy barks and licks her face.

Doug, excited by the turn of events, laughs again, "I take that to be an affirmative."

"Mom, we have some paperwork to fill out."

Doug proceeds to explain a few of the details about adopting a pet as they walk up to the front desk. Feeling a bit bashful, Claire makes the announcement to Stacy. "It seems things have shifted just a bit here. My mother, Margaret McCurdy, wants to adopt Daisy."

Stacy laughs and nods knowingly. "I've seen this happen before. No surprises here. We can easily change the home inspection address and keep the same time. Mrs. McCurdy, how about we…"

Perplexed, Margaret hesitates. Glancing at Claire, Stacy

begins again, "Mrs. McCurdy, we want to do a home inspection to ensure Daisy is being placed in the correct home. We want to confirm the integrity of the adoption by making sure Daisy is safe. We can come by your place tomorrow afternoon, say 2 o'clock? Additionally, by law, Daisy must be spayed before we can finalize the adoption."

"We can schedule Daisy to have her procedure this afternoon. She'll be good to go late tomorrow afternoon, providing you're approved for the adoption and barring any complications. For this to happen fluently, all of the adoption procedures should be completed by tomorrow afternoon, and I'll call you as soon as you're approved."

At that point, Margaret looks overwhelmed. "Mrs. McCurdy," Stacy says, "Don't you worry. This is all standard procedure. Everything will go smoothly. You'll be fine. I'm sure of it. Anyway, I'll call you tomorrow as soon as I know. If approved, can you pick her up around five tomorrow evening?"

Margaret pales, "Oh, my, this is happening so fast. I'm not sure." Claire and Margaret look at each other. Claire speaks first, "I know. Wow! You never know when a surprise may come your way, do you Mother?"

Stacy, seeing Margaret's look of concern, decides to address the elephant in the room. "Mrs. McCurdy, Claire told me of your recent loss. Getting a pet may seem overwhelming, but Daisy will be a great comfort to you. Even so, we don't want you to feel like we're bulldozing you into any decision. If you aren't sure, we can leave it as is." Stacy looks to Claire for help.

"Stacy, let me talk with my mom for a few minutes in private."

"No problem. I have a phone call to make. If you will excuse me, I'll be back in a couple of minutes."

Claire waits for Stacy to leave the room before speaking. "Mother, I don't want to push you into adopting Daisy. But I couldn't help watching you with her. She loves you, and you're so good with her. It's like you're a perfect match for each other. You're meant to be together."

As if an entirely different person has taken over, her mother asserts, "Claire, her name is Miss Daisy, and I want to go ahead with the adoption." Then she searches Claire's face for reassurance. "My place is a total wreck. Can you please help me out with the cleaning?"

"Sure Mom. I'd like to call Alex and see if… Oh God, I just remembered! I have to call Alex. He's at my place this very minute installing the doggy door for Daisy. I'll be right back."

It takes five rings before Alex answers. "Claire. I was just about to cut the hole in your door. What's up?"

"Alex, I'm so relieved I caught you in time. There's been a huge change in plans." Claire explains that her mother is now adopting Daisy—Miss Daisy. She hears Alex laugh.

"I know, right?"

"Should I drive to your mom's house to install the door?"

"No, right now, I'm not sure of anything. I'm sorry. I'll call you later with an update. You should see my mom with Miss Daisy. I'm so grateful. I should go, we're about to begin the application process."

"Okay then. We'll talk later. You call me, okay?"

"Sure thing, Alex."

Turning back toward the desk, Claire sees her mother in the inner office, sitting down and filling out the paperwork. Her body language reminds Claire that her mother is not yet totally recovered; she's still fragile. She doesn't want to push her mom any more by introducing Alex right now. The doggy door will have to wait.

Looking up at Claire, Margaret concedes, "Claire, I want to finish this, but I'm so very tired. Maybe you could answer these last few questions for me? After I rest for a bit, we can figure out how to get everything done in time."

In the car, they talk about some of the changes that will inevitably occur. Then to comfort her mother, Claire says, "Mom, we'll get everything finished in time. I assure you; I'll help out. After all, I love Miss Daisy too. If she ends up being too much of a handful, I can always take her. I'll be the one who does the dog sitting. I wanted some company, but now, because I'm dating Alex, I'm not so lonely anymore." Pushing her luck, she continues, "Cross your fingers Mom, he may be the one."

That evening Claire decides to stay in to get some rest. Tomorrow will be very full. Calling Alex, she promises that she'll make time for him after the adoption is complete.

Chapter Twenty-Six

Everything worked out perfectly. She went to her mother's early to finish cleaning in time for the inspection. At 2 p.m. sharp, a middle-aged woman, Cynthia, came to do the inspection and the interview. After the walk-through, Cynthia gushed, "Margaret, your home is lovely and perfect. So many beautiful antiques. I absolutely love your quilts. Did you make them?"

Margaret is tickled that Cynthia showed an interest in her quilts. "Yes, I did. Thank you."

"You might consider moving some of your treasures to a safe place until Daisy is a little older. In a sense you can consider her a toddler. She needs to mature a bit. You remember how rambunctious toddlers can be?" Not waiting for a response Cynthia continues, "Truly, though, your home is large enough that Daisy can wander around but not so big that she'll get misplaced." She chuckles at her joke. "Seriously, you'd be surprised at how many dogs go to homes without yards. You're fortunate to have one. Nonetheless, when Daisy fully recovers from her procedure, it'll be highly beneficial for her to go on daily walks. She needs the exercise, and getting outdoors will help her use up some of her energy."

Later that afternoon, Stacy from the kennel calls, "Margaret, everything is on schedule. Will you be able to pick Daisy up tonight, say a few minutes before five? We close at 5:30."

Margaret looks at Claire and repeats the question. Claire gives her a thumbs up. "Yes, we'll be there."

"The doctor wants to watch over her as long as possible today, allowing Daisy to rest. She'll recover surprisingly fast because she's young, but she'll nap most of the time. Keep a watchful eye on Miss Daisy's mood, keep her stitches clean and dry, and try to make sure she stays calm. No throwing balls or playing chase until a full week has passed. A quiet week will serve perfectly as a transition period for both of you."

After making sure her mother and Miss Daisy are settled at home, Claire says her goodbyes. "Mom, I need a day to rest before I go back to work. But, if you need something, call me. Remember, Miss Daisy will want to sleep most of the time. From the looks of it, I'm sure you both will do fine."

At home, Claire calls Alex to fill him in on the latest developments. They both feel it's best to let Mom settle in with Miss Daisy for the first week before mentioning the possibility of a doggy door. That will be a great time for them to meet. That is, if Alex is still in Boston.

"What have you been doing?"

"I am focused on a new project."

"Oh, what is it?"

"I'm not ready to talk about it just yet. It's important that I maintain that mysterious edge." They both laugh. "There may always be that element to me," he says. "Claire, I'm at a crucial point. I have to keep working."

"That's fine. I have plans for tonight anyway."

Claire decides to take a shower and put on the most comfortable clothes she owns—her PJs. She makes enough popcorn to fill the largest bowl in the cupboard, mixes in lots of butter and salt. Before she sits down in her overstuffed recliner to enjoy an old flick, *It Happened One Night,* with

Clark Gable and Claudette Colbert, she lights the fireplace. The entire weekend has gone nonstop. She just wants to relax.

Before she starts the movie, thoughts of the situation with Charles and Alex play in her mind. There's nothing definitive with Charles' status, which Alex finds troubling, and so does Claire. It's unusual for a patient not to respond to the medication to increase the production of white blood cells. For a few minutes, she stews over the possibility that the doctors may be missing something—some tiny detail that could change the course of his treatment. But she's sure they will figure it out.

Just as she settles in for her movie, she's startled by a loud thud. The noise sounded like something hit a wall or fell in the kitchen. She can't imagine what it might be. *Now, would be a perfect time to have a watch dog. What was I thinking when I agreed to let my mother adopt Miss Daisy?*

Claire looks everywhere for the source of the noise and finds nothing. Does she have a ghost?

Wanting to forget about the noise and life in general, Claire sits down again. She gets comfortable, ready to get on with the movie, when she hears the same racket again. This time, it seems to have taken on an air of urgency. *Can a noise even convey urgency? Weird.* She still doesn't go to investigate; she knows she'll find nothing tangible.

She reaches for the remote to turn off the TV. For some reason, the movie no longer interests her. Instead, she closes her eyes to meditate. Without intending to, she quickly slips into a state of grace as love and gratitude pour through her. She's especially grateful for God's benevolence that has been bestowed upon her during this past weekend with Alex, her mother, and Miss Daisy.

With these emotions running through her, she increases her vibration. She feels the heavy load she has been carrying fade away, replaced with a sense of renewal; she's ready to continue on with her chosen endeavors.

Claire laughs at herself and says a silent, *thank you* to those who watch over her. In that exact moment she hears the thud for the third time. In a clear voice, she acknowledges, "Okay, I'm ready to know the source, the reason for the noise. I'm pretty sure it's not the result of some freak accident; I have a guest here. Maybe there's something you want me to know, or perhaps you want to be invited to watch the movie with me? It's a really good one."

Claire feels unsure of herself, acknowledging that talking out loud like this sounds odd, yet the way things have been going lately, she feels it may be wise to be open to the possibility of someone or something being here.

She closes her eyes again and waits, willing herself to be one with the source, whatever it is. Relaxing into it, Claire feels ripples of energy moving from the top of her head to the bottom of her feet, over and over again. The feeling is wonderful, and Claire prays, "Don't stop whatever this is, please continue."

Then without intending to, Claire asks, "How is this happening? Who is doing this to me?" Deciding that it's pointless to ask any questions, she lets go, no longer caring how or why, only that she's grateful for this sensation. Tears of gratitude stream down her face. At last, the feeling slows down, tapering off until it completely stops.

Claire hears a voice telepathically speaking to her. "Claire, I have come for you."

"What? Who is this? What do you mean, 'you have come for me?'" Claire is reminded of Harry and Frank. "You mean it's my time?"

"Be not afraid. I am one of those who watch over you. I am one of your spiritual guides. I am Hannah. I have come to introduce myself to you, although we have always known each other in the higher realms of Light. The time has come—you are ready for more."

Chuckling, Claire concedes to the irony of it all. "More? Do you know how many times I've heard that exact phrase in the past week? Is this what Frank meant? I thought he meant more in my life." She finds herself whispering. "I thought he meant with Alex and helping out at The Manor with the patients. I had no idea he meant I would be receiving house guests."

"Dearest Claire. This message, as all messages, is intended to be understood on a multi-dimensional plane of consciousness. Let me explain. Our messages always have multiple meanings—a deeper meaning so to speak. A plane in your third-dimensional realm is flat, usually large, and usually barren. This particular plane that I speak of, unlike what you are accustomed to, has many levels. I merely use this as an example to give you imagery that will assist you with understanding my explanation."

Hannah stops speaking, allowing Claire time to study the three-dimensional illustration she projects, slowly rotating it in Claire's mind. The image, much like a blueprint, shows the basic lines of a large area, free of obstructions with many levels and corridors. None of the corridors or floors are closed as you would find with an architectural drawing. It looks like a maze, open and inclusive, allowing freedom of choice to take whichever direction is desired.

"Look closely at your choices," Hannah continues. "There are many possibilities, dear One. Life is not what it seems. There were times in the past that you felt limited in your choices. This is not the case. You have been given a great gift to assist others in their time of trial and transition. You are being honored at this time for your expansion. This gift is yours to accept if you so choose. We know your heart. We have seen a great impetus to be of service to others. Know, yet, the choice is always yours to make."

"What do you mean *the gift*? Is it to receive the messages from those like you?"

"Yes, to receive messages and so much more. The gift is to have an expanded understanding of life, and the ability to use it to the betterment of your community and your world. Always, as I mentioned, it is your choice to serve in this way. To give is to receive. You have given, dear One, with an open heart. It is time that you receive expanded modalities such as telepathic communications and expansion in other areas. I speak of extra sensory perception—sight, sound, touch, and so on. You are ready to receive more."

Claire, in awe, is at a loss for words. "I believe I understand," She hesitates, "…at least a little bit." Suddenly, her eyes flutter open, like something or someone other than herself is controlling her reflexes.

It's then that Claire sees Hannah standing before her—a glorious, angelic being, radiating golden white Light. Her resplendent dress shimmers like a thousand suns. Easily, she fits the description of a fairy godmother in a child's storybook. Claire is held spellbound.

Her attention is drawn to Hannah's beautiful, long, golden tresses with golden pearls woven into it. Finding herself in awe of Hannah's perfection, she stares, unable to take her eyes from her.

Hannah's oval face is utterly flawless, reminding Claire of the sculptures carved from alabaster in the various museums she's visited. Looking into her deep azure eyes, Claire feels Hannah's love and compassion. Hannah's nose is slender, emanating a regal quality. When Hannah speaks, Claire notices her full ruby lips and perfectly shaped, dazzling, white teeth. Realizing that she's only seeing portions of Hannah, her perception instantly broadens as if she has physically stepped back to take in the whole of her. Claire now sees Hannah floating inside what looks to be concentric circles. She wonders if Hannah is radiating the spheres?

For some reason, Claire isn't apprehensive. Instead, she's drawn in, captivated, ready to receive this love for all eternity. Claire feels completely calm, peaceful. "Hannah?"

"Yes, my dearest Claire. How can I help you?"

"How may I contact you? There have been times that I felt I needed guidance, for example, with Harry and his family. I understand…" Claire catches herself, realizing that Frank approached her concerning Harry. Will Hannah be able to answer any of her questions?

As if reading her mind, Hannah says, "Dear One let me answer you."

"But I didn't ask you anything."

"Ah, but you did. I know your concerns. I hear your thoughts. Yes, I know of your mission to assist Harry in identifying the source of his anger, and why he feels his life is futile. It is the desire of the All to assist in his healing and to repair the family unit before he transitions to the next plane. There is nothing that you can't speak to me about. Know that I Am One With the All.

"I see that my words confuse you. The All, dearest Claire, is All That Is. In your realm, there are those who describe this as God. Know that you can call upon me at any time. I am always nearby. I know and hear your thoughts, your voice, your frequency. All you have to do is set your intention, focus on me, and I will come."

Breathing deeply, Claire nods. Not knowing what is appropriate, she says, "Thank you, Hannah. I hope that we can talk again."

"Dearest Claire, I know of your union with Alex. Be not afraid. In the mind of the All, you and Alex are committed to one another. You are in wait to announce your love for one another to your family and friends. Be it known that in the mind of the All it is done. You are married and shall share the remaining years of your lives together in support of one another. The two of you are watched over—always.

"I ask that you speak to Alex about this gift. In other words, I am reminding you to be open with your beloved. Your journeys are eternally interconnected. It is time that the two of you exercise these gifts as you minister to the sick."

"Hannah, please, I don't understand what you mean."

"Use the power of prayer not only with your patients but in all of life's situations. God is the Way, the Truth, and the Light. Know that it is God who ministers through you to these people. Invite God to bring forth the measures of healing energy that are for the highest good to all those who are in need.

"During your daily walk, you meet many people, all of whom require healing on some level. Remember, dear One, people heal in a multitude of ways. Many troubles go undetected by the everyday bystander. You must give God, shall we say, permission to work through you. This is how it is done in higher realms.

"God gave you, humanity, free will. This is to let you choose of your own volition to act accordingly to the Divine Will, to surrender to the Source of all Life, giving of yourself as a conduit for God's healing Grace. I am Hannah, the Angel of Divine Intention and Will. I am here to teach you how to best use the gifts that have been bestowed upon you. I am with you always.

"Breathe in the Light. Feel how the Light lifts you up toward the heavens. You feel as if you are floating. I tell you that your etheric body is floating. You have bodies more than one. The etheric body is your Light body, which has joined the physical body for this journey and experience here on this lower, three-dimensional plane called Earth.

"It is a collaborative effort to be sure. It is a journey to experience free will, of course. But also, your journey is, like all of humanity's, about expansion, taking you to a full understanding that you are the essence of God having taken human form for this special experience.

"What a joyous and wondrous gift to experience this—to know, Claire, that it is your choice to follow God in all that you are and do. You do this because you are the One.

"Claire, know that this was your choice before you came to this Earth plane. Now, it is for you to choose consciously to do this and be this."

Astounded, Claire listens as Hannah continues, "It is time

I take my leave. Remember my words, dear One. They are meant to guide you. Remember also that you can always call upon me, and that you are not meant to traverse this world alone."

After Hannah fades away, Claire ponders over Hannah's words. Hannah had said that Claire is to choose, that she has free will to choose. Thinking about it for a moment confirms what Claire has always known as truth. She has always believed this in her heart. She knows exactly where she stands, her *choice* is to serve God by helping the sick. She watches over those who are in need. Then Claire hears Hannah's sweet angelic voice, "Thank you, dearest One for serving, you are kind beyond words."

For hours, it seems, Claire sits in her recliner. Finally, she looks at the clock. A mere hour has passed. She's compelled to find a journal to write her experience.

Chapter Twenty-Seven

The next day at The Manor, Claire barely sees Alex. Neither of them is able to find time to talk with each other. There was one moment that he winked at her, smiled, then mouthed, "I love you." Her heart melted. She misses him.

Later she sees him in the hall and hurries her pace to catch up with him. "Alex, can we talk after work?"

He nods. "Meet me at the nurse's station at 7 o'clock if you can. I'll wait for you." Then he's off.

As Claire catches up on some paperwork, another nurse, Wendy, interrupts, "Claire, Harry has become extremely cantankerous and unpredictable. Watch out for yourself."

Claire chuckles, "Wendy, you possess an unusual flare for drama." Not wanting to alienate her, though, Claire adds, "He's in a foul mood to be sure, but you're making it sound like he's dangerous. You really don't think that, do you?"

"Make no mistake here, Claire. Harry's sworn, many times, that he's going get out of this joint even if he has to walk out stark naked. He's gone so far as to threaten some of us. He's going to be transferred to the psyche ward if he doesn't get himself under control."

Claire decides to have a chat with Harry to find out what's troubling him. She knows there's another side to this. The staff is caring for him, and they deserve his cooperation and his respect, even though they're busy with other patients. A conversation is in order. Things must be set straight. The staff doesn't need to feel afraid of the residents—ever.

As soon as Claire walks into Harry's room, she wants to turn around and leave. The stench is that bad. Taking in as little air as possible, she calls out, "Harry, you doing okay in here?" She doesn't wait for a response. "Did you have an accident? Here, let me help you." As she works to assist him, she asks, point blank, "Why are you giving some of the nurses so much trouble? What's going on?"

His voice sounds scratchy, like he may have a sore throat, yet she unmistakably hears the animosity oozing from his voice. "I want to get out of here."

Seeing her name tag, he softens his voice, "Claire, where the hell have you been? It's been near a week since I've seen you." Taking notice that Harry slipped into a different speech pattern leaves her wondering and feeling a bit more cautious. *Wendy may have known exactly what she was talking about.*

Claire makes sure to enunciate every word, "Harry, I took my usual weekend. Everyone needs a little time to rest. I work really long days and then take long weekends. Crazy I know, but that's how it's done here." She pauses for added effect, "Guess what?" Again, she doesn't wait for his response. "You remember Alex? He was one of the nurses that helped you out when you first arrived. His last name is Malone!"

Grabbing his cup, Harry coughs up phlegm, then spits into the cup. "What? Who cares?"

"Harry, is your throat sore? You sound like it's difficult to speak."

"Right, it hurts."

"I'll order a culture and see what's going on."

Knowing Harry's irritability isn't only caused by physical illness, Claire is mindful of all of his facial expressions and behaviors. Watching for any change, she says, "I was really excited, knowing that your beautiful Patti Jo and Alex share the same last name. He might be related. Guess what? I'm going marry that man so that may make us related as well. Wouldn't that be something?" Then she changes the subject. She likes the idea of giving him something to mull over.

"Harry, I think we need to get you in the shower. A sponge bath isn't going to do the trick this time. Why didn't you call for help?"

Looking defeated, Harry murmurs, "Claire, what I do is none of your business."

"Harry?"

Harry refuses to look at her.

"Harry? Some of the nurses are complaining. If they're complaining that means we, you included, need to do things differently. We all have to get along."

Harry raises his voice despite having a sore throat, "I don't like it here and you know it."

"I sure do. But Harry..., Harry? Look at me, will you?"

Harry raises his eyes to meet Claire's.

"Thank you. We are both here for the long haul. We want to make the best of it. If you don't call us to help you when this happens and then you have visitors… well, think about that. When you have visitors, is it your aim to chase them away before they even come into your room? Is that what you're doing? It's a plan, but not a good one. The idea is to get you well. If none of us can stand to be in here long enough to help you, you may end up staying here forever. God help us all.

"If I were in your situation, I'd change that attitude in a hurry. It seems you'd rather go home to do as you please, but instead you're doing things to prevent that from happening. I'm going to revise your plan. Listen up now." Claire paused for additional effect, "Do you know which nursing aid is here today?" She knows but believes it might be a fun to get Harry thinking too.

"Nah, I don't know. Who cares?"

"Harry, come on. Use your good old-fashioned common sense. We have the good aids and the *good aids.*" She winks, hoping Harry takes the bait. "You remember Janet? Is she here or is it the other one, Diego? No? How 'bout Christine? Do you remember her?"

"Claire, I don't feel like playing any of your silly games. I don't feel like a shower either."

Claire patiently replies, "Harry, remember the first time we met? I asked some male attendants, including Alex, to assist you? Wouldn't it better if you chose who helps you into the shower?" Harry crosses his arms over his chest. His expression doesn't change.

"Nope? Well then, I guess you're stuck with me. Meanwhile, let's see how you're doing with your exercises."

"What exercises?"

Harry's attitude along with the smell begins to get on Claire's nerves. She knows relaxing in these types of situations is key. "Remember? You need to practice the breathing exercises to help you reduce your anxiety."

She sees by his confused expression that he doesn't have a clue what she's saying. "I'll tell you what. After your shower, I'll get Janet to come in here and work with you. We want you to go home, if at all possible. Harry, don't you want to go home?"

Harry moans, then says, "Claire, you know I'm never going to get well. We both know I'm never going home."

As much as Claire hates hearing it, she knows Harry is speaking the truth. For the first time, she realizes the extent of the situation—Harry has no hope of recovery or of going home. To him, there's no reason to try or cooperate. Claire looks Harry in the eyes, "Has Frank been here bothering you again?"

Harry's color transforms to a ghostly white. She clearly hears the dread in his voice. "You know Frank?"

In a lighthearted manner, she says, "Sure I do. Doesn't everyone?"

Harry is speechless. Wanting to offer him a shred of hope, she decides to plant an idea into Harry's head, "You know,

Harry, I've been thinking. It's quite possible Frank sometimes gets mixed up with who he *thinks* he's going to take out of here and who needs to stay."

Harry squints at Claire, his mind spinning out of control. He's afraid to talk about this because, well, everyone thinks he's crazy. But now, what is the point in hiding it. "Frank told me I had to go with him and that I should get my affairs in order. Period. End of story."

"And did you listen?"

Confused, Harry asks, "Did I what?"

"Get your affairs in order?"

Ashamed, Harry looks down and quietly says, "I need my kids to do that. As far as I know, we aren't speaking."

Claire feels his pain. Despite his body odor, she gives him a hug. When she backs away, she meets his gaze and says, "Harry, first things first. You're in control. You *can* control your attitude. This helps us help you. Will you at least try to cooperate with us? Take your shower, practice your breathing exercises, take that much deserved nap, then have a wonderful dinner."

Trying her best to entice Harry, Claire uses food as a power play. "I heard, by the way, that Salisbury steak and mashed potatoes are on the menu tonight. Oh yeah, there's also green beans. I know, green beans aren't the greatest, but the Salisbury steak is good. By then, you'll be ready to sleep. Tomorrow we can figure out a plan so you can have a conversation with your kids. How does that sound?"

Harry complains of being tired. Claire plunges forward, "I know, I know. Harry, I'm counting on you, and I believe you're going to get through this ordeal. It may not be the easiest thing you've ever done, but we'll pull *together*. Remember one day at a time. Okay?"

As it turns out, Janet is not available, so Claire asks Sherry, a newer aide, to help Harry with his shower. Sherry fully understands the situation by the way Claire explained it. Even though Sherry is newer, she has learned that Harry is one difficult man. Wanting to make the experience a little less overwhelming, Claire offers to get Janet to come in and assist Harry after Sherry helps him with his shower.

Part of Claire's job is to help the aides gain experience. Janet wants to become a nurse. For this reason, Claire looks for opportunities to place her in situations to force her to face her fears. Nursing is a messy business, to be sure, and working with residents who are difficult intimidates some of the aides.

After finding Janet, she tells her, "Instruct Harry to watch the monitor when he does his breathing exercises. That way he can begin to put together how deep, even breathing can slow his heart beat, helping him to calm down."

Taking a deep breath, Claire adds, "Janet, it's okay to flirt with Harry a little. He's one lonely, sad, and angry man, but he just wants to be loved. I'm sure you can make him smile."

With wide eyes, Janet merely nods and says, "Claire, you're the boss, but just so you know, your order may be too much for me to carry out."

"Janet, I realize 'my order' may be overwhelming but look at it this way, he'll be clean this time." Claire laughs as she watches Janet squirm. "It's our business to help our patients. Sometimes, it makes the process a whole lot easier if we encourage the residents to have a little fun."

Claire can see by Janet's expression that she isn't changing her attitude. "Oh, I get it Janet; he's definitely a tough sell. Do your best, that's all I ask. Let me know how it goes."

As Claire attends to other residents, thoughts of Alex creep into her mind. Then Charles pops into her mind, and she instinctively knows there's something horribly wrong. The knowing is so strong that she immediately sets out to find Alex.

On her way to the break room, she looks into every room with an open door. With no luck, she loops back to the nurses' station hoping to find Alex there. Disappointment sets in as she sees Derrick instead. Claire practically begs him to find Alex. "Derrick, I haven't been able to find Alex anywhere. This is *really* important. If you see him, please tell him I'm looking for him. He needs to call his brother, Charles, or his brother's doctor ASAP."

In a rush, she scribbles a note to leave on the counter at the nurse's station in case Derrick doesn't find him.

Alex,

Feeling that you should call Charles, NOW.

Love, Claire

It isn't until their shift ends that Claire and Alex finally connect and talk for a minute. "Alex, did you get my note?"

"Geez, Claire." Alex takes a deep breath, running his hands through his tousled hair, "There hasn't been time to breathe let alone call anyone. What happened anyway?"

"I had a strong sense that Charles may be in trouble, Alex. I've learned to pay attention to these feelings."

Unemotionally, Alex agrees, "I'll call now. Will you wait for me? Let's go for a coffee after. Okay?"

"Sure. This gives me an opportunity to check in with my mother." Claire feels nervous about what's going on with Charles and wants an excuse to keep from hearing Alex's phone conversation.

After three rings, her mother answers, sounding tired, but it's obvious that her spirit has rallied. "Claire, is that you? This pup is a feisty one, and even though she's recovering, Miss Daisy is sure keeping me busy. I'm fortunate that she takes long naps."

"How are you doing with getting her trained to go outside?"

Margaret sighs, "She uses these doggy pads they gave me at the kennel, but she's had a couple of mistakes. You should see her face when I tell her 'No.' She knows what I'm saying. She's intelligent and sensitive. I've been taking her outside when I catch her sniffing around. She knows she should go outdoors."

"What about a doggy door so you don't have to be on the lookout? Alex can install it. He says they're easy to do. Besides, it would be good for the two of you to meet."

"Alex? This is the fellow you've been talking about? You're

that sure about him that you want to bring him around?" While she listens to her mother speak, she imagines her mother sitting on her floral-print upholstered rocking chair, wearing her mauve robe and padded slippers. "You think it's time I meet him?"

Claire thinks her mother may be teasing by the way she asks the question, although she isn't sure. She thinks her mother is digging at a sore spot. Knowing how she feels doesn't stop her from reacting. "Mom, honestly, I told you I need your input, someone who is objective; that would be you. We've had this conversation before, remember?"

Softening her voice, Margaret says, "Claire, of course I remember, and certainly I want to meet him, but ultimately it's you who has to decide. How do you feel when you're with him? Listen to your heart. Your heart knows."

Exasperated, Claire sighs, "I know Mom. It's just… well, I start thinking he'll do the same thing Tom did. I don't want to be hurt like that ever again."

"Of course, you don't, honey, none of us do. Sometimes we have to take a chance, though. With your father, I found that the longer I was married to him the more I loved him. Oh, I have to stop talking about him or I'll cry." After what seems to be a couple of long minutes, Margaret continues, "What I'm saying is that love grows, deepens over time."

"I want to try with Alex. I really do. Kiss Miss Daisy for me. I miss you, Mom and thank you for your wisdom. I'll talk to Alex about the doggy door. How about we have dinner at your place while he installs the doggy door? I'll cook."

"That's a great idea. But give me just a little more time. I'm still adjusting. I'm really tired right now."

"Sure Mom. Just want you two to get to know each other. I'd feel better all the way around. I love you. Talk later."

"Love you too. Good night."

During their conversation, Claire notices that Alex has turned away from her. He's still talking but in a low voice. Still, Claire can't help but hear a few words here and there. After a few more minutes he hangs up and sinks into the swivel chair as if he's gathering the strength to turn and face her. When he finally does turn around, she sees tears in his eyes. "There are complications, Claire."

She feels her heart take on his burden. Fearing the worst, she asks, "What do you mean? What's happened?"

"Charles was hospitalized today. Heart attack, moderate though, and he had a reaction to the meds on top of that. He isn't stable. Renal failure as well." "You know the way it goes. They're doing all they can. They refuse to do the surgery now. I need to get out there. I want to be with him. I want to fly out immediately. I don't think I should wait."

Alex is quiet for a few moments, then stands up and says, "Let's go get that coffee. I'll drive."

Feeling his conflict and his fear, she senses that it may be better if he isn't alone right now. She asks, "How about you stay over tonight? You have extra clothes with you, right?"

"Thanks, I could sure use your company. Yup, I have clothes. I felt like I should be prepared. I'll call the airline from your place. Just need to get a reservation and a taxi for the airport. Can I leave my car at your place?"

Claire's heart aches for Alex. "Yes, your car will be fine."

As they walk out together, she feels the heaviness, the pressure of all the decisions he needs to make and quickly. "Will Charles be alright, Alex? He has a chance, right?" Then she remembers the message Hannah gave her.

Silently, Claire petitions Hannah. *Where are you? God, I don't know what your plan is for Charles. All I ask is that you take care of him. Comfort him, please. Give him peace as he goes through the treatments. Inspire the doctors to know exactly what the correct treatment is. Please, God, heal the body if it is in your Divine plan.*

Please give Alex peace as he makes his decisions. Press it upon me to be the support that Alex needs now. And please, show Alex the way. Let him know in his heart that You are in charge and that You know what is best.

After they step off the elevator, Claire moves over to the side to get out of the way of foot traffic. "Alex, God is in charge of this. He knows what's best for all concerned. I know all of this, but I still pray that the doctors will find an answer so Charles can have his life back if that's God's divine plan."

Alex puts his arm around Claire, pulling her closer to him. "Claire, the situation seems dire at best. God does some really miraculous things to be sure. We've both seen that on so many occasions. I have to remind myself that, yes, God is in charge. I have to do my part, though, whatever that may be. I want to be okay with however this turns out."

Giving her a hug, he says, "Now let's go get some coffee and let go of the day."

"Do you want to go around the corner or go to my place?"

"I'm feeling like a hazelnut latte. How about you?"

"Sounds like we're going around the corner then."

Chapter Twenty-Eight

After an uneventful drive and they have settled into Claire's home, Alex calls The Manor to schedule his leave and gets on the computer to make a reservation with the airline. "They have a seat in the morning at eleven; that worked out perfectly. All I have left to do is arrange for a rental car and prepay a couple bills before I go to the airport."

Alex pauses for a few moments as if deep in thought. "Was there something else you wanted to talk about? You asked to meet me earlier today?"

Claire laughs, "Well, I was missing you something fierce. But now, yes, there is something else." Hesitating, she wonders if it's a good time to talk about Hannah. "Alex, I haven't gotten to a place that I feel safe or comfortable talking about this subject yet." She takes a breath to calm herself. "I had another visitation."

"Oh?" Alex meets her gaze. His eyebrows arch and then he asks, "When did this happen?"

"Last night. I had everything all organized. Had my shower, made my popcorn, and I was ready to watch a movie. Then…" She takes another deep breath and then one more, worried that he may react like Tom. *Oh Hanna, Frank, where are you?* "Like I said, I was all ready to watch this great flick."

"I noticed the bowl of popcorn. Which flick?"

His question irritates her. "Really? Are you trying to make this more difficult for me?" Then she sees his smile and laughs. "You!" and jabs him in the ribs.

Alex grabs his side, pretending to be hurt. "Ouch! Why did you have to go and do that?"

Not buying into his drama, she stares at him. "Look, an angel came to talk to me. Her name was Hannah. She told me to be open with you about my experiences, Alex.... This is so difficult for me to talk about."

"Claire, I told you I have an open mind. This isn't new to me." Then, as if it's no big thing, he asks, "What did she say?"

"I tried to write it all down. Maybe you can just read it?"

"No, Claire, tell me. It would be good for you to talk about this. The more practice you have, the easier it will become, and it'll help us bond, don't you think?

"Claire, we have to learn to talk to one another about everything. At least that's what I think married couples do." Trying to lighten the mood, he adds, "Or is that merely another one of my many delusions?"

Ignoring his poor joke, Claire takes another breath, looking deeply into Alex's eyes, she hopes that by connecting with him like this she'll magically gain the strength to continue. "Okay, you're right. I know!" She inhales again, deciding to quit stalling.

She tells Alex her story while anxiously waiting on the edge of her chair for him to react. For what seems like several minutes, Alex rubs his chin as he thinks about the message. "It seems that you're moving forward in the healing field, but you're doing it in a way that is spirit guided. Is that fair to say?"

Surprised at his concise summary, she replies, "Well, yes. That's exactly what's happening. Wow, I like the way you put it. Hannah also said to use the power of prayer for healing and to give God permission to work through me. Thank you so much for helping me understand it in a way that doesn't frighten me."

"Claire, why does all of this frighten you so much?"

"This is hard for me to admit, but I've been afraid that I would be ostracized, judged, and even deemed crazy. I just haven't heard many people speak about having these types of encounters. Have you?"

"No, not really. But consider this, what you're experiencing is extremely personal—an intimate gift. To tell anyone? Well, quite honestly, it's none of anyone's business. Some people will criticize you and some will be afraid of you or even for you. Some will even be jealous. Generally, people are afraid of things they don't understand. They have their own ideas of how things should be. I guess you can say those ideas make them feel better about themselves, maybe even more powerful.

"You need to figure out who you want to share this information with. Isn't that true for any topic? We need to use discernment in all situations. You'll have to learn about it and decide how you want to handle it. Claire, everyone is different. We all have things that make us special, unique."

As Claire has witnessed dozens of times, Alex swiftly transforms into another persona, one more innocent and childlike. His demeanor lifts her mood. She knows that his purpose is to remind her what they share. "Me, unique? Because I know you're interested in what makes me special, right?" She rolls her eyes upward toward the heavens. "Oh Lordy, should I get my boots on yet? It seems to be getting rather deep in here."

Like a game, she counts on Alex's facial expressions to give her clues as to where he's going. His excitement is infectious; she can't prevent herself from playing along. "Okay, Alex, what is it that makes you special?"

His face softens, revealing an inner beauty that is rare to witness. Perhaps, he too, is an angel. Taking a breath, she waits. His voice is vibrant, yet clouded with emotion. "Claire, I know I'm special. I have you by my side. I'm blessed to have such a beautiful, intelligent woman as a part of my life. That, my dear Claire, makes me special."

Her breath catches as tears collect like a storm ready to let loose. Unable to speak, she looks down. Taking another breath, she gathers the courage, "Alex, you sure know the right things to say to make me feel better. I love you. You know that. I'm just beginning to realize what we have here."

"Claire?" Like a child, Alex rubs his eyes, coupled with an impressive yawn. "I'm pooped. I think I want to hit the hay, but I want to take a shower. You want to go first, or do you want me to?"

"Have you seen my shower? It's big enough for two. No discussion needed about who goes first."

Alex stands up, reaching out for her to take his hand. "Will you join me then, my lady?"

Rising to join her knight in shining armor, they walk down the hall.

Chapter Twenty-Nine

Claire is up before dawn. Wanting to let Alex sleep as long as possible, she quietly shuts the bedroom door behind her. Her morning routine is fairly simple, but she needs to pack her lunch and find some snacks that will fill in the holes during the day.

As she's making a sandwich, Alex quietly creeps up behind her. He wraps his arms around her waist, snuggles into her neck, breaths in her scent and kisses her. "Good morning. I smell coffee. I sure can use some."

"Umm... Alex, I sure could get used to this. Coffee is finished. You want an omelet or something?"

"Not ready for food yet. I just want coffee." Then he turns her to face him for a passionate kiss.

"Best be careful with those lips or I'll be tempted to stay home."

"Nah. You would never do that. You're too committed to your work." He holds her at arm's length "Or, would you...? Umm... oh, dear Claire, you look lovely wearing your poker face."

"Alex, I do love our little games, but I have to finish packing my lunch. Would you pour me a cup of coffee too? You remember where the cups are?"

"Sure. You want any cream?"

"Straight up."

"Woman of my heart. What time are you heading out?"

"I have twenty minutes.... I talked to Harry yesterday. I told him about your last name being the same as his wife's, and because I'm going to marry you, we may end up being related. He was a real grump yesterday. I don't know if he'll take the bait or not. But that man needs a strong dose of love. This is one way I can show him that I like him and that I care."

"Claire, you have a great plan. I bet he thinks about what you said. How can he not?"

"I've found people inherently want to be needed; they want to be a part of and contribute to society. With his life's situation, having no wife to take care of, I wonder if he feels needed or even wanted. Then, on top of that, he has all of those medical issues, and his children are angry with him so much of the time. To be included in society and in the family unit and to feel you have something to offer is important to the human psyche. Unfortunately, I haven't quite figured out how to make him feel like he's needed or wanted." Then an idea begins to develop in Claire's mind.

"What about that truck you're working on? Harry owned a body shop, but I don't know exactly what he did. Alex, you and Harry have something in common." She pauses in thought, then says, "Oh my God! He would absolutely love to talk shop with you."

"*That truck* is an Apache."

"The Apache then. Good grief."

"Claire, your forehead is wrinkly. Is this how I tell if you're upset or if a plan is formulating in that mind of yours? It looks to me like your sole ambition is to get me involved."

Determined to show Alex who's in charge, she places her hands on her hips and stares at him fiercely. "Why on earth would you need to question such a thing? Of course, I want you involved! We're a package deal, right?"

Straight-faced, he concedes, "Oh, I see how this is going

to run. I guess I'll just throw my hand in. I fold. You know how to play alright."

Laughing, like she has planned the entire scenario, Claire kisses him square on the lips to reward him for his part. "Alex, I want to change the subject. I want us to somehow stay connected while you're away."

"When I get settled tonight, I'll try to call you. No promises, okay? After a day or so, I hope I'll have some sort of schedule where we can talk at a specific time." His forehead creases with concern, "I really don't know what to expect."

"Some sort of schedule sounds great." Glancing at the clock she says, "Oh gosh, Alex. I've got to run."

But before she walks out, she gives Alex a kiss and stands back to look him over, wanting to memorize every detail.

Chapter Thirty

The day went exceptionally well even though earlier Claire saw an angel standing vigil in room 412. Claire did her best not to stare; on the other hand, she was curious how the angel would respond to her if she talked to him. Would he be polite and say hello or ignore her?

After the third time walking past the angel, Claire looks up and meets his eyes. As if an angel being in the room was an ordinary occurrence, she says, "You must be new around here. I haven't seen you before. I'm Claire."

Nodding, he smiles. Without hesitation he says, "Yes, Claire. I am fairly new to the Boston area. My name is Angus. Our girl Nancy will be coming home shortly. We are planning a big welcome home party for her after the transition." He smiles knowingly, "Won't she be surprised."

"Yes, I expect you'll have a big party." Noticing his accent, Claire asks, "You are from Scotland?"

"I am at that."

"By the way, have you seen Frank? He works here sometimes."

"Frank?" Angus pauses. "Oh, Frank. No, I have not seen him around. He is a busy fellow, that one."

"Well, thank you, Angus. Nice chatting with you."

Harry, much to everyone's misfortune, remains in a foul mood—even after his shower. Janet gives him a large dose of encouragement to boost his morale, and his throat culture didn't show anything serious. Even so, Harry just isn't doing well.

He, like the other residents at The Manor, ride the tide of daily pain and loneliness. Mood swings are, of course, common. Some patients are simply better able to cope with it all.

Then, having unfinished business such as not having one's legal affairs in order weighs heavily on some. The way Harry talks about needing his children to assist with this aspect of his life reveals his dependency on others.

Looking in on Harry, Claire asks him what type of work he did at the body shop. He tells her he liked to do body work, "You know straightening, patching metal, and painting a little." He shakes his head and says in disgust, "Course, these days cars are mostly plastic."

"Alex is working on a '59 Chevy Apache." Nonchalantly, she includes, "Short bed, heavy on the chrome…" as if she's an expert.

"Then you know your makes and models?"

Chuckling at the thought of her knowing anything about old cars, she confesses, "Oh, I'm a student, taking my first class. Short bed, heavy on the chrome is how Alex describes it. He's so excited about *his* truck. But he needs a place to work on it." Shrugging, Claire wonders if she should keep talking. "I had an uncle who was into the classics. I guess that's what you would call them. I do appreciate the talent it takes to work on them."

"You should tell your friend to come talk to me. I have an idea that may interest him."

"Oh? Well, it'll have to wait. Alex, just this morning, flew to Phoenix. His brother is very ill. I sure hope that everything works out for the best and he's able to come home soon. I miss him already."

With genuine concern in his eyes, Harry asks, "So his brother is sick? What's wrong with him?"

Remembering his wife Patti Jo died of cancer, Claire is especially mindful of her choice of words before she replies. "He has cancer. They're considering surgery but won't do the procedure until his white blood cell count is up. Not looking good for him. I've been praying for him, but you know what? God sometimes has very specific plans on where he wants his people. I've never met Alex's brother, Charles, and Alex is really concerned about him. I sure wish things were different."

Claire watches Harry's eyes darken as grief takes hold. He knows firsthand what it's like to lose a loved one.

"Harry, do you have a picture of Patti Jo? I'd like to see her."

"Nah, I don't carry one with me. They're all at home, sitting on the mantle."

"Harry, by the way, how are your exercises coming along?"

"I'm learning."

"Good. Let's practice now."

Frowning, Harry bluntly declares, "And the point would be? I'm a dying man. Probably be gone in a few days' time anyhow, so why?"

Looking Harry straight in the eyes, Claire chastises him, "Never, ever, give up. We're here to do our best to help you get better. By the way, have you seen Frank in the last couple of days? I want to talk to him. If you see him, will you give him a message for me?"

He studies her as if he just can't quite figure her out. "You're kidding, right? I know everyone thinks I'm whacko. I even wonder myself sometimes."

"Well, that's where I disagree. And don't you repeat this to anyone—I see angels too. If other people knew, especially the staff here…" She thinks of the implications for what seems to be the one thousandth time. "Do you know how much trouble I'll be in if you blab?"

Laughing to ease the tension, she quietly adds, "This is our secret. But really, just tell Frank I'm looking for him. Harry, I have to check in on another patient, but you're doing a great job. Practice your breath work. When you get that under control, you'll begin to feel much better."

As Claire leaves, she thinks about Harry's well-being. Unmistakably, Harry has mastered the art of how to sidestep some of Claire's questions. Having avoided her question several times regarding seeing Frank proved that. She respected his reluctance to be honest because for Harry it's a matter of survival.

If she were the one being prescribed certain medicines with so many unpleasant side effects, she would be suspicious of everyone as well, especially those in the medical field. There's a strong likelihood that the meds are actually preventing Harry from seeing Frank. At least, Harry is aware that she knows about Frank. Perhaps he'll begin to trust her.

Frank has been out of touch for quite some time. Claire considers how ill Harry is and can't help feeling apprehensive about how much time she has to help him. The doctors here have done about all they can, and Harry's evaluation period has nearly ended. By law, the doctor must write his diagnosis for insurance purposes. Heck, Harry may be transferred to another facility soon. *Where is Frank in all of this?*

Then it hits her, maybe this has all been a ruse to get Harry into the mindset that time is running out. If there's something that needs to happen and you think you're dying, well, most definitely, that would light a big enough fire. But then, on the flip side, Harry is positively sick.

Claire shakes her head, wanting to empty it of the one-sided dialogue. There's one thing she's certain of—she cannot second guess any being from the angelic realm. All the same, the thoughts persist. Maybe she still has time to help Harry. Maybe Harry has enough time to help Alex with his truck and maybe Patti Jo is related to Alex. She wonders what happened to make Harry so angry?

Claire thinks she should get in contact with Harry's kids; maybe they can help her. But then, she decides, no, it would be important for Harry to call them himself.

Her thoughts turn to Frank. Is he an angel of death? Is there such a thing? Claire never knows what to call the angels in wait. Can Frank help out in other areas? She has so many questions. Claire silently pleads, *Please Frank. Please come and talk to me about all of this.*

She's surprised to hear Frank's answer so quickly, "Claire, part of life is about the excitement, the wonder, the sheer joy of living through the experience. If you are given too many answers, where will the surprises be? Relax into knowing that you are to have fun while you are here. Harry will be fine long enough to restore his faith in humanity and to heal his family relationships. He is worthy of this blessing.

"Yes, dear One, I am Frank. Yes, I assist others in their journey to the next realm, but I help in many other ways. Be open to the experiences where magic happens. All is well. You are on the correct track. Continue onward, dear Claire."

"I understand what you're saying, however, it would be nice to know what my role is in this and how I can accomplish it."

"Claire it will work out fine. Trust me."

Claire feels a sudden shift in the energy and knows that Frank has gone just like that.

"Claire, what did you say?"

Startled, she turns around to see Derrick watching her, his eyebrows arched. For some reason, his hair catches and holds her attention. *What a wild mess it is.* "Oh, you know me. I sort out my thoughts out loud. I thought we all did that." Partly to hide her embarrassment, she laughs. "Derrick, how the heck are you today?"

"Very well. You?"

"Very well, also. Thank you for asking, Derrick. Have you checked on Nancy in room 410? I was just there a few moments ago. She needs an aid."

"I'll see to it," Derrick responds, then he's gone.

Glancing at the clock, thoughts of Alex come to mind. He's probably at the hospital by now. She wants him to call her, thinking that hearing his voice will ease some of the anxiety that's has been building. It's as if there's a huge cloud hanging over their heads. Having several patients pushing their call buttons all at once doesn't help matters either. Even though they have six nurses on staff at any given time, it still feels like they are always short-handed.

Time flies, and before she knows it, her shift is finished. As soon as her patients' files are in order, she walks down the hall to the window, where she can be alone.

Tonight, from her vantage point, the city is in a deep sleep. *Thank God the wind has finally stopped its incessant howling.* Now the water is relatively calm, giving the impression that all has been laid to rest… at least out there. Here, at The Manor, there's rarely time to be quiet, to really relax. She imagines she's out there, walking along the harbor with the brisk, sweet breeze caressing her face. She has no worries, no thoughts. The ocean waters give her all she wants, all she needs. It washes away her doubt, fear, and fatigue, restoring her peace and faith, which keeps her going.

Thinking of Harry again, she decides to stop and check on him before she goes home. It's still reasonably early. Maybe she'll catch him awake. She wants to talk to Harry about making a family tree on the Malone side as a gift for Alex.

Harry's door is open, so Claire walks on in. He's watching a rerun of *Mayberry R.F.D.,* with Andy Griffith. "Oh, wow! It's been years since I've seen this show. Maybe I can watch it with you?"

She can easily hear Harry's annoyance, "Really? Don't you have anything else to do?"

Cheerfully, Claire says, "Nope. I'm off. Finally, I can sit down and relax."

During the frequent commercials, she talks about her new plan to research the Malone family. "Harry, what do you think? I want to gift Alex with a family, if indeed there's a connection. Of course, I'll benefit as well. Will you help me?"

Harry grumbles, "Girl, you never stop, do you?"

Humbled, she puts her hands over her heart. "You know, Harry, I only have my mother left and a handful of relatives I rarely see. I've always wanted a large family. That's probably one of the biggest reasons I'm a nurse. I love people."

What she's doing, she knows, is intruding and probably considered a form of harassment. Yet, one more time she pleads, "Will you help me? Tell me what you know about Patti Jo and her family. For instance, where she was born and who were her parents?" Then she looks at Harry closely and lowers her voice. "Am I bothering you? Maybe I shouldn't ask this of you."

"No, that isn't it. We have the family history all mapped out. It's at home. I have no way to get it for you and…" Without warning, Harry snaps, his anger as much as slaps her across the face, hard. "Claire get out! I want to be alone!"

Trying her best to ride out his anger, she persists, "Harry, please, maybe you could ask your kids to bring it in? Alex may lose his brother. Would you please consider…"

Harry cuts her off, demanding that she leave now. Hurt, she agrees, "Okay then. I'll see you tomorrow."

CHAPTER THIRTY-ONE

Claire walks out of the hospital, feeling as if she failed or pushed Harry too far. All along, the signs that he wasn't in a receptive mood were there. Why had she not heeded them? It was such a great idea, though.

For a good five minutes, Claire waits for her car to warm up. Tonight, Boston is grappling with temperatures in the single digits. She's in no hurry to make the drive home or to even be there. No Alex. No Miss Daisy. She compares her situation to her mother's, thinking *this must be how my mother has been feeling since my father's transition—empty, flat.* Maybe some tunes will cheer her up. She turns on the radio.

On the way home, she remembers the dog that she almost hit and how that incident had tipped the scale, providing her with the fuel to change her life. She's amazed to think that one little near accident actually brought about two fairly major life changes. Visions of Miss Daisy with her mother, calmly sitting together watching TV, remind her that their lives are changing as well. Miss Daisy is making the difference in her mom's routine, bringing her mother back from the dead. For that, she's forever grateful.

At home, she calls her mother to see how she's doing. She

sounds exhausted. "Claire, I don't know about all this. I bet I took Miss Daisy out at least a dozen times today. Would you consider taking her for a day or two on your days off?"

"Sounds like you may be ready for the doggy door. Alex flew to Phoenix this morning, Mom. I have no idea when he'll be back. Sure, I can get her in a couple of days. Can you wait that long?"

Margaret inhales deeply before answering, "Not sure, but I guess I'll have to. She's a cutie though. She wants to be in my lap, to be held and cuddled. God knows…, " she sniffs. "I'm just tired, Claire. I'm not used to having a little thing to take care of. I'll feel better tomorrow."

"I'll call tomorrow after my shift to check on you two. You know, there are dog sitters. If you want, I can find one so you can get some rest."

"No, I'll be fine. I wouldn't feel comfortable leaving her with a stranger, now would I Miss Daisy?"

Claire asks, "She's in your lap now, isn't she?"

"Of course, she is. I have to go Claire. Miss Daisy is whining. She wants something."

"Probably just your undivided attention, Mom."

"Claire, do you think she's manipulative? She's a baby. She just needs someone to love her."

"Right, Mom. You're going to spoil her rotten. It's time for me to hang up. Tomorrow then?"

Claire decides to give her mother a week. By then she'll be fine. She just needs to catch on to the new routine.

Respecting Harry's wishes, Claire doesn't mention Alex or the family genealogy a single time the next day. But she does ask how the show ended. His response was classic, "I didn't finish it."

"Harry, I'm so sorry I crossed the line and disturbed you last night."

Knowing there's a chance Harry may transfer to another facility soon, Claire thinks about bringing up the family genealogy again. She tells herself, *Hold on Claire. It isn't your place to talk to any of the residents about where they want to live after they are transferred. You know the social worker and the family will figure it out.* But because she feels on edge, like she's literally running out of time, she breaks the rule.

"Your doctor is recommending that you have full-time nursing care. That means either you stay here, or you transfer to another nursing facility, it depends on your resources. The doctor wants a treatment plan in place before you leave. In order to do that, living arrangements must be finalized."

Confused by her sudden statement, Harry mutters, "What? I don't understand."

Wanting to explain his circumstances, Claire says, "Up to this point, you've been in rehab and being evaluated to determine what you need in the way of medical treatment."

Without warning, Harry begins coughing and sputtering. Standing nearby, Claire waits until he's calm enough to speak. "So, there's no chance I'll be going home."

"It doesn't sound that way. But remember the orders haven't been written yet." Feeling a sense of urgency, she takes a chance and asks again, "Would you please call Robert or your daughter? What's her name?"

"Augusta."

"Yes, Augusta, sorry. I don't know why I forget, such a beautiful name. Maybe one of your kids can bring in the book? Are either of them interested in the family history?"

Harry takes a huge breath, aggravating his lungs and begins coughing again. It seems several minutes pass before his lungs are quiet enough so that he can take a sip of water. "Look, if I call Augusta, will you get off my back?"

Claire recoils as though he has literally hit her across her face. The words fly from her mouth, "On your back? Do you think I'm on your back? All I want is to find Alex's family. Look…" her anger surges. "…I like you, Harry Delany, even if you're a pain in everyone's ass."

As soon as she says the words, she instantly regrets it but continues anyway; the anger is that strong. "There are

other people in this world who care about having a family—
who would give anything to have one." Claire wipes a lone
tear that has slipped down her cheek. Hoping that Harry
hasn't seen her weakness, she asks, "Please, just call Augusta
or Roberta and see if they can help me."

Claire, like all nurses, is trained to be observant, to
watch for every scrap of evidence to help them know how
to best care for their patients. Alarmed, Claire says, "Harry,
you don't look so good." In a matter of mere seconds, his
skin has turned pale with a grayish tint.

Instantly, Claire lets go of the anger and moves into high
gear. She knows at this point Harry's in trouble. Giving him
directions to follow is useless. Instead, she uses a soothing
voice that tells Harry she's increasing the flow of oxygen.
"Harry, breathe slowly, like you practiced. You'll feel better
in no time, I promise."

The tension is thick, heavy. Claire moves quickly, yet
she feels sluggish. In a flash, she realizes that since the day
that Harry arrived, she has been walking on egg shells. Every
move has been calculated to keep him calm. It's what a nurse
does. But this is different.

Harry has held her captive for the entire time he's been
living at The Manor. Finally, Claire feels she has broken
free. Suddenly, Harry grabs his chest and gasps, "Oh God,
it's happening again." In a rush, Claire hits the intercom to
make the call as she watches the monitor.

It's during moments like these that Claire feels as if she
has left her body, as if she's in a dream, watching herself
from afar. Everyone's movements are sped up, but Claire
feels like she's slowed down, watching herself perform all
the necessary steps to save Harry's life. In a flurry, the crash
team arrives.

A little later at the station, Claire is talking to another
nurse who assisted with Harry. She expresses her amazement
and gratitude, "Jillian, thank you for coming so quickly."

"Yep, he's in pretty bad shape," she replies.

Momentarily, Claire reflects on the conversation with Harry before his heart attack. She says to Jillian, "It's been a while since I nursed a patient that sour. Undoubtedly, he's the most stubborn man I've ever known in all of my twenty years of nursing. If only he would cooperate a little and not be so belligerent."

"I hear you, Claire," Jillian replies. "Although Harry's temperament doesn't surprise me, not one bit. I think he's been this way for a long time. You know, many people who suffer great loss and trauma sometimes resort to trying all sorts of tactics to prevent further pain. His case is classic. They try to stay safe by controlling the people around them, not giving in to them."

Claire closes the file she's updating and takes a deep breath. "I'm aware of that as well. But Harry's just angry and plain ol' mean."

"He's mean and angry because that's his way of trying to control his situation, his life."

"Right. You're so right. He also pushes people away." Alex was right; she's emotionally involved. Not good. Why didn't she listen to him?

Jillian continues, "As I said, this is classic. He fears getting close to people because he's afraid of losing them. So he takes care of the problem head on. No fuss, no muss."

Impressed with the way Jillian presented her assessment, Claire mutters, "Wow."

Jillian shrugs and nonchalantly says, "Psychology minor," like she has something on Claire.

Not having the heart to remind her that they all take psychology classes in order to get to where they are, Claire merely says, "Got it. Although, I sincerely wish there was something more we could do to help him."

"I agree. If you're talking psychology, I think he needs someone who'll commit to helping him learn to trust again."

Claire nods. Harry isn't the only one who's working to trust again.

Chapter Thirty-Two

Claire decides to request an additional shift. Her place feels empty without Alex.

She watches Betty, the supervisor, cock her head and eye Claire suspiciously. Claire's sure Betty will eventually agree to her request. Someone is always calling in sick or has another legitimate reason for not coming in.

Betty isn't speaking out loud, but surprisingly, Claire is listening to Betty's thoughts. *We've been through this before, Claire. We schedule the shifts the way we do for a reason.* Claire, a bit annoyed, silently recites, *so we have more time off to recuperate and are able to serve the patients in a healthy manner, and so we can enjoy life a little.*

Realizing she has been staring at Betty, Claire blushes and lowers her eyes to look at the family photo on Betty's desk. Claire doesn't want Betty to suspect what has just transpired.

Claire thinks she hears Betty say, *"But Derrick called in sick. I need someone to fill in for him."* With a jolt, Claire raises her eyes and blinks in surprise. Did she hear her speak? "Did you say something, Betty?"

Looking up to meet Claire's stare, says, "Is something wrong?"

"No. I just thought I heard you say something."

Betty answers, "No, Claire, I'm just thinking. It looks like I do need someone to fill in tomorrow." Betty chuckles, "Saved again. Thanks Claire," as she scribbles her signature formally approving Claire's request. "How did you know I had a scheduling conflict?"

Dazed, Claire begins to question her sanity. Did she hear Betty's thoughts or was it a mere coincidence? To cover up her confusion, Claire laughs, "Oh, don't you always? It always seems to work out, doesn't it? Besides, I love it here. Don't you?"

"Claire, I need to caution you," Betty counters. "I know you've been nursing for a long while now, but nurses are no different than doctors—you can burn out. You have witnessed that how many times now. As much as I appreciate you bailing me out, I simply ask that you pace yourself. Will you do that for me or, more importantly, for yourself?"

"Sure Betty. I'll watch myself. Thanks for the advice. Are we all set here?"

"Yes, thanks again, Claire. See you tomorrow."

Alex finally phones Claire on his second day in Phoenix. Sounding overly cheerful, he asks, "Claire, how are you doing?"

"Alex, I'm fine. It's you I worry about—you and Charles. Tell me everything."

Alex lets out a deep sigh, "I miss you, Claire. I sure wish I was with you instead of being here in the middle of this mess. It's grueling being at the hospital all the time. "I've taken over his health directives. I've searched for every document possible to help with the financial piece. I need to hire a lawyer for this."

Claire hears fatigue and frustration seep through as he speaks, "I'm holding up. I never dreamed…"

Claire's heart expands as she aligns with his concerns. "This has got to be difficult for you."

"Yes. Charles has not rallied. After testing, they reassessed his prognosis." Alex's voice becomes softer, more contemplative,

"He's not well enough for chemo, and the risk is too great for surgery. They're in a wait-and-see mode." Alex pauses, "Charles has stopped eating and he's in so much pain."

Thoughts swirl in Claire's mind. She avoids saying what she's thinking, *Charles is declining quickly.*

"I talked to Charles about his options and so did his doctor. At the time, he wasn't able to focus on what I was saying. Heck, he hasn't been able to focus on anything."

Alex sighs again. "He keeps asking for pain meds. He knows his situation is extremely dire. He's unable to relax and neither can I."

"Alex, I'm so sorry to hear this. I'll keep you in my prayers."

"Thanks, Claire. Listen, I've to get off the phone. I need a shower—bad. I'll call later. I love you."

"I love you too, Alex. Get some rest, please."

Chapter Thirty-Three

As Claire promised, she calls her mother every day to check on her progress with Miss Daisy. Claire's pleased to hear the strength returning to her mom's voice. "You sound like you're feeling better."

"I am. I imagine that getting outdoors is really helping me, even if it's bitterly cold."

"I'm sure the brisk fresh air is stimulating your endocrine system and probably Miss Daisy's."

"Oh, right, brisk. Claire, you know it's freezing out there. I can't even breathe normally."

"Well, something is helping for sure."

Claire runs a hot bath, pours a glass of wine and steps into the tub. As she allows her body to relax into the warmth, she feels as if she and the water are one.

Although health care is Claire's business, she still finds it difficult to grasp that a person can be disciplined to maintain a healthy balance in their life, and then instantly forget everything they know to be true when trauma comes knocking at their door. She has known of all sorts of accidents and life situations that cause people to drop into depression and quit taking care of themselves. It's a complicated issue.

Feelings of gratitude expand as she realizes she has maintained her balance during the rough patches in her life. Claire went through her brother's death, her divorce, and then the latest incident, her father's passing.

Of course, all the events were laced with sadness and despair. Fortunately, she had her nursing to lean on. She was forced to continue her daily schedule and interactions. Learning to trust a man again, however, is another issue.

Claire considers that each person is unique, assimilating his or her own individual experiences to create specific manners and routines to get them through life. Then, there's something akin to an inner clock that directs the process of creating thought to not only adjust one's methods when needed, but to expand and align with the higher mind.

Learning to live without Tom, to get past the hurt was difficult. Her father's death, ironically, wasn't as big an upset. Sure, she misses her father, but she understands that people simply move on to the next plane of existence.

When her father passed, Claire's feelings were bittersweet. She was happy for him, so very happy that he could go forward. It was almost as if he was stifled, unable or unwilling to live up to his full potential while he was married. Even so, she was sure he had gone through untold experiences and attained a higher understanding of his spiritual nature during his life.

Perhaps all along, she's been looking at all this incorrectly. Claire's father loved serving Margaret. She never heard him complain. He had a simple existence—provide for and to make Claire's mother happy.

Claire steps out of the tub, puts on her nightgown, and hears the phone ring. She so hopes it's Alex. Her heart leaps in anticipation.

Chapter Thirty-Four

Alex feels like he's dropping the ball concerning Claire. He spends every conceivable moment with Charles at the hospital while unearthing legal documents for the attorney he hired.

Alex senses that Charles will not remain on Earth much longer, but he has avoided calling Claire. He doesn't have the energy or the desire to unload any of the details on Claire.

He loves Claire. Although she's a strong woman, sharing too many details is an unnecessary burden. He puts off calling as long as possible. But then, as he drinks a cup of hot tea, he feels a strong, unexplainable urge to call her. He cannot delay the conversation any longer. "Claire? Is it really you?"

"Alex! Oh, I'm so thankful you called. You've been on my mind constantly."

"Oh, honey, I apologize for not checking in sooner."

"I have been on pins and since you left."

Working to keep from becoming emotionally distraught, Alex sticks to the business side of the situation. "Charles has been going through lots of tests, and the diagnosis is clear; the cancer is extremely aggressive, already metastasized. The doctors are discussing what action to take, if any at all. They're not in agreement with one another which, of course, postpones any course of treatment.

"Charles is in so much pain that they have prescribed a morphine drip, and he's sleeping more. I think the cancer is too far advanced; they won't be able to do anything to save him. The doctors are going to discuss options again tomorrow."

Anger slips through the tightly knitted cracks that preserve his ego. Sarcastically he adds, "Unless, of course, they continue to argue among themselves." Then he catches himself, "Oh, Claire, I'm sorry. Please forgive me. I've become increasingly frustrated with the medical team here.

"The crux of the matter is, if they decide to not go forward with any treatment, Charles will be transferred to a hospice facility until he leaves this embodiment. I could stay with him, of course, but I have bills to pay. Well, anyway, I'll call you tomorrow and tell you what the plan is."

"I sure hope that God wants the same thing we do—that Charles regains his perfect health."

As Claire examines the situation more closely, however, she has the uncomfortable feeling that they have relied solely on the doctors' strategies instead of on God. It feels as if Charles's life and theirs have been put on hold until *they* receive God's guidance.

Unfortunately, the likelihood of Alex coming home any time soon is slim. Alex could take an extended leave of absence from work, maybe borrow against his IRA to meet financial obligations. Claire doesn't know if he has any personal savings that he can dip into instead of taking out a loan, but he does have the house. She doesn't know if he has any equity to borrow against.

As she sees it, he could stay until Charles is either able to go through treatment or passes from his body. Her heart aches for both of them. Charles being forty-seven is much too young to have this happen, but cancer is impartial.

After they say good night, Claire wants to lose herself in quiet meditation, coupled with candles, soft music, and wine.

She focuses on peace, bathing Charles and his health issues with its light. Then she surrenders the outcome to God.

Her mind moves forward to the situation with Alex, seeing him home again, beside her. They're married and extremely happy together. Then, she sees a baby in her arms. They have a little girl. Finally, at peace with her life, Claire goes to bed and sleeps soundly through the night.

Chapter Thirty-Five

The next morning, Claire calls to check on her mother. After several rings, her mother answers out of breath. "Claire, is that you? Oh, good grief. I almost tripped over Miss Daisy, set me off balance."

"I almost hung up. Are you alright?"

Laughing, she says, "Just a minute. I'll check." Claire waits. "Mom, what's going on?"

"Oh, I'm looking at my leg. I banged it pretty good. But I'm good to go. Nothing broken."

"That's a relief. Hey, I'm calling to tell you that I'd like to visit today, probably in a couple of hours. If that's okay with you."

"Oh sure, come on over. We'll be waiting for you."

At her mom's home, Claire lets herself in as always. She's greeted by Miss Daisy who's barking furiously as if Claire is a total stranger. "Miss Daisy, don't you remember me? I'm Claire."

Miss Daisy begins wagging her tail and runs toward her. "Wow, look at you! All settled in and now the legendary guard dog. Mom, I had no idea she would be so protective."

Claire sees her mother's weary but proud smile. "She lets me know when something is amiss all right. Especially when the squirrels are on the deck, which is a good portion of the time." Her voice softens, "I tell her, 'No. They're our friends.' Then she flashes those beautiful brown eyes at me as though she understands exactly what I'm telling her. And, I think she does. But then she goes and does the same thing again. She just can't help herself. Yes, she has absolutely taken the role of a guard dog."

While Margaret talks, Claire assesses her mother's overall appearance. Her gray hair has lost its luster, and she hasn't had her hair cut and styled since she lost Dad. Yet, her skin has a healthy glow, and there's an enthusiasm in her manner again.

"Mom, I think you know what you're doing, and it's going to take persistence and repetition to get Miss Daisy to learn. She's a very intelligent, and she wants to please you. Keep disciplining her. I bet she'll get it sooner or later." Then Claire asks, "You're not sorry that you took her, are you?"

"Never in a million years, Claire! I know I made the correct choice. Even though she has a few undesirable behaviors, she's adorable, aren't you Miss Daisy?" Daisy barks in agreement, wagging her tail rhythmically. "Claire, to be honest, this little ball of fur saved my life. I wouldn't have it any other way."

Claire realizes how far her mother has come. She appears content, even happy; she's enthusiastic, she's come back to life.

Margaret watches Miss Daisy who appears to be listening to their conversation. Her ears are perked, and her eyes have an expressive awareness. "I have an appetite again." Patting Miss Daisy on the head, Margaret fusses, "Course, you always think you can share what I'm having, don't you."

"Sounds like one of those obedience classes that Stacy talked about might be helpful."

"I'm thinking the same thing. But the weather is frightfully bitter now. I think it may be best to wait until the temperature warms up a bit. Don't you?"

"Mom, the longer you wait, the more ingrained Miss Daisy's undesirable behaviors may become. At least call and see what they have available."

"You're right, as usual. I have a friend, Pauline. You remember her?"

"Umm, Pauline. Is she the woman who has those two adorable tan pugs?"

"Yes, and they do as they're told. I want to invite her over later this week and ask her how she trained them. That'll get me started."

Claire is relieved to hear of her mother's plans. "Mom, Miss Daisy is keeping you very busy. Why don't I do the vacuuming for you?"

"You did it already. I'll get it done in a few days. No rush."

Deciding to give her mother a final test before going home, Claire baits her mother. "I guess you have it under control, but wouldn't you appreciate a day or two alone? I'd be happy to take Miss Daisy. Give you some time off."

Margaret laughs, playfully waving the proposal away, "What, and miss all of this excitement?" She pauses, "I admit that after caring for Miss Daisy, I've been tired to the bone. But it's a good tired. I've earned it by taking care of her, not sitting here crying my eyes out because I feel sorry for myself. Claire, dear, adopting Miss Daisy is the best thing I've done since Leon passed on. I still think of him, but I find myself thinking of his absence less and less. What about Alex? You've barely mentioned him. When is he coming home?"

Wondering if she wants to expose her deepest fears, she rises from her seat and walks to the window as if something caught her eye. Claire swallows, "Alex says the doctors don't agree on Charles' prognosis. They have another meeting today, and we hope that they'll come to a decision on his treatment. One doctor says that the cancer is too aggressive to treat. Charles isn't doing well at all. I'm praying for him.

"If Alex stays there, it may be weeks or even months before I see him again. I feel like I'm on a roller coaster, knowing full well that God has this under control. Then, when I contemplate the idea that Alex may stay in Phoenix for so long, well, it's all so unsettling."

Being open and honest with her mother feels foreign and uncomfortable, yet a weight lifts, freeing Claire's mind and ultimately, her body. Her defenses are down, and the words spill out, seemingly of their own accord, "I just found Alex and then, wham, just like that, he's gone. When am I going to have a relationship that lasts? Am I meant to live my life alone?

"Mom, he proposed to me. I didn't tell you because I wanted you to meet him first."

"He proposed? Claire, I had no idea."

"Yes, and I said yes." Feeling she has been somehow targeted to be forever single, she cries, "Thing is, I don't know if I'll ever see him again. I think I'm cursed."

"Claire, you're tired. You should go home and go to bed. Your outlook isn't positive. You know that's because you've been under too much pressure lately."

"I slept really well last night. I felt rested and relaxed when I got up this morning." Claire wavers before confessing, "I worked an extra shift because I feel so alone at home. Mom, I feel like if I keep busy, I won't have to think about all of this, but it isn't working." Claire shakes her head as if shaking off her feelings.

"Of course, you feel like keeping busy is the thing to do. But, honey, you have to remember to pace yourself. That means balancing your days on and off and getting the proper rest.

"The other part of this is that you're afraid that you may lose someone after you have come so far. And you have come a long way. Tom did his best to convince you that you aren't normal. That's a tremendous weight on your psyche, especially coming from your spouse. When someone tells you something like that, there may be a part of you that actually believes it. That little piece of you that believes you aren't good enough keeps on whispering those very same words, 'you aren't good enough.' It creates an imbalance that continues to emotionally drain you until at some point, you realize you've been listening to the wrong voice.

"It's impossible to become stronger until you understand this false idea was imprinted in your mind. In other words, you can't change something that you believe to be true until you know it isn't."

Margaret looks off into the distance, "It's exactly what I've been doing. I've been listening to the wrong voice." A tear rolls down her cheek, then another. "I wanted to die."

Margaret's eyes lock onto Claire's for a few moments. "That voice said, 'Margaret, you aren't worth anything without Leon.' We did almost everything together. In retrospect, it's as if I didn't have an identity, wasn't whole without him, like I've been just a half of a person for all of these years."

In a low voice, Claire exclaims, "Wow, Mom, this is huge."

"Right, I know. I know! I took him for granted. I thought he would always be with me. Who am I? I don't even know. For months, I listened to that part of me that told me I can't go anywhere without Leon. He protected me. I was even feeling paranoid that no one liked me. The walls were closing in on me. Then I began to not care, and well, somewhere I began to feel sorry for myself, and I wanted to die. I haven't felt strong enough to go anywhere and, believe it or not, I haven't felt safe. It's a good thing I have you to watch over me and Miss Daisy." Giving Miss Daisy a hug, Margaret says, "Miss Daisy, you changed my life, truly!"

Miss Daisy whimpers and paws at Margaret's arm. Margaret looks up, searching Claire's eyes and whispers, "Thank you, Claire."

Suddenly, Claire imagines herself on a small boat in a vast ocean, her emotions rocking her to and fro as she processes the revelation that has taken place. *Her mother had wanted to die?* Deep down, Claire had known this all along. Why didn't she intervene before now? Then her heart opens with an expansive sense of gratitude. She peers at Miss Daisy who has been instrumental in unlocking her mother's heart.

Claire and her mother have shared something special, intimate, and for them extremely rare. This is a new beginning for Claire and her mother. Not at all sure she's able to articulate what has just transpired, Claire simply moves back to the couch where her mother and Miss Daisy sit. She gives them both a big hug.

"Thanks for sharing with me. You have no idea what this means to me. I'll go home and think about what you said and take it easy for the rest of the day. Maybe I'll watch that movie I..." Claire quickly stops herself to make sure she doesn't bring up anything related to her experiences with Frank and Hannah.

Concern etches Margaret's face, "Claire, what is it?"

Sighing, Claire says, "Oh, nothing. I wanted to watch *It Happened One Night* with Clark Gable and Claudette Colbert the other night and, well... I was interrupted. You remember that movie, Mom?"

"Oh sure. That was a cute movie. You have that on DVD?"

"No, it's available on one of those movie channels." Silently, Claire congratulates herself for successfully redirecting her story and not mentioning her experience with Hannah.

"I need to go home. I have some things to think over. I appreciate our conversation. Thanks."

"As do I, Claire. Thank you for listening."

Chapter Thirty-Six

All the way home, Claire thinks about how open and honest her mother was about her feelings, but she doesn't understand why she hadn't been totally honest herself.

Instead of going home to rest and watch a movie as promised, Claire clears out the spare bedroom, places a tarp on the floor, and assembles her easel. She has an extra table in the closet that she'll use for her paints and brushes. Then, she looks for her old familiar work apron. She begins to sketch the main features of a seascape. The activity totally consumes her until she hears her phone ringing. She hurries down the stairs to the living room finding her cell phone beside her recliner where she left it.

Claire sees the caller ID, and momentarily freezes. Emotions of doubt and desire became a messy mix. Certainly, she wants to talk to Alex, but at the same time, she's afraid of what he might say. She eases herself down into the recliner. The phone continues to ring until she gathers enough courage to answer.

After a short exchange of pleasantries, Alex discloses the information that will soon change their lives. It isn't long into his update when Alex stops mid-sentence.

Claire imagines Alex rubbing his temples and forehead to smooth out the tension while he breathes deeply in a valiant effort to stay detached and focused. "Claire, Charles hasn't rallied, and the oncologist, who even consulted with another oncologist on staff, feels that the cancer is far too advanced. They can't help him. The doctor has gone so far as to give a rough estimate of how much longer Charles has left."

"Oh God." Claire whispers. Alex's world is falling apart. "I am so sorry, Alex. What can I do?"

Then, as if the tide suddenly and unequivocally changes course, Alex's voice brightens, sounding hopeful. "These things are so iffy. You know that as well as I."

Claire hears what he said and agrees with him, but the result of his shift in manner is so sudden that she feels confused. Waves of emotion overcome her as she listens to Alex process the ordeal. "Charles is in so much pain that he isn't even coherent most of the time. I feel torn, Claire. I want to spend time with him." She listens to him breath, "But I think I'll come home."

Disappointment and gratitude collide, flooding Claire's consciousness. It's impossible to discern which feeling is greater. "Is it the money? Surely, we can figure out something to make it happen." Claire rushes on, describing some of the financial options that may allow him to stay with his brother until he transitions if that's what he wants.

"Claire, I've thought about the financial aspect of this, but it isn't just that. Charles has been pretty much out of it and doesn't know who's taking care of him or even speaking to him. That's not likely to change." Then his voice lifts as if he has been freed from a nightmare filled with despair; it's Alex who has rallied.

Claire hears his determination, strength, and acceptance as he admits, "Claire, Charles is dying. He is my brother, but hospice will take good care of him until he goes. I can't nurse him back to health. What I can do is come home to you. We need to be together.

"If I'm gone for an extended time, we'll have to start all over. I want to marry you. I want to be with you, Claire. I've waited for years for our time together. I'm confident that I'm making the right choice." He repeats with more conviction, "Claire, I want to come home to you!"

"Alex, there's nothing I want more." Claire pauses to work through her conflicted feelings. "I don't know. It isn't my aim to make you feel guilty. Charles is your only brother." Claire nearly slaps herself. *Claire, he knows that.* "Are you sure you want to leave him now?"

"I'm sure. I'll be home in a couple of days, tops. I'll stay until he's transferred and help him get situated. I have another appointment, tomorrow with that attorney I told you about. You know that he's going to have a shitload of bills come in. Of course, I can do nothing until he..." Alex stops. "No need to talk like this. I'll call you with the flight plan when I have it. I love you, babe."

Getting through the conversation with Alex without crying was a major accomplishment for Claire. After all, Alex coming home is what she prayed for, but not under these circumstances.

Claire finds it difficult to wrap her head around Alex's decision. She stares at the crackling fire. It doesn't seem right that Alex has chosen her over his dying brother. He should stay there, see it through. Will he end up resenting her for this? Will he have to fly out there a third time for the final arrangements and to empty the house? She wonders if there are services that do that sort of thing.

Returning to her *new* studio, in a trance-like state, Claire cleans her brushes, tidies up and makes coffee. The rich nutty aroma of the coffee brewing helps bring her back to the present moment. After filling her cup, she walks to the living room to sit in silence.

She barely gets comfortable when she hears a voice.

CHAPTER THIRTY-SEVEN

"Dear Claire, close your eyes and rest for a moment."

Claire asks, "Who's speaking?"

"It is I, Hannah."

Ripples of love flow through Claire's body, lifting her to untold heights until the tears begin to flow. She wipes her face, knowing this action is useless.

"Claire, I have come to you because I want you to be in a place of comfort and peace. Relax your mind. Come with me. I will show you the way."

Hannah directs Claire to breathe deeply, and slowly as she radiates oscillations of energy that raise Claire's vibration higher. She suspects Hannah is assisting her in relaxing in order for her to let go of her perceived troubles.

"Yes. You are correct. I am channeling a flow of energy through you. Your energetic body is being flooded with the frequency of love, yet you are feeling it with the physical body. Dear One, all of the fear you've previously experienced is a reaction to Alex's decision to come home. You feel fear because subconsciously, your belief is that you do not trust your dear husband to be."

Claire protests. "But I do trust him, Hannah."

"Not completely. You fear that he has not made a wise decision in leaving Charles and coming home, and you're afraid his choice will ripple outward, negatively affecting his psyche and your relationship. Being a couple brings you into this unfolding drama.

"Claire, at a subconscious level, you feel you will somehow pay dearly because he will soon come to regret his decision. You believe his choice is solely a result of his consideration for you and your relationship. Once he returns, he will realize his choice was incorrect. This may cause him to become bitter, therefore, he may come to resent you.

"You do not trust his choice, so you do not trust the chooser, Alex. Claire, remember, he is responsible for his choices, all of them, as is every soul incarnating on this earth plane. You, as his helpmate, are to support him in all ways, and this means to honor his choices.

"Know this. Charles has fulfilled his earthly contracts, which he agreed to prior to this incarnation. Be not sad that he is leaving this world. Rejoice that he is moving on—Charles lives on.

"He is an eternal being of light, just as you are. In his heart, Charles understands why Alex has made his decision to return home to you, Claire. And, Charles rejoices for his brother, that he has connected at last with his beloved—you, dear Claire.

"What Alex and you have declared, is just and ordained by those in the higher realms of Light. I say to you, be grateful for his choice. Be honored that it is you he chooses to spend his days with. What a lovely couple you are. Know that you are both blessed beyond measure."

Claire takes another breath and notices the vibration in her body tapper off until she no longer feels it. She asks Hannah, "Are you going?"

"Yes, Claire. It is time I take my leave. Remember that you are worthy of receiving this love that I speak of."

Deep in thought, Claire stares at the flames in the fireplace and then notices that her coffee is cold.

Chapter Thirty-Eight

The next morning, Claire finds her new studio doesn't have sufficient light to paint by. Boston winters are much too dreary with little sunlight during the day. She decides to postpone painting and goes into the kitchen. Alex will be coming home, and she wants to prepare some meals for the two of them in advance. She tunes into Pandora, then searches the cookbooks for tasty recipes ideal for freezing. Basically, Claire wants to stay busy, to keep her mind off the *things* that she can do nothing about.

After preparing several individual meals, Claire checks the studio finding the light bright enough to paint by, at least for a little while.

Methodically, she moves through her project, focusing on the shapes and colors. It isn't long before the shadows overtake the room again. Claire knows there's no point in continuing, so she cleans her brush.

Evaluating the ocean, the sleepy harbor, and the low-hanging clouds in the sky in her painting, Claire is pleased with her progress. As she studies the scene before her, she begins to examine her motive for painting.

Is painting merely a pastime or does she paint because she

loves the process of choosing colors and brushing them on the canvas to create something beautiful?

Examining her questions more closely, Claire concludes that for her painting serves as a type of meditation, a way to develop a stronger focus. She can lose herself in the activity completely. The endeavor is certainly pleasing and valuable in many ways. She decides that painting is a satisfying pastime, one that helps her develop artistically as well. Sure, oil painting is a challenge, but rising up to a challenge is what keeps any project interesting. *Right?*

Taking a deep breath, she focuses on her body. She feels energetic, vibrant, and at the same time, at peace. She realizes she hasn't felt this way since Alex flew to Phoenix.

Quietly shutting the door so as not to disrupt the calm ambiance, Claire walks into the kitchen and takes in the beautiful color of the walls and how it makes her feel: content, grateful, and proud. The colors she chose are perfect. The new look uplifts and renews her spirit.

She remembers the night that Alex had been thinking out loud about how to go forward with their two properties and how she had reacted to his bold reasoning; Claire cautiously considers the idea that somewhere deep down, *she* is unsure of her choice to marry Alex. But Hannah had not gone so far with her message to say that it was *she* who she didn't trust.

She agreed to marry Alex, yet she wasn't entirely sure she was even able to make that choice. Claire's only experience in marriage had been with Tom. *Look what happened.*

Sure, Hannah had stated that their union "is just and ordained." What Claire also wants is her mother's opinion, does Alex have the traits that would make him a good husband? In Claire's mind, her mother had a successful relationship with her father, they made it work, so her mother's opinion is unquestionably more valuable than her own. Of course, her mother knows best. She has good old-fashioned experience. Claire doesn't. Aw, that old stamp of approval that makes everything seem alright.

Claire laughs at her own outrageous notion. Is she so naïve as to trust someone else's opinion more than her own?

She wonders why she needs her mother's approval when she has Hannah's blessing. Would her mother's support make their marriage magically harmonious? Her mother's opinion has nothing to do with how their marriage will work out. But she admits that her mother liking Alex is as good as giving her a green light, confirming that she's safe to go forward.

Studying her thoughts more thoroughly concerning this *stamp of approval*, Claire comes to understand that what she's pursuing is nothing but a false sense of security. Her mother isn't the one who will be living with Alex—she is. Claire decides it's time to trust her own instincts and her choices. Now, she has to figure out if marrying Alex is *really* what she wants.

Alex is correct in saying that they would have to begin again if he stayed in Phoenix for an extended time. As a result of his prolonged absence, Claire might create more excuses to put off going forward with her commitment to him. She might become the one who harbors feelings of resentment because he chose his brother over her. Wow!

This ego stuff is really something. There are so many twists and turns. One has to be on the lookout at all times to see what aspect is in control.

There's no doubt that Claire enjoys being with Alex. But are they good for each other? After careful consideration, Claire believes they are. Then, she asks the question again, working to dig deeper, but realizes in a split second that she's arguing with her ego. Her ego is afraid and wants to play it safe; it's looking for justifiable reasons to not go forward, to grow, or to marry Alex.

How *does* Claire feel about Alex? When she puts her attention on her heart, she knows that she loves him.

Again, Claire laughs at herself. A relationship should be built on love, not second guessing the other person or oneself. Claire has almost fallen for one of the oldest games—self-doubt.

Chapter Thirty-Nine

Three days have gone by since Alex returned to work, and he has scarcely laid eyes on Claire. Heavy fatigue from his trip is clearly written on his face, which he can't hide. He's plagued with triggers brought on by hearing words like *cancer, death,* and *brother,* causing him to tear up. Overwhelmed by the unwieldy surges of emotion, Alex avoids talking about his situation. He isn't able to manage his workload, which causes more stress.

When he was away, his water heater quit, and he hasn't been to the grocery store yet. Not having a hot shower or fresh produce isn't helping matters. At work, he has to stay on task. That leaves sorting out how to handle replacing the water heater until late at night, or it has to wait until his days off. Alex wants to change out the water heater himself to save a few dollars. Although Claire is constantly on his mind and in his dreams, there isn't enough time or energy to bring her back into his reality just yet.

Meanwhile, Claire stews over their lack of communication. *Has Alex lost interest?* She so wants to tell him how she feels about their relationship, about him. Logically, she understands that he's sorting through his feelings about Charles. She knows that processing anything personal when you're caring for patients isn't good and shouldn't happen. One must be fully present with the residents or they won't get the level of care they require and deserve.

Claire concedes that their relationship is temporarily on hold, causing her to feel like she's low on Alex's priority list. Aware that her feelings have become unpredictable, she avoids talking about what's going on in her life. She wants to give Alex space to move through his ordeal, but the words he spoke to her when they last talked continuously replay in her mind—*Claire, I want to come home to you.*

Claire is unable to shake the feeling of abandonment. The longer the silence continues, the more uncomfortable Claire becomes. As a last resort, she begins to examine Alex's character, wanting to find some serious flaw.

She wants peace. She knows better than to invent a reason for Alex's behavior, but she feels there must be more to what's happening or what's *not* happening. *Why is he avoiding me?*

Claire begins to wonder if she should say something about it—do something—make a move. Perhaps, for some obscure and unexplainable reason, Alex has changed his mind about their relationship.

For a while, she uses her patients to keep her busy so her thoughts don't dwell on Alex. When sweet memories of their love making unexpectedly erupt, her face flushes and tears threaten to fall. For the love of God, she prays, *help me!*

Harry continues to put up his usual stubborn resistance, and Claire isn't going to attempt to tear it down. She has no doubt that God will reunite Harry with his children, so she stops thinking about it. When the right time comes, everything will fall into place.

She reminds herself that when several people are involved in anything, it usually slows down progress. People require time to work through their thoughts and emotions in order to adjust their minds for positive change.

Another two days go by, and Alex is still detached. Claire wonders how long she can wait for him to come around. Her heart aches, yet she knows that the situation with his brother is probably causing him to re-evaluate his entire life. Even so, he said all those things about wanting them to be a couple. How much longer must she continue to wait?

On her day off, to keep her mind off of Alex and Harry, Claire decides to visit her mother. While she's there, she may confide in what's happening, and see what her mom has to say about it.

When she steps back to look at the pieces of her life, she sees that things are not proceeding the way she thinks they should. She feels a sense of impatience.

God, I don't know what the problem is. It could be me that's preventing some of these people from going forward. I want to help Harry and his family. I want to be with Alex. What can I do to encourage Alex to talk to me? What can I do to help Harry? I understand that people want to feel safe. If they don't feel safe, they'll generally dig a hole as deep as they can and crawl into it to prevent interacting with others.

As she prays, the words pour from her heart. She doesn't know where the part about *feeling safe* comes from. Who doesn't feel safe?

"None of you do."

"Wait just a minute," she says. "Is someone talking to me?" Claire waits for an answer, but nothing comes. *How odd.*

At her mother's, she pretends that everything is fine and that she's there to visit and play with Miss Daisy. After she's been there for a while, she questions why she wanted to come to begin with. Without warning, an invisible force takes control, and she hears herself speak out, "Mom, it seems like everyone around me is avoiding me. I've waited patiently for Harry to call his kids to get one of them to bring the Malone family history to The Manor."

Feelings of despair mixed with frustration rapidly build as Claire explains her situation. "Alex's last name is Malone.

They may be related." Claire thinks back, remembering Alex's discouraging response to her idea, *I have met dozens of people with the same last name, very common name here, you know.*

"Go on Claire. It sounds like you've hit on something here."

"In the beginning, I was so excited. Alex doesn't have any family left except his brother. Needless to say, the possibility of Alex being related to Harry is slight. Yet, the last name is a common thread they all share that could work to bring Harry's family, and possibly Alex, back together. Except, Harry just gets angry every time I bring it up. Harry won't let anyone in. He doesn't trust anyone. It's all rather sad when I think about it."

Claire's eyes widen with wonder, and she looks expectantly at her mother.

"Claire, something has come over you. What are you thinking?"

Claire doesn't immediately speak; her mother may think she's lost her mind. Claire inhales deeply and exhales before she speaks. "Mom, you could come to The Manor. We can have lunch together and maybe you could stop in to visit Harry. Maybe you could get to know him?"

Claire listens to herself while watching her mother's expression. Is she going too far? Of course she is! Who in their right mind would do this for her?

Claire doesn't wait for her mother to answer or even tell her what she's thinking. Instead, she dives in, "Alex is home from Phoenix. You know that situation. What you don't know is that the doctors have given up hope that Charles will recover, there's nothing more they can do for him. Alex came home to be with me. He told me on the phone that he wanted to be with me, that he couldn't do anything for Charles. Hospice will take care of him, he said. He's on a morphine drip and sleeps all the time. Well…"

Claire stops and looks at her wringing hands, then she looks at Miss Daisy, silently pleading for help, for comfort. All this time, Miss Daisy sits at Claire's feet, attentively watching her.

Claire wants to hold her, to feel her soft fur. "Miss Daisy? Will you let me pick you up?" Timidly, Claire reaches for the pup, and immediately the dog comes to her. Claire places Miss Daisy on her lap and caresses the dog's long, silky, black-and-white coat. "You are such a sweet girl. I'm so glad you're here with us."

She rehashes her troubles as if repeating them will somehow help her sort them out. "Alex is home—has been for several days now. He has not texted, called, or even taken me aside to speak to me at work. I feel he's avoiding me." Pausing to review her rant, she adds, "Yes, he's going through a challenging situation, but really?" Claire looks at her mother for answers, "Maybe you can help me sort through it all?

"Claire, for heaven's sake! When are you going to let people figure out what they want on their own?"

Like a small child who has been shamed, Claire, stunned, blinks at her mother's choice of words. Then, she lowers her eyes, regretting that she's been so open and trusting. Her thoughts shift to anger, "Well, Mom, I don't know.

"I was asked to help Harry reunite with his children. Then Harry goes and has another heart attack, and Alex goes off to Phoenix. While he's there, he says he wants to come home to be with me. I heard him say those words, plain as day. He sounded sincere. Then he comes home and hardly speaks to me. Is there something wrong with me that causes people to want to distance themselves?" Claire doesn't stop there. She has lost her balance, her reserve. "Even you, the person I count on the most, you do the same thing."

Their eyes meet. The pitch of Claire's voice climbs to an all-time high. "Mom, I feel like I'm lost in a world where everyone wants to deny their real feelings—to deny the truth."

Margaret narrows her eyes, rubs her temples, then she holds up her hands to stop Claire's onslaught. "Claire, please stop. We both know that I'm not an expert. I probably shouldn't have said what I did, but there are times that people just have to think through whatever they're going through, Alex included.

Are you mixing up Alex and Harry avoiding you, with avoiding something in their own lives? I have a strong feeling that you want to say something to me. What did you mean by *I do the same thing*?"

Shaking her head in frustration, Claire stands to walk to the window, wishing that she had kept her mouth shut. However, she knows the opportunity has finally arrived to speak her truth. Turning to her mother, she lowers her voice and pleads for forgiveness. "Oh, I messed this up big time. Oh God, I'm so sorry."

Yet, Claire feels she must continue. Her voice drops to a whisper, "Mom, I've backed off. For days, I've backed off giving them both time to think through what they're going through. I feel like I'm running out of time. I'm out of patience, I guess. I wanted to feel my way through these relationships, to listen with my heart." Claire laughs, "but no one is talking." She bows her head and slowly asks with tears in her eyes, "How long must I wait for the truth to come out?" Suddenly, Claire's patience runs out. She can no longer take this. "Mother, when are *you* going to speak the truth?"

Her eyes widen as Margaret looks at her. "Claire, what are we talking about?"

"I've waited years for us to have a conversation about Steve, my little brother, about when he died, how he died." Claire's heart aches and tears stream down her face. "He as much as killed himself, Mother. When are we going to talk about that? It hurts so much to keep it all inside."

Margaret face and neck redden as the shadows of agonizing pain cross her face. Yet, Claire won't, can't stop herself. "I want you to know what happened. Do you know what happened to Steve?"

"Claire, I know what happened. He was a very unhappy boy. Your father and I, we talked. I understand."

Aghast, Claire cries out, "What? You know? Why didn't you tell me? All these years, and you said nothing! I always thought you believed it was an accident."

"No, Claire." Margaret wipes the tears from her eyes. "Oh sure, I wanted to believe his death was an accident. It was months later…, you remember how long it took me to clean out his room. I found pages and pages of dark ruminations. It looked as if Steve had been trying to sort out his feelings. The writings said it all. But even before that, deep down, I knew the truth."

Claire murmurs, "I was at the university. I wasn't here."

"Right, I remember now. Knowing that what Steve did, he did on purpose, makes it all the worse. I felt like I failed as a mother. I just had to face it."

"Claire, I need something to drink. I'm sure you'd like something as well. Please don't think that I'm running away from this. I'll be back in a minute with some hot peppermint tea for both of us."

Minutes later, she returns with a tray filled with cheese and crackers and hot peppermint tea. For a few minutes, they both sit in silence, savoring their snacks.

At last, Margaret asks, "Claire, is it the circumstances surrounding Steve's death that you've been holding on to all of this time? I didn't want to make it worse by talking about it. You felt bad enough as it was. He was gone and buried before I knew for sure that it was…" Her voice drops, unable to say the word that they both know.

Nodding her head, afraid of saying the wrong thing, Claire looks at her mother as she silently reviews her mother's heartfelt confession. "You failed as a parent? How can you say that? You raised us the same. I didn't turn out that way. All of these years I've been dancing around that event, literally petrified to speak of it, to say his name for fear I would upset you more. God, yes, all of this time.

"Every time that event came to mind, I felt like another little piece of me was dying. I had no peace, none at all. I wanted us all to be on the same page, so we could talk openly about Steve, about everything."

"Claire, sometimes people get stuck, like me, for example.

I thought I knew best by keeping it to myself. I was stuck. I know it, and I knew it at the time. I felt sorry for myself, I lost my son. I felt like I'd failed, that I was a terrible mother. Then my husband dies. Leon made me feel safe, comfortable. He took care of things, and we did things together. I was not alone. When Steve passed, I had Leon to lean on. Like a child, I hid behind him. He made the decisions that affected our lives—kept us going. He was there to buffer some of the harsh realities this world throws at us, like Steve's death."

"Now I get it," Claire says quietly. "Harry is sick, real sick, Mom. He isn't going to recover. Before he leaves this world, it would be better if he lets go of some of his pain, his fear that he dumps on others. I'm supposed to help him in some way."

"Claire, you keep saying that. Why are you responsible for him in any way except to care for him while you are on duty? Earlier you said someone asked you to help him. Who was that?"

"Mother, you know I want to share everything with you." Claire takes a deep breath and sighs, questioning if she wants to talk to her mother any longer. She's suddenly weary of all the drama. *Does she really want to tell her?* Then, it seems as if the dam finally collapses, pouring out at last to free her of the weight that she has carried for so long.

Nervously, Claire laughs to prolong the inevitable. "Yep, I'm as guilty as the next guy. You remember when Tom and I split? Do you remember why?"

"Well, he didn't agree that you should be working at the hospital."

"Mom, the reason we didn't agree was because I saw an angel with a patient before the patient passed. I told Tom about what I saw. He thought I was mentally unstable, having that kind of experience. I love my job. I love my patients. And I still see angels when a patient is about to pass. But...," Claire waits for an indication of how to proceed.

"Claire, oh honey. All this time you had these experiences, and you felt you couldn't talk to me about them?"

"Well, yes. I was afraid that you, like Tom, would think I'm crazy. It doesn't feel good when your family members think this way. Not at all, so I kept my mouth shut."

"Claire, my own mother had similar encounters."

Shocked, Claire stares at her mother, "What? No way. Are you serious? Are you sure?"

"Oh, I'm quite serious. We didn't talk about it for the very same reason."

"Mom, it hasn't stopped. I still see the angels. Now they speak to me. Frank, he's one of the angels, he's the one who asked me to help Harry."

Very quietly, Margaret says, "Oh, I see."

"That's why I feel frustrated. I see and hear all of these angels, and I thought I knew what I was doing. I thought I had the perfect idea to help Harry, but it just hasn't panned out, not yet anyway."

"Claire, really, the family history is an excellent idea, and I believe well worth your efforts to pursue. It would serve several people if you can help connect them. But, dear, you cannot force Harry or anyone else to change their course. Even with your gift, it doesn't change the fact that for some people, death may be a painful experience. To be sick and to know that you won't overcome it, would be like staring death in the face. Can you imagine the strength it would take to have that knowledge and remain calm? I, for one, don't know how people hold themselves together. Of course, maybe there are some that are relieved and welcome it, death that is." Margaret visibly shivers.

"Harry doesn't want to die. You're right. I can't force anyone to change their course. I just want to help Harry's family see the situation from a different perspective. I understand that part.... Then, there's Alex..." Claire frowns as her words trail off.

"Claire, give him another day or so. I'm sure he could use some extra rest after being away. Besides, there's been no closure for him; Charles is hanging on, still connected. It's a heavy weight to carry. Alex is grieving. Remember when my father was sick for so long? It was a stressful time for everyone.

I've also learned that many people go through a time of deep inner reflection when a loved one is about to pass or has passed. There's something about death that makes us stop and ask certain questions about life. We want answers instantly, but we may have to wait for them."

"But Alex and I go through this stuff at work all the time."

"Claire, this is Alex's brother. He may question his decision to come home and leave his brother to pass without family. So many of us come to doubt our choices well after we make them."

"Mother, how do I make those choices from my heart? Is that even possible?" Miss Daisy licks Claire's face as if to reassure her that it's possible.

"Well, that's a tough question," Margaret begins. "I know we want to feel confident that we're making the best choices, the ones that bring us peace, but sometimes, there are factors that prevent us from choosing what we truly want, what is really in our hearts."

Claire and Margaret stop to look at each other. "Claire, I'm trying to come up with an example for you. I guess the easiest one would be illness. Say, I'm ill and homebound, and someone I love dearly, who lives in another state or even in the same city is about to pass. There's nothing more that I want than to be with that person to express how much they mean to me, the difference they made in my life, and to say goodbye. Unfortunately, I'm prevented from fulfilling my wish because of my own health issues. I'll have to say goodbye another way. We all do the best we can, considering the circumstances."

"Yes, I understand now," Claire responds. "Thanks for talking this through with me. This has really helped. I'll just give Alex a couple more days to rest before I do anything."

"I think that's what I would do; although, there may be another reason why he's avoiding you." Margaret's eyes dance with delight as she smiles, "It's just an idea. But, could he be playing hard to get?"

Disheartened and put off, Claire glares at her mother.

"Really, Mother, I was fine with waiting for a couple of more days and then you say that."

"Well, it's a possibility. Or maybe he just wants to see how much you love him by waiting for you to come around."

Shaking her head in utter disbelief, Claire lets go of her harsh reaction to her mother's suggestions. "Well, there are always other possibilities. I should get out of here before you come up with something else equally appalling."

Laughing at her mother's audacity, Claire looks at Miss Daisy as if she could somehow rescue her. Miss Daisy's ears perk up and she whimpers. "Mother, you know I love you. Thank you for being so open and honest with me. This conversation has really helped, especially about Steve. I really miss him, Mom."

"I know honey, and I love you too, Claire. I hope that in the future you'll be able to speak openly about your experiences. That's if you want to. Some things are private, of course, and I want to respect that."

Chapter Forty

At home, Claire prepares to settle in for the night with a good book and a glass of wine when she hears her phone ring. Seeing it's Alex causes her to hesitate. She had finally made peace with having a few more days of silence.

As a result of Claire's conversation with her mother, she had mentally surrounded herself with a shield of protection that felt like a thick, fluffy blanket, giving her the comfort, she needed. She isn't sure she's ready to or even wants to talk to Alex.

Working to rearrange her mind to accept this new development, Claire takes a deep breath. Then, trying to sound like she isn't anxious, she says, "Alex, hi!"

"Claire. How are you over there?" Alex sounds stronger than the last time they had a real conversation. Cheerfully, Claire answers, "Just sitting down with a good book." Noticing a bad connection with the cell service she asks, "Where are you?"

"I'm on my way home. I just finished a major haul at the grocery store. Cabinets have been stark bare for days. Thought I'd better check in. This week has been rough, and I just wanted to be alone. This thing with Charles turned out to be, well, what I mean is, I wouldn't have been good company. I think I needed some down time."

"I wondered about that. I wanted to give your space, but quite honestly, I was beginning to think..." Claire doesn't finish her sentence. What she's thinking sounds immature.

Alex clears his throat, "Ah, so you thought I was giving you the cold shoulder, did you?"

"I didn't want to say that because it makes me sound like an insecure child."

"Well, it's obvious you're not a child. But now, I too wonder only because of what you insinuated, if you may feel a tad insecure?"

Sucking in a breath, Claire is not sure she wants to be honest. "Truth be told, yes. I haven't had enough time with you to feel secure. I realized through this past week that I don't know you, not really. Funny, I'm not sure I even know myself." Claire's voice catches, "Not really good to begin a relationship when I feel so, ah, unsure of things."

"Right, I get it. Do you wonder if I'm suddenly moody and sullen when I'm slightly provoked? That sort of thing?"

"Alex, really, all I know is how you are at work," Claire responds. "That's all."

"Claire, I'm the same person. Yes, I need rest, time to think and feel, and certainly now, I want to be hopeful that my brother will recover." He breathes deeply. "I need comforting because I know...." Alex doesn't finish his sentence.

Claire hears a measure of sadness in his voice, even defeat. Claire's compassion kicks in. "Why don't you come over here? I have room, I think, for your groceries."

A wisp of happiness flutters in Alex's voice, "I do want to see you, but I was totally out of everything. I would love to come over. Is it too late? I could take my stuff home and put it away, then drive over. It would take me an hour before I could get there. That would bring it to eight. Is that too late for you?"

"Not if you stay over. What did you buy? Anything good?"

When Alex doesn't answer right away, Claire thinks that the call got dropped. "Alex? Alex, are you there?"

"Yes, hang on. I'm thinking." With an edge of excitement in his voice, "I'll surprise you. See you in an hour or so."

She doesn't know much about this guy but she's sure she wants to learn.

Chapter Forty-One

The day begins with Claire on the run. Her mother phones to tell her she's sick, too sick to take the dog out. Can Claire come and get her? Claire can't imagine what would make her that sick. "What's wrong?"

"I have the flu or something, maybe food poisoning. Got to go." The phone goes dead.

Contemplating the situation, Claire shakes her head. Then she quietly sets about gathering her clothes so as to not disturb Alex who's still sleeping. For a moment, she watches him sleep, thinking how perfect last night was—all the bells and whistles. He came over with two pieces of dark chocolate cake, then promised to cook chicken cordon bleu for her today. Alex is beginning to settle in.

Claire writes a short note and leaves it on the pillow before going to the bathroom to dress. After she shuts the bathroom door, she mutters, "Just great." Ten minutes later, she's in her car, driving down Brookline Avenue.

When Claire arrives, her mom is in the bathroom. First thing is to get Miss Daisy outdoors. Miss Daisy doesn't waste any time doing her business.

Deciding to at least let her mother know she's here, Claire

gingerly knocks on the bathroom door and asks if she has any Pepto Bismol to calm her system down. Her mother moans, "Almost out."

"How about 7UP or Sprite?"

"No."

"I'll go around the corner. I'll be right back."

When Claire returns, Margaret is sitting in her rocking chair. She looks ragged. Her gray hair is stringy, and her complexion is ashen. Claire thinks her mother looks more fragile now than when she was depressed.

"I know I look frightful, Claire. I've been up all night."

"Mom, here's the Pepto Bismol. Let me get you a spoon. Until you feel better, Miss Daisy can stay with me. I have two more days off. Tell me how much to feed her, I'll figure out the rest."

Miss Daisy was obviously not thrilled about going into the carrier but that couldn't be helped. After they arrived at Claire's and she let Miss Daisy out, the pup was bouncing off the walls. *Oh boy, so this is what it's like.*

Alex walks into the kitchen wearing nothing but his boxer shorts. He whistles. Miss Daisy runs straight to him. He picks her up and, instantly, they are the best of friends. "Claire, the strangest thing happened to me this morning."

Interested more than concerned, Claire asks, "What?"

"It was like a really bad dream." Alex is playful, yet serious, like he doesn't know how to tell Claire what's troubling him.

"Oh, honey, it's okay. I'm here now." Claire is pretty sure he's just playing one of his games with her.

Alex begins with a straightforward synopsis. "I woke up. You were gone. That was not cool."

Not being sure of his motives, Claire follows his lead, "Does this mean we're now officially living together?"

"You think I'm kidding."

Claire has a queer feeling that he's honestly upset. "Are you...?" Claire looks at him with a critical eye, hoping she didn't misread him. "You're kidding right? Oops, nope, you're not kidding."

Alex puts down Miss Daisy and walks straight to Claire to take her in his arms. "Do I look like I'm kidding? Claire, come on. I want to live with you, forever."

Remembering the conversation Claire had with her mother about Steve, she pays attention to her body before speaking. "I know. My heart is really happy to hear you say that and I see no reason why we can't be together. Of course, there's a matter of homes. If this is the only obstacle we confront, I feel extremely blessed and I thank God for that."

During breakfast, Claire gives Alex a rundown on her mother's condition. "I should go over there and clean out her refrigerator. She's a pack rat, probably get some fresh food for her as well."

Then, as she thinks more about it, she realizes that her mother's illness may be a release of energy, resulting from their recent heartfelt conversation. It had been so intense that it manifested on a physical level. Claire feels that some of the negative energy is moving out of her.

Before Claire has the opportunity to tell Alex about her conversation with her mother, he says, "Tomorrow *we* can go clean out her fridge and do her shopping." Alex sees Claire's surprise and laughs. "Yes, Claire I said, *we*. I'm sure she won't want anything today. Maybe by tomorrow she'll feel well enough for me to put the doggy door in.

"By the way, while I was away, I did a little thinking about the house situation. Which place would you like to keep? I'm not saying we can't keep both of them, but we are both really busy with work." Alex shifts the subject, "And, oh, I bet this will surprise you. I had a talk with Harry. He said he has an empty stall in his body shop that I can rent, and he gave me some phone numbers."

Astonished, Claire shrieks, "Wait! No! His body shop?"

"Yep! He quoted me a figure, very reasonable. He said he likes my girl and wants to help us out. Imagine that! He likes you. That should make your day. Of course, I want to check it out before I agree to anything."

"Really, Alex? Of course, Harry likes me. What's not to like?" Suspiciously, Claire eyes him. "You made a reference to more than one phone number. What else?"

"He gave me Augusta and Robert's phone numbers. Remember the genealogy? He said there's a book. His wife worked on it for years, and it's extensive. We would probably find what we're looking for.

"He also confided that he thought this might be a good opportunity to get Robert involved in his business. He just wants the family to get along. He lost me, though, when he mentioned an incident after his wife died, which is causing all the trouble in the family. His kids won't let it go. He did something that didn't sit well with them when he was angry and depressed. I didn't press him."

"I don't believe what I'm hearing! Are you sure?"

Alex presented a Boy Scout salute. "Scouts honor. Later today, I'm going to make a few phone calls. It'll be interesting to see where this takes us."

Feeling a surge of relief run through her, Claire sighs. "Everything is finally changing for the better. There's so much to think about. It sounds like Harry's about to make some changes in his life. I'm so grateful. As for the houses, I like my stone work, but your floor plan is more open. You're the one with the garage, Alex. If you rent the stall from Harry then I could park in the garage too. Right?"

Then, Claire looks down at Miss Daisy, who has been sitting in front of her with those big brown eyes trying to get her attention. "What do you think of all the news?"

Miss Daisy barks and wags her tail. "She's such a sweetie, Alex. That's for sure."

Chapter Forty-Two

Later that afternoon, Claire's mom calls, "The trips to the bathroom have slowed down, and a while ago, I had some broth and a soda cracker. So far, so good."

Claire is relieved. "How about Alex and I come over tomorrow and clean out your refrigerator? We can bring Miss Daisy with us for a short visit if you're up for it. Are you missing her?"

"No, I haven't had any time to miss anyone. You and Alex are back together then?"

"Yes, Alex called last night. It was weird. I was starting to get comfortable with the idea of a couple more days of *me time* when he called."

"You mentioned that you want to clean out my refrigerator. Do you think this may have been food poisoning?"

"Who knows? I just want to be sure. Have you been around anyone? I have an inkling that it's simply an energetic cleanse. Remember when we talked the other day? We really brought some negative energy to the surface. Sometimes that sort of thing manifests as a physical release."

"Well, that's something to consider. Why don't you call me tomorrow morning? If I can keep my food down for the rest of the day and if I feel better, then I think it would be great for you to come over for a while. I should meet Alex. I want to meet Alex."

Claire lifts her glass for a silent toast, *Hallelujah. Here's to my mother's progress.*

"Right. I definitely want you to meet him, and I want him to meet you too." Letting go of all expectations, Claire simply says, "If not tomorrow, then it will happen when it happens. You sleep as much as you can and drink plenty of fluids. Call me if you need anything. Otherwise, I'll call you tomorrow."

For the first time in several days, Claire feels lighter, freer, more relaxed. Alex is finally home, truly home. They agree they want to be together. That means it's time to decide if they both feel Alex's house is the best choice, and if so, how to get her moved over there, and what to do with her place.

Claire, however, continues to stew over the possibility that what they are planning will ultimately fizzle out, leaving her stranded, homeless. She prays for guidance. Initially, she feels it's not logical to keep her house, but getting in a hurry could prove to be really foolish.

For some reason, Claire thinks of Harry. He may know more about property values and rental houses. The feeling that she needs to speak with Harry is persistent and so unlike anything she has ever experienced. She admits she barely knows Harry, yet intuitively, she feels he'll have the answers she hopes for.

Claire decides to drive over to The Manor tomorrow, before they visit her mother. She chides herself at going into work on her day off, but she knows this is what she must do.

The rest of the day, they divide their attention between discussions of where to live and playing with Miss Daisy.

Problem is, Miss Daisy doesn't want to play catch when they throw a ball to her. She wants to be outdoors. Never mind the arctic cold, the sun is shining. She finds that neither Alex nor Claire will let her out when she goes to the sliding glass door and whines. Instead, she sits in front of the door, her eyes glued on a squirrel's every move or on the neighbor's sassy cat sitting on the fence post for the shear purpose of annoying Miss Daisy.

Naturally, Alex and Claire's conversation, gravitate to topics dear to their hearts. "When Hannah was talking to me, she said I was to give God permission to heal through me, to invite God to bring forth the measure of healing energy that's for the highest good to those in my care. This shouldn't be limited to praying for a patient before we work with them but throughout our visits. It's like talking telepathically to God at the same time we're with the patient." They both agree that it takes practice to be conscious of the divine in action in every moment of their lives.

"Alex, I've been focusing on how my patients respond when I care for them like I would for a family member or a really good friend. It's amazing to watch how they begin to open up, as a beautiful flower, receiving the exact nutrients required to fully blossom."

"I get what you're saying. Right now, for me, all I can do is practice being more aware of their emotional needs, while I remain focused on their physical requirements."

"Alex, you're the most caring nurse I know. You have a knack for nurturing the residents and making them feel safe. You engage them in conversation. I've seen you in action too many times to discount your skill."

"You give me too much credit. I know I have room for improvement."

"I suppose we all do, Alex. I've noticed, on too many occasions, I operate on autopilot, doing only what's necessary to calculate the next course of action. And then, there's the endless administration of medications and documentation. At times, those tasks can become so wearisome. I know that's part of my job, but it can become rote, monotonous. I want to incorporate something that gives the residents a sense that I'm not only working with them on their physical illness but also working to support their mental, emotional, and even spiritual well-being. I like to give them the kind of care that tells them I'm listening, and I care; they are special."

"For me, it's too easy to be abrupt in my duties because I'm busy running from patient to patient. Some days near the end of my shift, I feel like I've gone into survival mode. I must preserve my energy and do only what's necessary. I go home and want nothing more than to sit down, have a beer, watch a show and zone out."

"I agree, Alex, at times the constant motion, going from patient to patient, makes me feel rushed, unless I consciously take a few minutes to connect in a deeper more personal way. I admit, there are days I just want to finish and go home, the demands exceed what I have to give on all levels. But Alex, I feel that there's nothing more I would rather do than be a nurse. I love these people."

"You're so right. It takes a certain type of person to love nursing. I've always loved my work."

Claire feels she's present with the conversation but there are moments when she admittedly, watches Alex's face for the sheer pleasure of it. As he speaks, he engages her with his expressive features, his eyes convey his emotion, the creases that line his forehead when he's in deep thought and the way he rakes his hair with his fingers when he wants to make his point, his easy smile when they agreed. At times, her eyes drift to his lips. She isn't aware that he even notices.

"Even though I love what I do, I have to release the pent-up emotion. That's why I go to the window to look out over the horizon and watch the reflection of the lights on the water. I feel like it's my sanctuary, where I'm infused with the beauty of a magnificent cathedral. I feel like I'm calling in all that splendor to take my troubles and transmute them, then to heal and balance me."

"So that's your secret?"

"You think what I do is a secret?"

"You seem to have an inordinate amount of focus and energy. I always wondered how you maintained that." Then, more seriously, Alex adds, "Our jobs are extremely demanding, Claire. Everyone needs some sort of outlet. The past few weeks we've been together have been so much better for me. I look forward to being with you—that's certainly uplifting. And, by the way, I saw you looking at my lips." He grins, a mischievous glint lights his eyes.

Claire throws her head back and laughs. "Alex, I can't help it if I'm enchanted by you, attracted to you, and I love making love with you." Claire clears her throat. "Yes, to have something to look forward to is good, but we still have to release the energy. If we don't, we'll end up sick. I'm pretty sure that's what caused my mother's illness."

"You mean that sex is imperative to releasing unwanted energy?"

Claire raises her eyes to meet Alex's and stammers, "Uh, I don't know how that works. We're building and releasing energy. So..." Claire's at a loss for words.

"Alex, I don't know. I do know, when I ask God to help ease the flow of my tasks, to help me stay relaxed, it helps. I ask for those special moments where I can make a difference and give each patient what they require in order for them to heal on all levels."

Claire crosses her arms. She knows she feels subconsciously defensive and wants to finish this conversation, "I know you also really care for your patients. That's one of the qualities that I've noticed that you excel in. In order to help them heal, or more accurately, keep them comfortable as much as possible, we want to care for them on a deeper, more intimate level."

Claire remembers all the patients that have passed while in her care. "When I bond with a patient and he or she passes, I can't help but grieve, even though I see them escorted out by an angel. Often, it's bittersweet. They're no longer suffering, but it's still difficult to see them go.

"Sometimes I just don't know what to do with my feelings. That's why I go look out the window and watch the lights. That helps me let go. What do you do to let go, besides having a beer and watching a show?" Claire looks up to find Alex smiling at her.

What Alex is thinking is clearly written on his face. "Oh Alex." Claire's breath catches. Shyly, Claire looks out the window to keep her mind off what Alex is thinking.

Laughing loudly, Alex stands up, walking directly to her. What happened next throws Claire off-kilter. Alex lowers his body into a kneeling position in front of her. Feeling his heat, she holds her breath. He leans in closer and lowers his voice, "That's when I concentrate on something physically demanding like...," He watches her face to see if she's taking the bait, then smiles.

Without wavering, Claire exclaims, "For the love of God kiss me, will you?"

Alex holds up his hand to stop her. "Claire, I was merely going to say that when I concentrate on something physically demanding such as a woodworking project, I lose myself in the activity."

Frowning, Claire slaps Alex's arm. Pretending to be insulted, she pouts, "Oh, like that truck or that mysterious project you were working on the other night?"

Laughing, Alex modifies her description, "The Apache. Yep, that's what I'm talking about."

"Right, the Apache."

They both know they're dancing around their sexual tension and where it's leading. Alex runs his fingers through his hair and stands up. Claire's half-closed eyes are glazed, accompanied by shallow breathing. He takes her hand, "Claire, let's go into the kitchen, get some coffee, and let Miss Daisy out."

In disbelief, Claire stares at Alex, "You, sir, have underhanded methods. You're toying with me!"

"Ah, so you have me figured out, have you? I promise we'll get to it soon, my dear Claire, soon."

By the time they enter the kitchen and let Miss Daisy out, they both have simmered down, but Claire sees how it is for Alex. "You're way more in control of your desires than I am. That is, I suppose, an admirable trait."

"I have had plenty of practice. Besides, anything worth waiting for..., you know the saying."

Claire, a stickler for semantics, gladly corrects Alex, "No, that's not how it goes. This is how it goes, 'Anything worth doing is worth doing right.'"

Claire makes a fresh pot of coffee and reaches for two cups, thinking of a way to shift the conversation to Charles. She wants to know if Alex has made any headway in Phoenix but feels she may be too bold if she asks directly, almost as if it isn't any of her business. She reminds herself that they're a couple, and therefore, she's part of the deal. "Alex, what about Charles? You remember Hannah?"

"Sure, I remember Hannah."

"Hannah told me that Charles is going home. He has finished his work here."

Claire is mindful of Alex's pain. She watches for signs of discomfort. Seeing none, she continues, "I wondered because I'm being guided to pray for the healing of our patients if that's what's meant for their highest good, then what about praying for Charles? Do you think that God will heal Charles if we pray for him?"

Catching her eye, Alex takes a swallow of coffee before he says, "I don't know the answer. You said Hannah told you that Charles is going home? Is it decided then?" Noticeably, his voice grows more subdued as he attempts to scour the message for hidden meanings, like he's trying to solve a riddle.

Claire knows that Alex is examining the possibilities and patiently waits. "When we pray for someone, that energy is reserved for that person. In my opinion, it's God's business when he chooses to use it. For instance, if we pray for Charles to heal and we don't see any improvement that doesn't mean there won't be any after his transition. Very interesting topic, you have introduced, Claire."

Claire values Alex's knowledge and opinion. Alex continues, "Do we, any of us, really know God's will? I want to think that there isn't any disease of any kind. But as I understand it, we, in our human imperfection, have created that very thing.

"There's free will, and we choose what we create. God, because of His infinite wisdom and love, uses all sorts of so-called negative manifestations to teach us patience, empathy, kindness, and forgiveness. I see that happening with not only the patients but also with those who are involved with the patients. Everyone is here to learn something."

"Thank you for sharing your perspective."

Wanting to expand on the subject even more, Claire adds, "I get how working with our patients assists us with learning to be more patient, compassionate, and so on, but I also think a way to expand or improve upon what we call God qualities and virtues is to identify the lower propensities and to correct them. You know, when I realize that I'm running out of patience, I'll work to become more patient, tolerant and forgiving. I strive all the time to be more tolerant, overall, I want to be a better person. I find that it's through balancing myself that I become a healthier person. Maintaining a healthy balance enables me to express more patience and compassion."

"Like with Harry?"

"Yes. And with any of the residents. I must be balanced in order to care for them. Not only that, but it's wise to remain neutral, yet supportive in how they cope with their situation.

"There's also the theory of karma. With everything we think, say, and do there's cause and effect. If we think negative thoughts and do negative things, we become more negative. We then draw negative energy to us. The outcome may be an illness or disease, unhealthy relationships, or so forth. Even with all of God's goodness and mercy, we create our own lives through our choices." Throwing up her hands, Claire professes, "I'm sure there's more to this."

"You know, Claire, I have prayed for Charles to heal and continue to do so. I know that his illness is not purely physical, although it sure appears that way. Charles needs spiritual healing as well, to let go and forgive past hurts. Personally, Claire, if it were my choice, I'd bring Charles home and heal him of this disease. There's nothing more that I want than for my brother to have perfect health. I know he would love to meet you.

"Then there's the possibility that we'll have children. Those children would love to have an uncle who lives in Phoenix. They could go visit him sometimes. But to know if it's God's plan for him to heal before he leaves this planet? I do not know."

Alex begins to pray, "God hear me now. If it's your will, heal my brother, Charles, of all illness and disease, be it of the mind, soul, or body. God, I know it's in your hands. I ask this in the name of the Father, the Son, and the Holy Spirit. May Your Will Be Done. Amen.

"He's my brother. I love him. When he's gone that side of my family is gone, except for me. It's a strange feeling to be left behind like that. But in the end, it's God's will."

"Alex, I just want Charles to have the opportunities he requires for healing and for him to be happy."

"Charles would need to examine some of the things that bother him, that he has fixated on for so many years. Those very things have kept him from being truly happy and going forward in life."

Perplexed by Alex's comment, Claire asks, "What are you talking about?"

"There are relationships that have been broken because of trust issues that I believe to be a direct result of the loss of our parents. You wouldn't think a person would harbor such a deep fear of abandonment that it would prevent the ability to have a healthy relationship with a woman, like for instance, in marriage. Charles has been in four separate relationships that I'm aware of. He claimed to love each woman and he proposed to each of them. Then, just days prior to the wedding, he sabotaged the relationship."

"Alex, that pattern may be a result of past embodiments as well. It could have been a momentum he created from everything combined."

"Past embodiments?"

"Well, sure."

"I'll be honest, Claire, I haven't given that any consideration. But, I suppose, you may be right about that. I wasn't sure you were into that type of thing."

"Definitely. I see angels consoling patients before they're escorted to the next realm. They're in between embodiments, going in for a rest and re-evaluation. I know they're being counseled as they prepare for the next life."

"Claire, I have a confession to make."

Claire fixes her eyes on Alex. Being unable to read his expression, "Well, you certainly have my attention now."

"I have had dreams about you. I'm pretty sure we were married before in a past life."

At first, Claire thinks he's joking. She cocks her head in contemplation. Trying to make light of his disclosure, Claire asks, "Are they nightmares by any chance?" She can tell by his expression that he's quite serious.

"In the end, they were nightmares. You end up dying in childbirth. Our lives where full of meaning. In my dreams, we were dedicated to each other and very much in love. We complimented one another. Financially, we had more than enough to see us through. I believe it was the Victorian era. We had three children, two boys and a girl." Alex looks in the direction of the staircase, his tone taking a different quality, one of sentiment, as he says again, "We loved each other very much and were totally devoted to one another and the children. You loved to cook. You baked bread, pies, and cakes." He chuckles, "You made these meat pies that were absolutely delicious. Your hair was long and brown."

His eyes take on a dreamy, far-away look. "You braided your hair every night and fixed it up in this bun thing during the day." Then he says, "Claire, I loved your hair."

"Is that why you make so many comments about my hair?"

"Well, sort of. And I do like teasing you, Claire. But truly, your hair was down to your waist. I... well... you know how sexy that is?"

"I died in childbirth. Wow! Was I in pain? I mean did I die quickly, or did it drag out? How did that affect you, your life?"

Alex got up to refill his coffee cup. "Slow down there. I just get pieces. I just know you died. I took care of the kids after you died."

Uneasily, she asks, "Did the baby die too?" After Claire asks that question, she stops to think about it all. "I'm almost forty and have never been pregnant. There have been times that I felt this uneasiness about having children. But I always dismiss it."

Alex's forehead creases as he stares off into the distance. "No, the baby lived. She lived. Her hair was strawberry blond. I have the sense that we picked out her name before she was born." Her name was Amarisa." He shrugs. "At least, in my dreams, that's what I called her."

Claire repeats the baby's name, letting the syllables roll off her tongue. "Amarisa, what a beautiful name."

"Her hair had this natural curl, little ringlets. I've had dreams enough that I feel a sense of dread in some of them. Like I know what's going to happen."

Claire feels his sorrow deep in her heart, "How on earth did you manage?"

"Oh, I don't know. I must have had help. I was a doctor. My office was at home."

"I'm sorry, Alex."

"This time is different. That won't happen."

Feeling morose, Claire offers, "It's much easier to have children when you're younger." To lighten the mood, she says, "Now, I think it's time to let Miss Daisy back in."

Then they indulge in a good home-cooked meal.

Chapter Forty-Three

Alex and Claire decide to take Miss Daisy over to her mother's and clean out her refrigerator in the early afternoon, with the possibility of taking her mother grocery shopping afterward. Claire phones her mom.

When Claire suggests going grocery shopping, her mother is uncomfortable with leaving Miss Daisy. "Miss Daisy is not trained yet. Yes," Margaret says, "I've been working with her to get her accustomed to being in the kennel at certain times of the day so I can rest. At first, Miss Daisy adamantly resisted, but I'm seeing some progress."

"Mother, she'll be fine. To be safe, Miss Daisy should stay in the kennel when you're gone. I'm sure she'll be fine."

"Oh, Claire, I'm sure she will be okay. I just don't want to leave her like that."

"Mom, I have some things to get finished before we come over. It's going to be a busy day. We'll see you later, then."

Alex is determined to go home and work on his *project* for a couple of hours. When he doesn't readily disclose his plans, Claire arches her brows and peers at him. Alex laughs, "It's something special for later. If you're simply patient and trust me, it'll all work out for the best."

Alex wraps his arms around Claire's waist, snuggling into her neck. "Claire, honey, it's okay. It's a surprise. By the way, would this be a good time to take a load of your things over to my house? It's going to be a big job. We might as well get started with your move." With a sly look in his eyes, he adds, "My bed is better anyhow."

Claire grins, "Yes, I can get some things together. But it's going to take a little effort to figure out what I want to take. Remember you have a fully furnished home, Alex."

"I want to swing by The Manor. Can we meet at Mom's house, say, at one o'clock? Would that give you enough time to do your thing?"

"Sure. No problem. Just pack some of your things, and I'll take them with me. But The Manor is out of the way for you. Can that wait?"

"No, I want to take care of some things as soon as possible." Claire sees his curiosity peek and appreciates his ability to refrain from prying.

Chapter Forty-Four

Claire stops at the nurses' station to let them know she's just visiting. Slipping off her coat, she walks straight to Harry's room, lightly knocks on the door, and cautiously enters. Today she's wearing blue jeans and a yellow, oversized, pullover sweater.

Harry is busy eating his lunch of spaghetti and meatballs and barely notices that anyone has entered his room. When he sees her, he frowns at the intrusion. He doesn't recognize Claire until she speaks. Quickly, his confusion is replaced with a friendly smile.

In all the days that she has cared for Harry, Claire has never felt so welcome. She walks over to the bed and takes his hand. "Harry, you look fantastic. Is it the spaghetti or not having me around that makes you so happy?"

"Claire," Harry stammers, "what... are... you... doing? You aren't working, are you?"

"Nah, I came in to see you. Do you have time to talk? Listen, I'll go get some coffee while you finish lunch and come back. Would you like one?"

"Not supposed to drink that stuff with my heart meds. You know that Claire."

"Well, maybe for you, some hot cocoa or lemonade? I sure could use the coffee though."

"I'm good. Go get yourself what you want. Don't think I'm going anywhere."

Unable to restrain herself, she bursts out, "Harry, I see you have a new attitude." Claire glows with pride. "Very nice."

When Claire returns, Harry's plate is empty. She takes time to evaluate his numbers on the display monitor. Nodding toward the monitor, "Harry, your display is impressive."

"I feel terrific, Claire. Better than I have in a long while." Suspiciously, he looks at her and asks, "Just why are you here, anyway?"

"I have a problem, well, sort of. You know Alex and I are getting married. Well, not yet. We're moving in together for now. Thing is, we both have our own homes. I'm moving in with him, so I thought I'd sell my house. Then I got to thinking, what if it doesn't work out, and Alex bails on me and I'm left homeless. Quite frankly, I'm a little scared. My first husband ditched me really fast."

Feeling hypersensitive, she nervously rambles on. "Harry, I don't know what to do. I wanted to talk to you. Maybe you have an idea or some advice for me."

Quizzically, Harry asks, "Why me? Don't you have parents to talk to?"

"Ah, Harry. Mom is recently widowed. She's not someone who I'd ask for advice. Not this kind." Claire pauses, mentally creating a list of people she can rely on. Frowning, she answers, "No, not really. In matters like this, I have no one."

"I don't know much about what you're asking. In the beginning of our marriage, we rented, then saved enough to buy a house. Then later I bought the shop. I still have both."

"Yes. Alex told me about your proposal. That's so awesome, Harry. He really wants to work on his truck. I'm sure he'll check out the shop soon. This thing with his brother, well, I guess you probably know that the doctors aren't expecting him to make it. Alex is a little distracted by it all. He's grieving and he's taking care of all the details which is a heavy load, but well…, you know. I hope you can be patient with him for a while longer.”

“Claire, my shop is fairly small, but it would be perfect for Alex. Heck, right now there’s not much going on.”

Hearing voices in the hall, Claire asks, “Are you expecting anyone today?”

“Nope.”

She walks to the doorway and sees Robert, Bridget, and another woman. “Hi, I was just talking to your dad. He’s doing really well. Are you Augusta?”

The young lady answers, “Yes, who are you?”

“Oh, sorry, I’m Claire, one of the nurses here. Off duty today. I met Bridget and Robert a couple of weeks ago.” Looking in their direction, she asks, “Do you remember?”

Robert looked at her suspiciously, “No, I don’t remember you.” Then he turns to his wife as if asking if she remembers. Bridget has the sweetest smile as she exclaims, “Yes, Claire. How are you? Pops says you would like to look at the genealogy book.”

“You mean Alex didn’t call you? He, I guess, hasn’t had time. Yes, he, we, are most interested in your family history. He’s a Malone like Patti Jo, your mother. I want to help Alex find some family. He doesn’t have anyone left.”

“I’ll bring it in tomorrow. Pops told me a little of what is going on with Alex. Seems Pops has taken a liking to you.”

Nervously, she continues, “Alex and I are trying to make a go of it. Everything is new and undecided still. I feel like I don’t have a clue about what I’m doing. That’s why I came by to talk to Harry. I don’t have a father to talk to. He passed recently. Oh God.” Claire exclaimed, “I’m sorry. I’ll leave you all to visit. This is awkward. Harry, I’m here tomorrow if you have any insights about my dilemma. Maybe by tomorrow, you’ll have an idea or two. Oh, I’m rambling again. I’m truly sorry. See you tomorrow.”

Harry narrows his eyes, like he’s about to witness Claire going over the edge. And that’s exactly how she feels. Claire has a gnawing feeling that she's somehow connected to these people, and they will always be friends even if Alex isn't closely related, but she's in a precarious position concerning all of it. She feels especially guarded, not wanting to blow it.

"Claire." Harry tries to get her attention. "I have the perfect solution for you. I'll tell you when I see you next time."

"Sure." She waves and then walks out and down the hall. Feeling perplexed, Claire stops to take a deep breath, shakes her head, and mutters, "What just happened?"

Later, Claire meets up with Alex at her mother's. Margaret's color is normal, and Miss Daisy is unmistakably overjoyed to be home as she runs full speed to Margaret. You'd have thought they had been separated for months.

After they all settle down, and they're able to hear themselves talk, Claire introduces Alex to her mother. "Alex, you remember my mom, Margaret?"

Margaret gives Claire a sideways glance that she's unable to read. Then Margaret turns her undivided attention to Alex and begins a pointed dialogue to Claire's amazement. "So, you're Alex. I've heard a little about you. No doubt you're a hard worker or you wouldn't be here today, of all days, unless you're on a mission to impress Claire and me. With me being ill and this being your day off, that is."

"Mother, how could you?"

"Margaret," Alex laughs at her tenacity. "Claire and I go way back, and I *am* a hard worker. When I see that someone can use a hand, well, it's in my nature to pitch in. I want to install the doggy door. But just so you know, I do not offer my services for free." Margaret remains silent.

"Claire says that you can cook. How about a home-cooked meal on one of my days off?" Still silent, he eyes her skeptically. "Really, Margaret, you know that you could use a door for Miss Daisy, and we should get to know each other. I'm sure you have a notebook, near full of questions to ask me, right?"

Clearly, Alex is playing her. He's wearing his poker face. *Oh, this ought to be fun.*

Margaret smiles, "So you have a sense of humor and aren't near as puny as I thought you would be. I know you have your eye on my dear Claire. But Alex, you'll have to earn my trust and my respect if you think you're going to run off with my daughter."

"Is that so?" Alex answers back. "Well, let's begin then. Can I take this door down and cut a hole in it while Claire works on your refrigerator? We'll make noise, Claire especially."

Just like a little old lady, her mother asks, "You're going to take the door down? It's mighty cold out there. Am I going to freeze?"

"Nah, we'll get you all bundled up. You should survive. Where are your blankets?"

Waving away Alex's offer, she says, "Alex, it's all right. I'll get one. I'm fine with a little noise. Having a door will cut down on all the trips I've had to make lately."

"You realize, Margaret, that you're going to have to train Miss Daisy to go out. I'm sure, though, if you tell her what you want her to do, it will make the process less grueling."

Almost in a panic, Claire's mom wants to know how to train a dog to go through the door. Attempting to ease her concern, Alex says, "Well, Miss Daisy will understand after she sees you go through the door first. You know you have to show her how. What did you expect?"

Margaret's face drops. In a flash, her expression changes. She knows Alex is pulling her leg and laughs. "You are a jokester, aren't you?" Looking toward her daughter, she warns Claire, "You'll have to watch this one."

Alex chuckles, casually offering, "Nah, really you just train her by putting a treat on the other side of the door and then open the flap a little so she can see it. She'll get the gist of it in no time."

After a hard day's work, they decide to take Margaret out to Bobby Brown's for a cheeseburger and milkshake and then head home. As they're eating, Margaret tells Alex to call her to figure out a day for his home-cooked meal. Claire is beginning to feel a little left out until Alex asks if he could bring his friend along.

Margaret, wanting to know who this friend is, asks, "Who?" But seeing the expression on Alex's face, she suddenly gets the joke and laughs, "Oh, darn it, Claire. He got me again."

Chapter Forty-Five

The next day, as promised, Robert brings the book of family history to Harry's room and even stays for a while. After Robert leaves, Harry informs Claire that they have begun to discuss how to handle the estate when he *kicks the bucket.*

Claire, a little shocked with Harry's candor exclaims, "Harry, this is what you wanted. I'm so happy for you."

From what Claire has gathered, the family had gone full tilt when Patti Jo passed, but Claire suspects that the family had been on shaky ground for a long time. When she passed, either Patti Jo had not given directions on how to handle her belongings or Harry, not being the sentimental type, had gone ahead and taken care of things on his own.

Augusta, who at that time lived with her parents, was especially upset over the handling of precious keepsakes. It seemed that regardless of what the children wanted, their father didn't consider their feelings. To give Harry the benefit of the doubt, though, he may not have understood how important those things were to his children.

Robert, feeling inclined to act as Augusta's voice, tried to protect his younger sister by insisting that Harry allow Augusta some time to go through Patti Jo's possessions before he so quickly disposed of them. The ramifications of that incident intensified over the years, spawning many episodes relating to how Harry had treated his family.

Recently, the anger has been put aside. Claire is hoping that Harry will apologize for his behavior.

In the evenings, Alex and Claire meticulously comb the family genealogy book for clues. "This is the third evening we've studied this book, and I still don't recognize any of the names or places."

Even so, they were able to find some good information and took plenty of notes to begin their own research.

Three days later, the doctor informs Harry that his condition is at the point where it would be beneficial to consider full-time nursing care. On the fly, Harry tells Claire, "They're kicking me out. I hate to leave you here."

"But Harry, I don't want to lose you. Where will you be going?"

"My kids want me closer to them. You know that place on 60th and Hawthorn? I think it's called Longfellow Nursing. That's going to be my new home."

"Oh, Harry. That's only a few blocks from where I'm moving, you know Alex's home. It'll be easy for me to visit you, that is, if you want me to visit."

Harry is rough around the edges and, sometimes, downright belligerent but for some reason, Claire really loves the old coot. Somehow, it no longer matters if they never find a family connection.

Claire surmises they share a valuable link, Frank. They're able to speak to each other about him. It's common ground. In reality, Harry has a soft spot that he just doesn't want others to know about.

At some point, Claire asks about his wife's passing, how he dealt with it. She's surprised that Harry handled her passing similarly to how her mother managed her father's.

"We were a couple," Harry explains. "Patti Jo was a great wife, mother, and cook. She took care of everything. When she died, it was as if a piece of me died too. I didn't know how to take care of myself, and to this day, I still miss her ham and beans and cornbread." He adds, "I miss her."

Claire thinks it best to act like a mediator—someone he can talk to who isn't personally involved. This gives Harry a safe platform to explore his emotions. Eventually, Claire asks him questions about things going on in her world that she feels he can help her with. They're learning to listen, respect, and trust each other on a deeper level.

Harry's idea for Claire concerning her home is to go ahead and move in with Alex. He likes Alex and thinks highly of him. Harry tells Claire, "You can depend on him. He's reliable, solid.

"Take your sweet time moving your things over there if that makes you more comfortable. You'll learn from it—the stress of moving in, getting to know one another, and making changes with the house and with yourself. This will show you just how well you two get along, teach you how to get along. The reality of a relationship is that, at times, you'll disagree. Heck, all couples disagree. Me and Patti Jo had some pretty big shakes." Harry sees Claire's perplexed expression, "Claire, you know, big whoppers."

"Oh, yes, whoppers. I got you now."

"It's how well you're willing to talk through your disagreements and settle your differences that proves a thing or two." But the one thing Harry tells Claire to bring it all home is, "Claire, no one is perfect. You know that. There'll be those days when nothing seems to go as planned, and every little thing he says irritates the heck out of you. You just want to ring his neck. You'll know for sure after that happens and he's still standing beside you, supporting you just like he promised. My dear, that is what we call *true love*."

Chapter Forty-Six

When Alex calls Robert to discuss the arrangements to rent a stall at Harry's shop, Harry's relationship with his son begins to change—for the better. When Harry hears that Robert agreed to show Alex around the shop, he knows Robert is showing an interest in the family business, something that Harry has wanted for a long time. He begins to relax. Harry is finally beginning to feel respected and honored.

Robert's action, in itself, pleases Harry. Harry, obviously relieved, openly declares that he wants to pass the business down to his son.

After Harry settles in at Longfellow Nursing, Claire runs into Augusta. They begin to explore what they know about the Malone line. Augusta reveals, "I would love to research the family more. My mother did it for years. She told me once that family research and documentation is forever ongoing. She thought I would like it when I was older. Well, I'm older, now."

Claire is eager to set up a time for them to go to the main library and to do some research.

Later that day, as Claire tells Alex about her conversation

with Augusta, he says, "You know, Claire, I think I would like to try doing some research and see what comes of it. I really feel comfortable with this family. It would be a good activity for us to do together, help us bond, especially when it's too cold to work on any of my outdoor projects."

After a couple of weeks of research, Augusta finds the missing link that connects them with Alex. They are forth cousins. That knowledge seems to fulfill something inside all of them.

It isn't long before things start to fall into place when Frank visits Harry again. By then, Harry is able to talk openly to Claire about Frank's visits. She isn't sure how to feel about any of it. She has grown fond of Harry. She finds that a part of her is sad, knowing that he's not going to be around much longer. She relies on his counsel. It's as if Harry stepped in to take on the role of her father.

During this time, Frank surprises Claire one evening at home. She's busy packing some of the last items to take over to her *new place*. For some reason, she's distracted and decides to take time to fix a sandwich. As she digs through the refrigerator, she hears Frank call her name, "Claire?"

Startled, she jumps, bumps her head and curses. When she's finally able to stand up, she turns around to see Frank standing there, as if neither of them has anything better to do than to talk.

"Claire, I wanted to come by and tell you that you have done a fine job with Harry and his family. It looks like we can begin the transfer soon."

"The transfer? What are you talking about?" Claire wants to remain forever ignorant, but in reality, she knows exactly what he's referring to.

"Harry is ready to transition to his new home. I just wanted you to know this will be taking place soon. Perhaps you can visit him and give him a heads up? He is a little frightened. Maybe you can tell him about Jerry and some of the other patients. This may ease his anxiety concerning his upcoming move. I am sure you will know exactly what and how to say it."

"Gosh, Frank. I really was hoping that he could stay a while longer."

"Claire, it is his time. Look at it as a grand gift that he is about to receive."

Tears pool and then spill over. "I've grown to love him as a father. But sure, I'll go over tomorrow and talk to him about the transition and some of my experiences. Is that soon enough? I can go over now if you feel I should."

"Tomorrow works best."

"Frank, I never did thank you for the letter you wrote to me. But truly…" Her heart swells with gratitude, and the tears begin to fall again. She isn't sure she can talk, so she grabs a tissue. "Well, thank you, Frank. While you're here, can you tell me about Charles? It appears, he isn't going to make it, is he?"

"Claire, your way of looking at death isn't how we view it. When you ask if he is going to make it, I know what you mean. But, dearest Claire, Charles is fine. Right now, he is resting, waiting to be released in fullness from this realm. He is not suffering. When the time comes, it is important that you go with Alex to take care of the remains. Alex is to have closure, and he will do better if you are at his side during this process. I'm sure that you both can take leave from your duties at work, sufficient to accomplish this task and to also close up Charles' house."

"I'll make sure that I go with Alex. And Frank?"

"Yes?"

"Will I continue to work with you like this? Or is this a one-time deal?"

"Dearest Claire, this is only the beginning. You are ready for more."

For a moment, Claire closes her eyes as if to prepare herself for the future. Instead, she feels a powerful love emanating from her heart and merging with Frank's. When she opens her eyes, Frank has vanished.

"Ah, Frank! Why do you keep doing that?"

About the Author

Kansas native, Nakala Akasie, contemporary Pleiadian Messenger, channel, and author currently resides near the spiritual mecca of Mt. Shasta in Northern California with her husband Ray El. Together, they serve as a bridge for those who reside in the Higher Realms of Light during the planetary and cosmic shifts currently taking place.

Nakala enjoys the disciplines of yoga and daily meditation. She and her husband also teach workshops on how to connect with spirit guides using a pendulum. Nakala loves to garden, watch the sunrise and sunset, create artistic projects, and go hiking on the sacred Mt. Shasta with her husband.

To contact Nakala:
WhenAngelsSpeak5@aol.com
PleiadianTraveler.com
WhenAngelsSpeakToUs.wordpress.com

Like Pleiadian Traveler on Facebook